A HIDDEN DANGER

There was something mysterious, and a little sinister, about that track which had disappeared into the brush. Campomoche stopped short and pointed his ears to the right, snorting and staring out among the trees. Cal reached for his gun as he saw a brush corral, hidden away in a thicket of mesquite. He rode in on it slowly, glancing nervously about for something he could not name. As he looked over the bars, he saw a bunch of J Prod cows, each one with a new-branded calf. The answer was plain and he reined his horse away. He had stumbled on a rustlers' camp.

Bitter Creek

DANE COOLIDGE

LEISURE BOOKS NEW YORK CITY

A LEISURE BOOK®

January 2006

Published by special arrangement with Golden West Literary Agency.

Dorchester Publishing Co., Inc.
200 Madison Avenue
New York, NY 10016

Visit us on the web at www.dorchesterpub.com.

Bitter Creek

Chapter One

THE SCORPION AND THE TARANTULA

There was a mirage on Dry Lake. All the world seemed afloat, bobbing dreamily in a sea of heat, and a bull, pacing moodily toward the ranch, loomed up like an elephant on stilts. Little bushes, banked with sand, rose up and became trees; distant trees disappeared in a blur, and all that was real on that endless sun-baked floor was two men, toiling along the road. One was a giant in size, but walking with a limp, fetching his left foot down with a slap, and the other, although he stood on his feet like a buck, was torn and bruised from fighting. He forged on ahead, muttering angrily to himself, his eyes fixed on a grove of phantom trees, until a shout from behind made him stop in his tracks and turn back with a guilty grin.

"Wait, man!" shrilled Peggy McCann. "Me poor stump is hurting arful . . . dom the day that I fell down that shaft! But ye will be hiking on and laving me behint, until I have to holler after you like a child! For cripes' sake, Watson, have some mercy on a cripple and don't be running arf there, ahead!" He sat down heavily, nursing his game leg in both hands, and Watson stood over him grimly.

"There was a feller back in Watsonville," he suggested helpfully, "that learned to walk on his hands."

"*A-ah*, you and your Watsonville!" burst out Peggy profanely, and with the cursing his spirit returned. "It's a wonder," he jeered, "you wouldn't go back there yourself, if it's all as fine as you say. The deepest shafts, the longest tunnels, the richest rock, the best of everything . . . and here you are, out on this desert. Did they have any trees there, where a man could cut a crutch? Because that's what I'm needing the most."

"We had a crutch tree," boasted Watson, "where you could take your pick . . . right up there by Curemquick Springs. Them fellers that came in to boil out their rheumatism used to hang up their crutches when they left."

"*A-ah*, of carse they did," scoffed Peggy, rolling up his overalls and beginning to unlace his stump, "or ye wouldn't be a native son. And are you the guy that misnamed this mine we're coming from and called it the Thousand Wonders?"

"I'm the guy," admitted Watson, "and I guess I'd ought to know whether there's anything on Bitter Creek or not. Didn't my old man come through here, going on to forty years ago, and make a million in six months out of the Golden Bear? Well, the Thousand Wonders Mine is on the very same vein, so what's to keep it from being a bonanza? I still maintain that, if we'd gone ten feet deeper, we'd've struck the Golden Bear ore. But this Eastern crook, Hunnewell, just bonded the property for an excuse to go out and sell stock. That's all he knows, the poor, ignorant baboon, and, if he'd had his way, he'd've bonded the Golden Bear. But that's one mine I'm holding onto. The old man told me it was rich, and I reckon he ought to know. I'm through with these promoters. The times have sure changed since old Sam Watson was here, working the Bear. I've tried to be honest and play the game straight, the way my father did before me, but you wait till I get my hooks into the next promoter and see if the fur don't fly. It's going to be like the case of the scorpion and the tarantula that met on the Bitter Creek trail . . . the scorpion jumped on the tarantula and the tarantula jumped the scorpion and the one that got his stinger in first, won. Say, Peggy, you've got water on the knee!"

"Hah . . . wahter, is it!" returned Peggy, giving over his effort to lubricate his artificial limb, "and how the divil will I git wahter on the knee when I'm so dry I can hardly spit? Nah, the trouble with me is wahter on the brain and listening to that blathering promoter. If it wasn't for him, I'd be at Larry's Place right now, blowing the top arf of a nice, big schooner. But, no, I was all for being a foreman . . . the same as you was for being a superintendent . . . and now here I am with me stump hurting arful, in the middle of the great Mojave Desert."

"Well, put on your cork leg," said Watson, "and stop knocking your betters, and I'll pack you into camp."

"Yes, you will, you jaybird!" Peggy cackled scornfully. "And me weighing two-seventy, with one leg arf? But who are these betthers that you say I'm after knocking . . . outside of yourself, of carse!"

"Why, Everett J. Hunnewell," replied Watson glumly, and Peggy raised a howl.

"What . . . Hunnewell, you say? That dhirty, lying hound! Didn't he skip out and lave us both flat? Didn't he say he'd be back with a truck load of grub . . . ?"

"That's it." Watson nodded. "We fell for it. No, there's no use knocking. We should have known better . . . whoever saw a mining man with a plug hat? But this bird comes out here rigged up like a corn doctor, with a plug hat and a Prince Albert suit . . . and we fell for him all the same. Wasn't he right there in front of me when I bonded my mine to him and took the first payment in stock? And didn't he beat you and me, and Pat Duffy and his gang out of every last dollar he owed? Well, that's what I call class, the triumph of pure intellect, the dominion of mind over matter. But when he skipped out without paying the men off, I will say I consider that low, because he knew they'd take it out of my hide. I wouldn't have minded, though, if they'd come on one at a time, but they ganged me."

"Ah, but, Watson," protested Peggy, "you mustn't be too hard. Didn't Pat and the byes do their best? Didn't they work day and night, and short-handed at that? And then to be beat out of their pay! It's the custom, you might say . . . on the desert side at least where these promoters are thick as fleas . . . it's the custom to collect by hand when it can't be done no other way. Take it out of their hide and then walk to town . . . but it's cruel hard, at that."

"Well, it'll be crueler yet, when I get into town and raise enough money to pay them . . . because I'm going to call those lads out one at a time behind the house and take my receipts the same way."

"*A-ah,* now Cal, me bye," soothed Peggy, rising awkwardly to his feet and surveying him with a fatherly smile, "you're low in your mind this day. But think if you was me, with one leg in the grave and sixty-nine years on your head. You've got your chance yet, if you'll take some good advice . . . but try to keep them lads for your friends. Because they'll be the divil and all if they git set against ye. . . ."

"Here," broke in Watson, "you lean on my shoulder . . . lean hard, now, and keep off of that stump. If it wasn't for me, talking you out of quitting, you would be heisting one at Larry's Place, right now."

"No, but, Cal," protested Peggy, "you've been beat up something terrible, and they kicked you in the ribs to boot."

"Never mind," replied Watson, "you can't kill a bonehead, and the ranch is just down the road. You can't see it,

10

but it's there, right in that bunch of mesquites, hid on purpose by the horse thieves that built it. Do you see that patch of white, 'way back through the trees? Well, that's the house . . . so get off your foot. There's an artesian well in that first corral, and after the big drink we'll eat!"

"Oh, we eat, do we?" cheered Peggy, striking his arm away. "Here, git out of my way . . . I can walk. I've had a heartache for two days . . . ever since we ran out of potatoes . . . but, Cal, are you sure they'll feed us? Pat Duffy and them stiffs have been there already and probably ate them out of house and home. Our welcome has gone to hell, with that gang before us to give us a dhirty name, and this Sol Barksdale, so they say down in Soledad, is a harrd-hearted man at the best."

"Leave it to me." Cal smiled. "You don't know Armilda. She'd feed us if we were horse thieves."

"A-ah!" Peggy leered, raising his inch-long black eyebrows and opening a cavernous mouth. "Ah, I see! So that's how it is! You're sweet on the gurrl and she'll feed you, anyway. . . ."

"She'll feed us," put in Cal, "and that's all you need to know, so get off your foot, and walk!"

"He says walk!" observed Peggy to the world at large, and ambled down the road with a grin. A broad lane appeared through the middle of the trees ahead, flanked on the east by the corrals and branding pen, and above the gnarled mesquites rose the green tops of cottonwoods, drinking deeply from the waters of Bubbling Wells. Hens cackled in the barnyard, the old bull was pawing and rumbling near the water gate, but the white adobe house, hidden back among the shadows, was ominously silent and still.

"They've seen us," quavered Peggy, wiping the sweat

from his face, but Cal Watson would not listen to his fears.

"You come on behind," he said, "and I'll go ahead. Maybe Armilda has gone to town." He smoothed down his rumpled hair and jerked a tatter from his sleeve as he strode on toward the gate, and all the time his lips wore a half smile and he kept his eyes on the house. It was familiar ground to him—many a time he had stopped there on his way from his mine in Soledad—and, as he peered beneath the trees, he thought he caught a flash of white, moving swiftly across the square of the screen door. But no one appeared and his smile became set as he glanced nervously from the bunkhouse to the barn, and then with a *ping* a bullet struck ahead of him and went ricocheting away across the lake.

He pulled up short, started ahead impulsively, and again a warning bullet cut the dust. He stared, and looked back to where Peggy was standing, gaping, then ahead to where the shots had rung out, but in the slack of his waistband he carried a pistol of his own and he kept doggedly to one gate. Not another shot was fired, but, as he reached out his hand to open the gate, Sol Barksdale rose up from the brush. He was a small, grim man with intolerant eyes that gleamed savagely through his glasses, and his lips, tightly clenched above a bristling bulldog jaw, opened and closed in spasms of excitement. Cal could see that he was swayed by some overmastering passion, although it seemed to have bereft him of speech, but, as his hand touched the gate, Barksdale leaped into the open with his rifle ready to shoot.

"Open that gate," he said, "and I'll shoot you like a dog. I don't want you here, Cal Watson."

"The hell you don't!" mocked Cal, and then he stepped back, for he saw the killing light in the man's eyes. A cold chill came over him—he had known Barksdale for years.

Could it be he had gone suddenly mad? Not since the day that his wife had run away—only to die, alone, in old Mexico—had Sol Barksdale, the tyrant, been even his former self. And yet he had not been insane, although he had been harsh and exacting, given to biting retorts and hours of sullen brooding. But now he was on the hair-trigger to shoot.

"What's the matter, Mister Barksdale . . . has something gone wrong? Haven't I always been your friend?"

"You get out of here," commanded Barksdale, "and don't you come back! If you do, I shall surely shoot you."

"Oh, you will, eh?" returned Cal. "Well, don't you ever forget that I've got a gun, too, Mister Barksdale. And I was out on this desert before you ever heard of it, so the chances are I can shoot. Now, if you will just kindly tell me what's the cause of all this . . . ?"

"You know very well, sir!" cried Barksdale in a fury. "Be off now, before I forget myself. And if I ever catch you talking to my daughter again. . . ."

"Your daughter!" yelled Watson, jumping as if he had been shot. "Why, what do you think you mean? Why, damn your black heart, you can't talk to me like that! You don't need to think, just because some man stole your wife. . . ."

"Not a word!" charged Barksdale, his hand trembling on the trigger. "Not a word . . . don't you speak her name! And now, Watson, if you value your life. . . ."

"All right," assented Cal, "I'll go."

He turned away quickly, but his heart was sick to think that he had gone so far, but at the same time his anger was boiling up again. He had been warned away from Armilda! Never once since he had known her had he given Barksdale the slightest cause to doubt his good faith toward his daughter, and now, if he left without protesting his innocence,

13

it would look like a confession of guilt. But if Barksdale was insane. . . .

He started off blindly, only to bump against Peggy, who was standing close behind him.

"Don't we git anny wahter?" queried Peggy huskily, and Watson whirled about again resolutely.

"Sure we do," he said, and headed toward the water gate, left ajar for the trapping of wild cattle. The artesian well was enclosed by a huge corral made of railroad ties bound together with old cables from the mines and the gate was so hung that a rope up the lane would slam the great gate and latch it. Cal had no more than started when the gate leaped on its hinges and closed in their faces with a crash.

"What the divil are you doing?" demanded Peggy indignantly, turning to glare at the man who had done it, but Watson made a jump and, unlatching the gate, hurled it violently back against the fence.

"Come on, Peggy," he cursed, "and get your drink . . . he can't refuse a man water on the desert!"

"I can . . . and I will!" cried Barksdale in a frenzy, advancing at a crouch down the lane. "Now you go, and go quick, or by the living God. . . ."

"They's two of 'em," whispered Peggy, grabbing Cal from behind and dragging him off down the road. "Come away, before we both get killed!"

Chapter Two

A RUN OF LUCK

Cal Watson submitted, for his mind was in a daze and Peggy was big and determined, but, as he stumbled off down the road, he called down curses on the man who had denied him water on the desert. And not only water, but shelter and food and a crutch for poor crippled Peggy, yes, and had besmirched his good name and, by implication, the good name of his daughter.

"The crazy fool!" he burst out. "Why, he must be crazy! What . . . shoot me for talking to his daughter? Why, I wouldn't hurt Armilda for anything in the world, and he knows it, too, the old walloper. He's been sitting around the house and looking down his nose and thinking about his wife and Simpson, until now, by grab, he's got the idea that somebody's after his daughter. I'll make him take that back if I have to ram the words down his throat."

"Yes, sure you will," soothed Peggy, still keeping Cal in front of him as he hobbled off to the south, "but who was that cowboy that closed the gate in our face, when we were only after a cup of water? May the curse of Cromwell. . . ."

"Cowboy?" cried Watson, suddenly wresting himself loose and glaring back toward the ranch. "Did you see a cowboy there?"

"Did I see him!" clamored Peggy. "Haven't I been telling you, all the time? He was a tall, slim lad with a big cowboy hat . . . it was him that pulled the rope and closed

15

the water gate . . . and I was just about to give him the cursing of a lifetime when I see him reach down for a gun. Up it come to his shoulder, p'inting straight at your heart, so I grabbed ye by the arm and saved you from getting kilt, though it's small thanks you've given me as yet."

"Oho!" Watson nodded. "So that's what it's all about. I thought it was damned funny for old Barksdale to start shooting . . . but I'll take care of you, Crump!"

"So you know him, eh?" said Peggy. "There's a ba-ad, wild lad, I know. He was laughing, the dhirty divil, when he closed the gate against us . . . may he roast a thousand years in hell!"

"Yes, I know him," muttered Cal, "the dog-goned Texas coyote. He's the new cattle detective that Barksdale and Johnson have hired to find out who's stealing their stock . . . but he looks more like a cow thief to me. I'll bet you Sol Barksdale never fired those two shots . . . that was some more of Crump's rough stuff. And if Barksdale had started shooting, Crump was figuring on drilling me. I'll have to keep my eye on that guy."

"Kape away from him," advised Peggy, beginning to limp down the road. But Watson stood gazing at the ranch. Since Wayne Crump, the swaggering Texan, had come to Bubbling Wells, he had noticed a change in Armilda. Perhaps it was merely because she was coming to be a woman, but he had noted how her eyes followed Crump. He was tall and handsome, in an arrogant way, and his saddle and spurs and fancy rigging made him the envy of the other boys at the ranch. And he had a way, too, of saying gallant things, and those things count with a woman.

But couldn't she see, behind that slow smile, the wiles of the professional lady-killer? And behind the iron mask of his hard-lined pokerface the devil that was plotting her undoing?

16

He was a bad man, indeed, in more ways than they had thought. But why should Crump try to murder *him?* What had Cal Watson, the prospector, done to Wayne Crump, the detective, that he should come out against him with a gun?

Cal asked this again as he hurried on after Peggy, and like a flash the answer came back. He, too, had admired Armilda; he, too, had won her smiles. Crump was simply getting him out of the way. But what desperate plot was in his mad mind to make him resort to such violence? Was this wild Texan trying to steal Armilda himself? The memory of fleeting looks, of a sinister smile, of sly laughter at whatever he said—all these came back to him in a rush of tumbled thoughts that left him staring back with scared eyes. This man from nowhere, this mysterious, flashy stranger with whom he had bandied grim jokes. In his absence he had stepped in and dared to claim Armilda—yes, and to oppose him and drive him away. His was the hand that had fired those warning shots and slammed the gate in his face, and his were the lips that had whispered in Barksdale's ears the poisoned words that had set Barksdale against him.

But what of Armilda? After all her father's warnings, after all that had befallen her mother, could she consent, could she even dream of running off with such a man? How was it possible for her to watch him, day after day, as he straddled about the place and not see the evil that was in him? But she was young, younger than she looked, and first love is blind to things that any stranger can see. And behind that shy smile which flitted across her lips there was a reserve that no insistence could break down. What she thought one never knew, unless she chose to tell, and that was not Armilda's way. She much preferred to smile and leave the words unsaid.

Perhaps Crump had taken too much for granted. Cal smiled to himself and drew a long breath. After all, Armilda could take care of herself.

Peggy McCann was staggering as he toiled on down the road, his round miner's hat bobbing slowly up and down as he heaved his leg forward from the shoulder. Then he threw his crashing weight upon the stump of his lost limb and flinched as he took the next step. Ten miles he could never go, or five without a crutch, and Cal Watson took the only way out.

"Here, you sit down," he ordered, "and take a little rest while I go and get you a yucca. It'll make you a crutch, and a good one, too, and then we'll cut across to the stage road."

"All right, Cal," agreed Peggy, sinking down in the sand. "I was jist about to sit down, anyway. But if you'll get me a Joshua, I'll make one more thry! But Cal, bye, I'm perishing for a drink!"

He stretched out on his back, pillowing his head on one mighty arm, and Cal Watson toiled off up the slope. It was a long and weary climb up the side of the sharp ridge that looked down on Bubbling Wells from the south, but halfway up the hill he gained the edge of the yucca forest that banded the whole valley like a beach line. Above that line, and its altitude, there were Joshuas by the thousand, below it hardly a one, but the dry, pithy stalks were as light as bamboo and strong enough to hold up a giant. Cal plucked three of the strongest and returned at a trot, for the sun was getting low in the west. And soon, with the cross-piece nicely padded with his coat, Peggy McCann was swinging off on his crutch.

It put new life into him to get his weight off the stump, and, besides, there was call for speed, for if they arrived at the road after the stage had gone by, it would mean a long night of misery, a dry camp, and no shelter from the cold winter wind that always sucked down through the pass, either that or the long ten miles to Soledad without a drop of water. But when they reached the road, the stage had not passed, for the mule tracks still pointed to the north. Only an auto had gone by, but which way they could not tell, and they sat down in the sand to wait.

The sun sank to the edge of the far western horizon whose blue peaks seemed 100 miles away, and then the gorgeous sunset set the whole sky aflame before it burned down and faded to a glow. Back at the ranch at Bubbling Wells they could see a pale light gleam out through the gathering dusk, and then the evening star hung itself up like a lantern, heralding the way for the lesser stars. The deathly hush of the desert was stirred by a chill breeze that grew to a rushing wind and the sweat had hardly dried on their clinging shirts before they felt the iron cold of coming night. Peggy stirred uneasily and rose, groaning, to his feet.

"I'm freezing," he complained. "Let's build a little fire, for there'll be no stage this night. Ayther it's gone by already, or it ain't coming at all, and, if it did come, that Mexican wouldn't carry us."

"Yes, he will," asserted Cal, "because I'll trade him my six-shooter if he won't take us any other way. But he's got to take you . . . you're crippled."

"Yes, crippled! Wasn't I crippled at the ranch, when they turned me away from the wahter? *A-ah*, what do they care for an old stove-up miner . . . come ahn, let's get out of the wind."

He led the way down the wash that crossed the road at that point and found shelter in the lee of the bank, and, while Cal went out to gather more wood, he started a puny fire.

"Oh, murdher," he sighed as Cal came back and laid a piece of sagebrush on the fire, "what the divil has come over us, annyway? It seems like iverything we try, no matter how simple it is, we fall down and lose out entirely. Here we had a good road to come over and ketch the stage and the dommed Mexican nivver comes by. Well, find me a smooth pebble and I'll suck it till marnin', like I've done before, manny's the time. And sometimes, when iverything in the world is ag'inst you, the luck changes and a man can't lose."

He slumped down by the fire, knitting his bushy black eyebrows and thinking of other days. Watson was just stretching himself in the sand when he heard the muffled *clink* of a chain.

"What's that?" he demanded, springing anxiously to his feet, and by the dim light of their fire he saw the stage gliding by, as shadowy and unreal as a ghost.

"Hey!" he called, starting to run up the wash, and Peggy added his voice to the clamor.

"Shoot your gun arf!" he shouted. "He can't hear ye for the racket! Hurry up . . . shoot your gun arf, I say!"

"Hey! Wait!" whooped Cal, still trying to catch the stage, and then he drew his pistol and fired. But the driver, already scared half out of his wits, let out a yell and laid the whip to his mules. They broke into a gallop, plunging off into the darkness, and Cal threw down his gun in despair. "Well, go to hell, then!" he burst out resentfully and made his way back to the fire.

"What's the mahtter?" wailed Peggy. "May the divil fly away with him for laving us out here to die! What the hell was you thinking about, running and waving at him that way? Sure, he thought you were another hold-up."

"Yes, holler your head off!" answered Watson savagely,

20

and cast himself down by the fire. Every muscle in his body seemed to ache and throb from weariness, his brain was too tired to think, and, as Peggy McCann ran on with his plaint, he closed his eyes and lay still.

There were times, as Peggy had said, when the simplest thing he tried turned out an absolute failure, when to get a drink of water or flag a Mexican stage driver was beyond his power of accomplishment. He remembered now that some months before the stage had been held up and robbed, and the sight of his running—and firing his gun in the air—had no doubt thrown the driver into a panic. But what a run of luck!

He sighed, and was dropping off to sleep when he heard a muffled throbbing in the air. It was so faint and far away that it might be the wind, or the guttering flames of their fire, but something about it snatched him away from the realm of sleep and warned him to rouse up once more. He rose up and listened dumbly, but the wind was in his ears, a great weariness seemed to drug his every sense, yet, just as he was dropping back, the throbbing came again, and he leaped to his feet like a buck. Bowing his head to the wind, he went charging up the wash, throwing his feet as if he were treading on air, and, as a spidery little automobile came rushing down the road, he stepped in front of it, holding out his hands.

"Stop!" he yelled, and with the headlights full upon him he stood there till it skidded to a halt.

"Well, what will it be?" inquired a mild voice from the machine.

Watson answered: "Water!"

Chapter Three

SOLEDAD

The luck had changed, as far as Watson was concerned, for the man in the automobile had water. He handed out a canteen as big around as a barrel head, and Watson drank—right then. If Peggy McCann wanted a drink, he would have to come and get it, because Cal had other business on hand.

"What's the chances for a ride?" he inquired briskly.

The mild little man, who nothing seemed to surprise, invited him to climb right in.

"But I've got a pardner," explained Watson, "who weighs two hundred and seventy pounds."

"Bring him on," said the man. "Plenty of room behind."

"Well, you're the kind of a man," exclaimed Watson approvingly, "that I've been looking for all day. These dad-burned snoozers that have come into the country lately wouldn't give you a drink of whiskey if you were snake-bit!"

"Take a nip," invited the gentleman, handing out a large bottle. "You seem to be playing to hard luck."

"I was," admitted Watson, "until I met you. Hey, Peggy, come over and meet a white man!"

Peggy came, throwing his limber leg ahead of him and swinging along on his crutch, and, when he saw the canteen, and the bottle of whiskey, too, he gave a wild whoop.

"Lave me to it," he cheered, "but for wanst in my life I'll be taking the wahter first."

"My name is Wiggins," observed the stranger, while

22

Peggy was kissing the bottle, "and I'm on my way to Soledad. Just climb in behind, boys. I'm in something of a hurry . . . you'll find some grub in one of those sacks."

He was very nice and friendly, this little man with the jack-rabbit car, but at the same time strictly business. From the way he opened up and went whirling down the road, Cal judged he was, indeed, in a hurry. But not too hurried to talk, or, rather, to listen, and, as they clung to the back of his seat, Cal and Peggy took turns in telling him all of their troubles. He said little or nothing, laughing now and then quietly, and, almost before they knew it, they had glided into Soledad and were being set down at Larry's Place.

"Don't mention it," he murmured when Cal began to thank him, and then slipped Peggy five dollars. "Good evening, gentlemen. Hope to meet you again, sometime." And with a thunder from his exhaust he was gone.

"Some guy," pronounced Cal, gazing admiringly after him. "He can have my shirt any time he asks for it."

"He's a gentleman," proclaimed Peggy, "if I ever seen wan. Come on, I'll introduce you to Larry."

They went in through the huge door that kept out the wintry wind, and there by the stove sat Pat Duffy. Yes, Big Pat and Little Pat and Murdock and Garrity—and Shay was over watching the games. It was the same Big Five that had ganged Cal at the mine and now they glanced up at him dourly. But they, too, had had a long walk and nothing to drink, so they took it out in scowling and muttering among themselves without offering any insulting remarks. Yet, as he shoved in by the stove and warmed his chapped hands, Cal could feel their hate rising like a wave. As for Peggy, he had headed straight for the bar, where Larry Kilgallon stood smiling, and, after a word in his ear at which Larry nodded amiably, Peggy jerked his head to Cal.

"Larry," he began, speaking the name like a caress, "this is Cal Watson. He's me friend, you understand, and, as we're both a little short of. . . ."

"That's all right." Larry smiled. "Glad to see you. It's kind of late for the cook . . . but how'd you like some ham and eggs? Hey! Jack! Give 'em all the eggs they want!"

He held up his hand in some signal to the cook, and Peggy crow-hopped across to the lunch counter.

"Gimme six eggs straight up and then six more turned over," he said to the glowering cook.

After Cal ordered six, the cook set out two egg pans and broke two eggs into each.

"Hey! Put arn me eggs!" spoke up Peggy insistently. "Didn't he say . . . 'Give 'em all the eggs they want?' "

"Yes, but did you moind his hand?" inquired the cook with a knowing grin. "He held up two fingers, understand?"

"No, I don't understand!" howled Peggy indignantly. "Put the eggs arn, I say, and do it now! Ain't I spint hundreds of dollars across Larry's bar, and nivver reached me hand out for the change? You're new here, I see that. . . ."

"Yes, and not so new, ayther," replied the cook without stirring. "Didn't he hold up two fingers? That means *two!*"

"Well, dom you and your impudence!" cried Peggy in a fury, reaching down and stripping the overalls from his game leg, and, slipping the finger through the hole into the interior, he hooked out Wiggins's five-dollar bill. "Now take a look at that," he exclaimed triumphantly, "and tell me how many I get?"

"You get twelve," returned the cook, catching another signal from Larry, and the whole barroom burst into a roar.

"Ain't I right, byes?" Peggy grinned, waving his hand at the crowd. "I'm a big man, and I've got to ate accordin'!"

"You'll do," pronounced Larry, joining in on the laugh.

24

"And eat hearty, Peggy. The drinks are on me!" He signaled again to his bar assistant who set out two glasses on a tray. Larry added the bottle and Peggy was drinking his good health when Big Pat Duffy drew near. Big Pat had had his eggs and a cup of coffee, and that was all for the night, for Larry had his rules and one of the strictest was that bummers should get two eggs and no more. Larry was watching them now, a sturdy, wrinkled old man with a great fluff of curly white hair. When he saw Big Pat edge over toward Cal, he laid off his apron and stepped out. For another of his rules was that those who were broke should not break in on the pleasures of the spenders. And Peggy, having flashed a five-dollar bill, had attained to the honored status of guest.

"So you're ating and drinking, eh?" observed Big Pat to Cal, leaning his elbows on the lunch counter beside him. "And this marning, at the mine, whin we asked you for our time, you rayfused to pay us a cent."

Cal glanced at him impersonally and went on with his meal, but Duffy was not to be denied. He had come there for trouble and trouble he would have, so he raised his voice a trifle louder.

"I want me pay!" he announced, bringing his fist down on the counter.

Cal slid down off his stool. "You'll get it," he said, "if you keep your mouth shut. Otherwise, you can collect by hand."

"By hand, hey?" howled Duffy, trying to work himself into a fury, and then a brawny paw took a twist in his collar and whirled him about like a top.

"Get out of here," ordered Larry, "and don't you come back until you learn to behave like a gentleman."

Duffy opened his mouth to shout, and then he thought

better of it and left by the side entrance door. Larry returned to the bar, and, after hiring a four-bit room, Cal retired and slept like the dead.

The November wind was howling and rattling the windows when he awoke to another day and, after thinking it over, he heaved himself out of bed and went down to view the town. The main street of Soledad—there was only one street—ran parallel to the railroad that made it, and facing the track, each with its false front brazenly painted, stood a shameless row of houses. After a succession of fires, which had swept down the line, they had separated, each place to itself: first a saloon, then a restaurant, then a pool hall and hotel, and lastly Johnson's Store. Whispering Johnson owned the hotel and pool hall as well—in fact, he owned the whole town—but the store was his pride, and, with the feed corral behind, it made quite a gash in the skyline. All the rest was desert, as dry as a bone and as level as the floor of the sea.

Larry's Place stood up the track by itself, the only building not on Johnson's land, but in spite of the social blight that such isolation implied it was not unknown to fame. In the first place, it had been built in the early days, when the corkscrew and the six-shooter were kings, and its walls were composed of some 40,000 bottles, laid neck to neck in natural cement. It stood like a great fort, its walls studded with gleaming bottle ends, its broad porch like the ramadas of old Spain, and from Albuquerque to Walla Walla, and south to the line, the old-timers brought their pay checks to Larry.

He was a hard man, they admitted it, taking his cut on everything, but he gave them what they wanted, and, when they were broke, he slipped them a bottle to sober up on. A bottle and a stake, to get their next job, and what more could any man ask for? So they came and went, hard-rock miners and desert rats, mostly Irish, a clique to themselves, and on his broad porch they gathered and talked, bringing in the news of every camp on the desert.

But Larry's was no place for Watson, as he knew very well, because the only man in town who could help him out of his difficulties happened to own the rival saloon. Whispering Johnson was a big man, and a rich man, too, a great character and a power politically, but the suppliant that came to him with Larry's whiskey on his breath was foredoomed to a peremptory refusal. Johnson hated the very ground that the old bottle house stood on, because it took many a dollar from his till, and the one sure way to gain his enmity for life was to buy a round of drinks at Larry's. There were those who even hinted that Bill Beagle, the town marshal, had two standards for judging inebriety, and that a man who would be drunk and disorderly at Larry's would be just getting mellow at The Keno. Not being addicted to such expensive habits as buying drinks across the bar, Cal could only judge such matters by hearsay, but to remove any suspicion of having gone over to the enemy he had his breakfast at Johnson's hotel.

But Johnson was not up, either to witness this show of fealty or to listen to his appeal for a loan. Knowing where he would go when he did get up, Cal turned into The Keno bar. The town marshal, Bill Beagle, sat humped up behind the stove, engaged in conversation with a Mexican, and, as Cal came in, he glanced over at him sharply, for there was no love lost between them. Beagle was an oldish man with a long, drooping mustache that he combed between two fingers as he talked, but at some word from the Mexican he straightened up with a jerk and laid his hand on his gun.

27

"How's that?" he demanded, turning abruptly to his companion, and the Mexican rose up, trembling.

"That is heem!" he cried, pointing his finger at Watson while his eyes bulged out with excitement. "That is the robber . . . he tried to keel me!"

"What's biting you?" inquired Cal, moving over toward the stove, but the Mexican mistook his intent.

"*¡Ai, cuidado!*" he shrieked, ducking down behind the stove and grabbing Bill Beagle by both legs. "Arrest heem . . . he is going to keel me!"

"Stop right there!" ordered Beagle, kicking the Mexican aside and drawing his pistol on Watson. "I arrest you, in the name of the law."

"All right," responded Cal. "What's the matter with your friend? Come out of there . . . I'm not going to hurt you!"

The Mexican came out, but now his black eyes were flashing and his finger was at a point. "I know you!" he hissed. "You theenk you're es-smart . . . you tried to hold up my stage!"

"Why, sure I did!" Cal laughed. "But you were so badly scared. . . ."

"You see?" clamored the Mexican, catching Beagle by the arm, "he admeets it . . . but I know it's heem, anyway!"

"Why, sure it's me," said Cal. "Didn't you see me going past you? We beat you into town in that machine. You're a hell of a stage driver . . . why didn't you stop when I ran out and tried to flag you?"

"He tried to shoot me!" spat the Mexican. "I know heem!"

"Did you shoot at this man?" demanded Bill Beagle sternly.

Cal paused just a moment before he spoke. Anything he

said could be used against him, and, of course, he had fired his gun into the air.

"No," he said.

As the Mexican began to jabber, Bill Beagle brought his pistol to a point.

"Put up your hands!" he snarled. "Ben, take that gun away from him. I suspected this all the time."

"You suspected what?" flared back Cal, his natural antipathy suddenly intensified by Bill's air of swaggering arrogance.

"Never mind," returned Beagle, "but I knowed very well you never made no living out of mining!"

"Well, what then?" continued Cal, as a crowd began to gather.

"You robbed that stage," snapped Beagle. "That's enough."

"Sure it's enough . . . or it would be if I'd done it . . . but I happen to have a couple of witnesses to prove that this Mexican is wrong."

"You can tell that to the judge," answered Beagle significantly. "Come on now . . . down to the lock-up."

Cal Watson drew back, and his lips went white—he had not thought of the lock-up. But as he glanced through the crowd, one face stood out, and he welcomed it like an angel from heaven. It was Wiggins, who had saved him before.

"Just a moment," spoke up Wiggins, working his way through the press and addressing the belligerent Bill Beagle. "I happen to know this young man, picked him up on the desert last night when he was suffering from lack of water. He had a miner with him, a one-legged man, and on the way in they told me quite circumstantially about the stage driver running off and leaving them."

"He tried to rob me!" cried the Mexican, seeing his case suddenly weakened.

29

A voice from the crowd said: "Oh, hell . . . turn him loose!"

The onlookers began to disperse. Only the stage driver and Bill Beagle remained unconvinced as Wiggins explained the natural mistake, but in the midst of the arguments a big voice boomed out and Whispering Johnson appeared.

He was a huge, powerful man, wearing a faded blue shirt and overalls that hung low beneath his paunch. When he saw Cal Watson, he made a dash and grabbed him out of the crowd.

"Come over here!" he commanded in the thunderous tones that had given him his name, "you're just the man I've been looking for. What's that? *Aw*, turn him loose!"

This to the vindictive Bill Beagle, who still clung to his prisoner, and for once Bill forgot who was king. One word from Whispering Johnson and Bill Beagle would be a fugitive instead of an officer of the law, but his blood was up and he ventured even yet to oppose the will of his boss.

"What's the matter with you?" demanded Johnson, turning to look at him coldly. "Turn him loose . . . didn't you hear what I said?"

"Yes, but. . . ."

"But, nothing!" bellowed Johnson. "You seem to forget something." And he led Cal Watson away.

Chapter four

BY HAND

"Now, here," began Whispering Johnson, leading Watson into his office and closing the door with a slam, "you've got a mine, haven't you . . . or a hole in the ground . . . that you call the Thousand Wonders? You know me, Cal. I speak straight out, no evasions. How much do you want for that mine?"

The wheels in Cal's head began to run like a mechanism, like an adding machine that calculates a total, and without delaying a second after that total was reached he blinked and said: "Five hundred dollars."

"You've sold a mine," announced Johnson, and, reaching down into his overalls, he fetched out a crumpled bill. "Here's twenty to bind the bargain."

"Good enough," agreed Cal. "I want the cash in my hand the minute I sign the papers."

"You'll get it," replied Johnson, "and the papers will be drawn up as quick as Judge Brown can do it."

They stopped and looked at each other like two shifty fighters who have broken away from a clinch, and Whispering Johnson laughed. Cal gazed at him grimly, wondering what was behind it all but unwilling to admit he was piqued. The mine was sold, that was all he knew—or needed to know, now that it was done—and $500 would put an end to the insults he had endured since the shutdown took place. It might seem quixotic, but he would rather pay off Pat Duffy than sell the Thousand Wonders for a million.

"Make it snappy," he said, and went back to The Keno, where Beagle was still holding the floor.

"I'll take my gun," Cal suggested, "if you can chop that line of talk. Precarious business, this apprehending of fugitives."

Bill glanced at him venomously, his caved-in chest heaving as he sought for some fitting retort. "I've got a good notion to arrest you," he burst out helplessly. "You're a dangerous character and I know it."

"Never spoil a good notion," observed Cal, smiling thinly. "How about it . . . do I get back my gun?"

"Yes, you get it back!" cried Bill Beagle petulantly, handing over the confiscated gun. "But I want to warn you, young man, you be careful what you do!"

"Yes, and you be careful," answered Cal defiantly. "Just because you ambushed Kid Benson and potted him for the reward, don't get the idea that you're bad. You can't run it over me, you old billy goat."

"Now, here!" boomed out Johnson, coming in from the store. "You boys cut it out, understand? I don't know what you're quarreling about, and I don't want to know. All I say is . . . cut it out!"

"Well, talk to him," said Cal, "I'm not hunting for trouble."

But Beagle answered never a word. He went out the back way, chewing angrily on his tobacco, and Cal glanced after him contemptuously.

"We had a bad man like him, back in Watsonville," he said. "Finally got run out of town by a Chinaman."

"*Aw,* don't stand around here telling stories about Watsonville," broke in Whispering Johnson impatiently. "The judge is over at my office."

He led the way back to the cubbyhole of a room where

he transacted all business of importance, and old Judge Brown, after spitting judicially into the stove, spread out a sheaf of blanks.

"Is this a patented claim?" he inquired in a weak voice. "No, I thought so . . . merely a possessory title." He glanced up at Johnson, but as he motioned him to proceed, he sorted out a quitclaim deed. "Any encumbrance on this claim?" he asked suspiciously. "You've had it bonded, haven't you, to Mister Hunnewell? Well, now, when you made out that bond and lease, did you take the precaution to advertise and record said lease, at the same time giving public notice that you would not be responsible for any indebtedness? You did not, eh?"

"No, I did not," admitted Cal, and again Judge Brown glanced at Johnson. But Whispering Johnson, for some reason or other, was not disposed to take his customary advantage.

"Fill it out," he directed, pointing to the quitclaim deed, and the judge obeyed the man who owned him. "Now!" went on Johnson, running his eye over the blank and scowling at the technical words, "here's a quitclaim deed to the Thousand Wonders lode mining claim, fifteen hundred feet, and so forth, together with all and singular, the dips, spurs, mines, minerals, dumps, and so on . . . for and in consideration of the sum of five hundred dollars and all the rest of it. Sign here and you get your money, after you've acknowledged your signature before the judge."

He dipped the pen, and, after looking the paper over, Cal signed it and acknowledged his signature.

"Here's your money," grunted Johnson, counting out $480 and laying it before him on his desk. "That's all, Mister Brown, we'll excuse you." The judge rose up meekly and slipped out through the door, at which Johnson recovered his voice. He had been speaking low, so that people in the store could hardly understand what he said, but now, with the quitclaim deed in his fist, he became his normal self.

"Well, sold a mine, hey?" he bellowed. "First one you ever sold, I guess. What about this bill at the store? Eighty-seven dollars for grub and tools . . . do you want to pay that now? All right, now what about that horse and mule that you've had in my corral for a month? Cost you a dollar a day apiece if you call it a full month . . . been in about twenty-six days. Well, that's my regular rate, or you can figure it by the day . . . dollar and a half apiece, at four bits a feed. Call it sixty dollars, eh? Now, what about your men . . . I heard you hadn't paid them, and their claim is a lien against the property."

"I'll pay 'em," answered Cal, "unless you think of something else. But if you crowd me much further. . . ."

"Here's your money," said Johnson, hastily shoving over the balance. "The mine's bought, that's all there is to it. But you get a receipt from every one of them men, or I'm stuck, according to law."

"I'll get it." Cal nodded. "Anything else, Mister Johnson?"

"Well . . . no," pronounced Johnson, after looking at him again. "Or that is . . . well, of course, Cal, you'll be wanting a little bill of grub. . . ."

"Don't worry," answered Cal, and shut the door.

This was the usual thing as far as Johnson was concerned, for he was known to be a close trader, but, coming as it did after a series of hard knocks, it left Cal a little ruffled. Not only were the sharpers like Everett J. Hunnewell out to strip him of everything he possessed, but Johnson, the store-keeper, and Judge Brown and Bill Beagle, all had gone out of their way to take a hack at him. There was something wrong somewhere, and, as he walked up the street, he counted off his enemies on two hands.

First and foremost there was Hunnewell, who had brought on all this trouble by pretending to buy his mine. Then there was Pat Duffy and the rest of the gang who had collected their pay by hand. At the thought of old Sol Barksdale, denying him water, he turned down another finger grimly, and the memory of Crump sent a shudder up his back and brought the fighting light to his eyes. Bill Beagle, of course, made a living by catching hobos and sending chance citizens to jail, but in this case he had been a trifle overzealous, and there would have to be a hereafter for him. Passing over the stage driver and meekminded old Judge Brown, there was Whispering Johnson, who made ten. Ten men in two days who had all taken advantage of him—his hands were both fists when he arrived at the bottle house, and he crooked a beckoning finger to Pat Duffy.

"Come out here, you big stiff," he challenged contemptuously, "and I'll pay you that money I owe you."

"Who . . . me?" inquired Big Pat, rousing up from his chair and staring about uncertainly, but the sight of a roll of bills overcame his better judgment, for Larry had cut him off at the lunch counter.

"Out behind the house," amended Cal significantly, and Pat followed him like a man in a daze. "Now," began Cal, when they were off by themselves, "I owe you sixty-three dollars . . . is that right? That's for eighteen shifts at three and a half . . . here's your money, and I'll take my receipt by hand."

He placed the money in Pat's hand and started a swing for his jaw before Pat could even double up his fists. All the resentment and blind fury that he felt for ten men was behind that one vicious blow and Big Pat went down like a beef. Cal Watson stood over him, a twisted smile on his lips.

"There's one of them," he said. "Now watch me get the rest. I'm from Bitter Creek, if you crowd me too far."

Chapter five

AND THOU . . .

There are times when the best two-handed fighter in the world has to acknowledge that they are coming too fast for him, and especially if he is up against the Irish. Watson had no sooner taken his receipt from Big Pat Duffy than the rest showed a marked tendency to gang him. Of course, he might have fought them, but his body was sore and bruised, so he paid what he owed and came away. The man doesn't live that can whip the whole universe, and he was sick and tired of it all.

He rode out of Soledad on his big bay, Campomoche, with a saddle gun under his knee, and, following behind, came Lemon, his sorrel mule, loaded down with light literature and grub. For man cannot live by bread alone, and in the long days to come, when he would not see a soul, Cal yearned to envision life as it should be. He desired nothing more than to forget all care and strife and, sitting in the shade, read story after story in which everything came out just right. Stories of chivalrous men who did not gang the boss, of brave people who did not shoot from the brush—and of young men like himself, fair-haired and blue-eyed, who didn't know how to lose. It was a dream world, of course, but who does not crave dreams when life is so sordid and drab?

The news agent at the train station, who had opened this gate to the world of dreams, had loaded him down with books and magazines, and to make it full measure he had thrown in a book of poems which someone had left on his hands. It was the "Rubáiyát of Omar Khayyám", and, as he headed north for his old camp, Cal lolled in the saddle and read:

> A book of Verses underneath the Bough
> A jug of Wine, a loaf of Bread—and Thou
> Beside me in the Wilderness—
> Oh; Wilderness were Paradise enow!
> Some for the Glories of This World; and some
> Sigh for the Prophet's Paradise to come;
> Ah, take the Cash, and let the Credit go,
> Nor heed the rumble of a distant Drum!

It was infinitely soothing, after his month of toil and strife and the jangle he had just had with Whispering Johnson, and, while Campomoche jogged along up the road, Cal heaved a great sigh at fate. What a thing it was, this essential something that molds our destinies like potter's clay, and how futile was all care and struggle, when tomorrow or the next day one must die.

> Yet, ah, that Spring should vanish with the Rose,
> That Youth's sweet-scented manuscript should close!

He sighed again and thought of Armilda—he would have to ride around the ranch. Always before he had stopped there. Campomoche had taken that trail today, but he had had to pull his head to the west, for Cal's welcome at Bubbling Wells was gone. It would be the stage road now, skirting around Dry Lake until at last they reached the old stage station at Bitter Creek, but what a long drag it was, and what a cheerless place to camp, when he might be back at the ranch. Yes, Armilda was the "And Thou" who, singing beside him, would make the "Wilderness Paradise enow." He had never thought much about it—because he had been very busy and she sang for him anyhow, at the ranch. But now that he was denied, he felt a hunger for her presence that was little short of pain. It was a month and more since he had gone by the ranch on his way to show Hunnewell the mine, and he wondered suddenly how she was doing with her singing, and the correspondence course on the piano. She hadn't needed the course, because she could play already, but that was one of the cranks that Sol Barksdale had developed and she had yielded without a word. But what cursed spite had made old Sol think that Cal was trying to steal his girl? Cal thought it over again, and, his mind wandering to Crump, he reined his horse out of the road.

The stage road that he had taken kept well west of Barksdale's, passing through the gap that had once drained Dry Lake, but the trail to Bubbling Wells went right over the ridge and descended like a toboggan slide to the ranch. In between, there was nothing but some dim cattle trails and the frowning cap of the *malpais,* the lip of the cup that had once enclosed Dry Lake when that great flat was a boiling volcano. There was no law of God or man to prevent California Watson from gazing down upon the home of his beloved! He was a free agent, in fact, entitled to go wherever he pleased without even consulting Campomoche, and, although that willful beast tried his best to circumvent him, up the lava ridge he went to the top. Leaving his animals in a gulch, Cal edged up to the rim and looked out over the vast expanse below.

To the north rose Frémont Peak, the great landmark of

all that country, beckoning him on as it had beckoned the famous pathfinder, for at the base of that granite dome lay the Golden Bear Mine, his sole heritage from a gold-mining father. Cal's eyes sought it first, for it was the beacon to his home, and then they swept the far side of the bowl. First they envisaged the long range of clay hills, once a mountain of volcanic mud, that ran from Mount Frémont to the east, and then the cone itself that had belched out all this mud, and the lava rim that circled to the south. Everywhere were blackened hills, the flanks of dead volcanoes half buried beneath a smother of windswept sand, and behind and beyond and all about the great circle rose the mysterious blue spires of desert peaks.

In the middle lay the broad lakebed, white and shimmering with alkali, veiled as always in a dreamy haze, and along its shores the drifting sand and salt grass showed tawny as waving wheat in the sun. Higher up from its shoreline the mesquite trees began, then the green of desert creosote and gaunt Joshuas, but the heart of it all, the precious jewel that it cupped, was the ranch at Bubbling Wells. Seen through the clean air, Bubbling Wells was at his feet, a cluster of white houses overshadowed by vivid cottonwoods set in a thicket of black mesquite. If Armilda was there, she was too busy cooking to come out for a look at the hills. Cal got out the glasses that he used in hunting horses and focused them on the yard, and, as he lay there watching, Wayne Crump came out of the kitchen and went striding across the open to the bunkhouse.

So that was the way that he earned his $100 a month— telling stories to Armilda in the kitchen. The gang of thieves who had been running off cows and stealing from Johnson and Barksdale need have no fear of this false-alarm detective who apparently never left the ranch. The man who caught them would have to do some riding and make a few dry camps, but Crump was satisfied to leave that to the cowboys while he made love to Armilda. Cal cursed under his breath as he saw the tall Texan come out and begin spinning a rope. It was a trick he had learned at the Wild West contests, where he claimed he had won money riding broncos. First he built a big loop, straddling his legs far apart as he tossed it up and down in the air, and then he leaped through it, as limber as a lizard, while Cal glared through the glasses at the door.

She came out at last, the girl of his dreams, and stood, watching the gallant show. Cal put down his glasses and looked up at the sky to ascertain if he had to stand for that. Then something occurred to him and he went back to his horse, where his rifle was slung on the saddle. It was unethical, of course, to take a shot at a rank stranger, and in some quarters it might be misconstrued, but Crump had fired at him twice and—well, anyhow, why be a worm? Why let this procession of sharpers and tinhorns pass over his frame in a row? Why not turn and sting them, play the tarantula to their scorpion, and see if they wouldn't go around him? He raised his sights to 800 yards, but Crump had disappeared into the barn.

Cal laid down his gun and picked up his glasses. The rope spinner was saddling up his horse. He rode him out the gate where Cal had been turned away and began to build what he called a wedding ring. As he came riding back, trying to jump his horse through it, Cal held well ahead of him and pulled. The bullet struck in the powdery silt, throwing up a plume of dust near the gate. When Cal saw he had shot low, he held a little higher, shooting twice, as fast as he could. But the first shot had been enough. After one startled look, Crump had ducked and spurred for the house.

The rush of his flight almost ran him into the bullets that had been aimed between him and the gate, and in the cloud of dust that rose Cal could not tell for a minute whether the Texan was down or not. The chances of a hit were practically negligible or he would not have fired at all, but, as he grabbed for his glasses, his heart missed a beat, because luck had been against him of late. But, no, the luck had changed, and he laughed to the brazen sky—Crump was running like a rabbit, unhurt.

Chapter Six

THE BIG NEWS

The Golden Bear Mine was in a formation that men liked—where the granite of Frémont Peak came in contact with the porphyry of the volcanic ground to the east—and yet after the first big strike the Golden Bear had never really paid, and the leasers had completed its ruin. They had robbed his pillars, letting the roof down here and there and rendering the whole mine unsafe. The best that the son of old Sam Watson could do was to burrow for stray stringers on the surface. Even the stringer ground had been worked and worked again, but after every rain some new gold would appear, and in a pinch he could go chloriding underground. And, since even foxes must have holes and the birds of the air their nests, Cal Watson made his home at the mine.

There was a cave house under the creekbank that was snake-proof and watertight, having at least eight feet of roof and a fireplace beneath the air shaft that served also as a chimney, keeping it warm on wintry nights. In the heat of desert summer it was the coolest place for miles—all the more reason for making it snake-proof—and a kitchen beneath the overhang of the quarried-out roof made an ideal place to cook. The tepid waters of Bitter Creek formed a pool below the house where dishes and clothes could be washed, and a five-mile ride to the old stage station below gave him the finest drinking water in the land. There was enough bunch grass on the flats and up among the rocks to feed his animals for months, and, except for the cattle that drifted in to drink, there was nothing to disturb his dreams.

The cattle belonged to Barksdale, and Johnson and Barksdale, the brands being J Prod and JB, and, as Cal rode up the cañon and found them hanging around his house, he sent them on their way with a yell. Nothing that belonged to Sol Barksdale or Whispering Johnson was welcome at the Golden Bear, and these same old cows on several occasions had broken in and raided his camp. Besides, his mood had changed, and every time he thought of Crump, he whooped until the silent places echoed. It didn't take long for the idea to percolate after that first bullet had struck up the dust, and, unless all signs failed, there was someone back in Texas that was looking for Crump with a gun. If by any chance, the cattle detective should discover who it was that had fired the shots, even then Cal was satisfied. Crump had fired the first shots, thinking to make his bluff stick, and this was to give notice that he was called.

A long week passed, a week of brooding peace, before the blood began to stir in Cal's veins, and then it stirred but faintly, for Omar Khayyám had put him under his spell. It was like the call of the lotus-eaters to one whose heart was sick, but at last he made a pretense at going to work. In the gulch below his house some long-departed Mexican ore thieves had built a stone *arrastra* for crushing rocks, and, after chloriding around the dump, Cal hitched his mule, Lemon, to the sweep and started him on his monotonous rounds. Attached to the other end was a heavy granite block that dragged ponderously around a trench paved with stones, and beneath this ponderous millstone the picked ore, submerged in water, was ground at last to mud. All the gold that it contained worked between the millstones, where quicksilver had been deposited to catch it, and, after the sump had been sluiced away, Cal could gather with a spoon little balls of blackened amalgam. This he placed in a buckskin bag, through which he squeezed the bulk of the quicksilver, roasting out the rest in a homemade retort.

Next to being a timekeeper it was the easiest job in mining, and it paid day's wages and more; only, of course, it led nowhere, beckoned on to no great future, held forth no dazzling hopes. It was a lazy man's job and, after his whirl at high finance Cal found it both satisfying and restful. There was no sense of wasted time, for his *arrastra* was producing, since the mule did the work, and yet after each clean-up he would have his bead of metal, virgin gold that had been wrested from no man. It came from the earth, where it had laid hidden for ages, until some crochet in man's brain had conjured up the myth that it had wondrous value.

Cal had built him a shade by the side of his *arrastra* with a couch where he could sprawl out and read, and, while Lemon, blindfolded, toiled dutifully around and around, the owner of the Golden Bear dreamed. The bell on Lemon's neck almost lulled him to sleep with its faraway, musical *tonk, tonk,* the muffled rumble of the millstone was infinitely soothing, and the heat made him nod as he read. Even *The Dalton Boys in Texas* failed to hold his thoughts, and he was dozing, when Lemon stopped. One lop ear was raised, pointing off down the cañon, the other ear was swiveled inquiringly toward the boss.

"Gyup," murmured Watson, reaching sleepily for a rock, and Lemon followed on after his leading string.

"Git up!" grumbled Cal as the bell stopped again, but this time Lemon gave a warning snort. Both ears were at a point, straight as a weathervane down the cañon, and at the tramp of a horse Watson jumped. Someone had ridden

44

clear in on him while he was asleep at the switch—he reached over and snatched up his gun.

"Hello, Lemon!" called a voice, and Cal laid the gun down again—it was Armilda, out riding the range. There were times when the stern discipline that her father maintained broke down with astounding completeness, and then she mounted Stranger and went racing across the flats until her lawless fit was spent. This was one of her days, and, as he rolled out of the shade, Cal felt that she had come with a purpose. There was something about her voice and the steady look in her eyes that told him she was camping on his trail.

"Well, poor old Lemon!" she exclaimed endearingly, dropping down from her tall horse to run to him. "Has he gone and blindfolded you again?"

She stripped off the old gunny sack and left Lemon blinking in the sun while she turned and looked at Cal.

"Well, your conscience is all right," she observed enigmatically.

Cal replied with a guilty grin. "Yes, no one looking for me," he hinted maliciously, and at that her face came straight.

"Don't be too sure of that," she admonished. "And, besides, your conscience isn't so good. Didn't I see you reach for that gun?"

"You might've," he admitted. "A feller shot at me a while ago. Maybe you heard about it . . . it was down at your ranch."

"Yes, I heard about it," she said, and stood gazing at him.

"What was the old man's idea?" he asked at last, and she shook her head and looked down. What she was thinking he could only guess, but when she looked up, there was something in her eyes that he had never seen before.

"I don't know," she replied, "but it wasn't my idea . . .
you're just as welcome as ever at the ranch."

"Yes, sure," he grumbled, "but he promised to kill me if
he ever caught me talking with you again."

"Then I don't need to look for you?" she inquired half
scornfully.

"I didn't say that!" he flared back. "I'm not afraid of
your old man, and I'm not afraid of that tinhorn,
Crump. . . ."

"Then what did you shoot at him for?" she demanded
instantly, and he saw that the fat was in the fire.

"What did he shoot at me for," he shouted angrily, "the
limber-legged, imitation bad man? And the dirty dog
slammed the water gate in my face . . . what do you think of
a trick like that? No, I don't care if I never come to your
ranch again . . . a place where they'll deny a man water . . .
but I'm going to come whenever I feel like it, just to show
that poor simp what I think of him."

"He knows," she said, fetching out three empty cartridges
and rattling them significantly in her hand. They were the
empties from his .30-30—someone had been up there and
found them—but something told him it was not Wayne
Crump.

"I suppose he sent you up there?" he suggested sarcastically,
and the hot blood leaped to her cheeks.

"That is none of your business," she stated defiantly.
"And I didn't think you'd do it," she added.

"Do what?" he demanded. "Take a shot at that jumping
jack?"

"No . . . suggest that he sent me," she answered.

"Well, now, say," he began, shifting his feet uneasily,
"you might as well tell me the truth. If you're in love with

46

that man, just say the word . . . come on, I want to know."

"That is none of your business," she said.

"Oh, blazes," he muttered and stood silently. That was answer enough, from Armilda. "Well, all right," he sighed. "I think you're making a mistake, but I'll never speak against him again. We've always been friends, Armilda, and we'll be friends yet. That is until . . . well, good bye."

"But I'm not going yet," she protested demurely, after she had allowed him to shake her hand.

"Oh? No, of course not," he replied, laughing shakily. "No, don't let me hurry you off. We've always been friends, and we're always going to be. That is . . . do you want a drink of water?"

"That's what I came over here for," she answered calmly, plucking his canteen down off its hook, and, as she took a drink, Cal gazed at her furtively while his heart went dead in his breast. He had thought he knew Armilda, but never again would he admit that he knew any woman. She was hardly more than a child, brought up out on the desert—and to carry it off like this! Not a tear, not a tremor, not a word of explanation, she just stood there and smiled and let him do the talking. But, then, that was always her way. When the smile would not answer and she had to resort to words, she could make them cut like a knife, but that was not her way; she much preferred to smile and let the world think what it would.

"Well, what's the news?" he asked, when she had seated herself comfortably, after loosening the cinch on her horse.

She glanced over at him teasingly. Somehow never in his life had he seen her more radiant, and there was a joyous glow back in her eyes.

"Haven't you heard?" she twinkled, and, when he swore he had heard nothing, she shook her head and smiled. "Not yet," she decided, "you'd lose all interest in me . . . the way you did before. After you went through to the Thousand Wonders you might as well have been dead. All you thought about was that mine!"

"Oh, no," protested Cal.

She brushed his defense away. "Don't say it . . . it will only make things worse."

"Well, what's the news, then?" he reiterated, although it made no difference to him now if the world had started to crumble at the poles. The point was that by his negligence, and working his head off at the Thousand Wonders, he had lost something that could never be regained.

"I've learned a new song," she announced. "It's the ninth one in the course. I just hate those finger exercises, but the song is called 'My Rosary'. It's wonderful. I'll sing it for you sometime."

"All right," he assented, although rather drearily. "When I get my new piano, I'll invite you over. How'd you come to find those cartridges?"

"Oh, I just rode around"—she laughed—"until I cut Lemon's tracks behind the ridge, and then I followed up to where you had been. I didn't think you'd be quite so careless."

"Little brainstorm," explained Cal. "Things had been kind of going against me. No offense, I hope, back at the ranch?"

"We-ell, I couldn't quite say that," she replied. "You'd better not sleep quite so much. When people get excited, there's no telling what might happen . . . we've promised to be friends, you know."

"Sure." Cal nodded. "Well, it's perfectly natural. But he shot at me first, you know."

"We weren't going to speak of him," she suggested reproachfully. "But, oh, I haven't told you the news I was going to tell you as soon as I got through talking about myself. But when am I going to see you? Can't you come down to the ranch sometime? You can wait until they're both away."

"Nope," he said, "might make you a widow or an orphan. Go ahead now . . . what's the big news?"

"Haven't you heard a thing . . . about your mine or anything? Oh, I don't believe you've been out of this cañon! But, say, when you see me racing around down on the lakebed, that means that I want to see you. If I'm wearing a white shirtwaist . . . otherwise, stay away from me, because I'm busy now, hunting up my calves."

"All right," he assented, "but why don't you come on over here? I might not be watching the lake."

"Well, watch it," she scolded. "Oh, I see you'd never do . . . and then you go and say . . . 'Oh, blazes!' " She laughed to herself as she stepped over to her horse and tightened his cinch with a jerk. "Do I look all right?" she asked, swinging lightly into the saddle and tucking her riding skirt in place. "You know . . . oh, I haven't told you . . . we've got some neighbors down below, and I'm going to call on Missus Polley!"

"Pol-ley?" repeated Cal. "I never heard of them before. You say they're camping down below?"

"Yes, down at the Thousand Wonders . . . haven't you honestly heard about it? But be sure you pronounce it Pol-ley! It's spelled Polley, you know, like a parrot or something. . . ."

"No, but listen," broke in Cal, "what about the Thousand Wonders?"

"Why, it's sold. Haven't you heard?"

"No, and I never will, the way you keep on stringing me. Make it brief, now . . . you bought it, and for how much?"

"Well, then, Johnson bought it . . . for five hundred dollars. And he turned around the same day and sold it for ten thousand to a. . . ."

"Ten . . . thousand!" yelled Cal. "I knew there was something funny or he'd have robbed me of every danged cent."

"Yes, and then that party turned around and sold it to Polley for twenty thousand dollars."

"Aw, you're fooling!" he protested.

She shook her head, laughing. "They're camped there, right now."

"Yes, but twenty . . . thousand . . . dollars! He must be a millionaire!"

"He is"—she nodded—"like you read about. A colored cook and a valet . . . four tents up already . . . and, oh, yes, his wife has got a lady's maid."

"What, down there?"

"Down at the mine. And they have a truck out every day, to bring them fresh provisions and ice. I'll have to hurry along or I'll be too late for dinner . . . shall I tell them that you'll be down soon?"

"Yes, sure," he mocked, "tell 'em I like my chicken à la Maryland. You're feeling real devilish today, aren't you?"

"Well, yes and no," she said, "but if you want to hear the truth, I'll tell it on a stack of Bibles. The day after you shot us up I went into town to visit with Ellen and Mary Johnson, and Whispering Johnson came over, and . . . well, you know how he is . . . he pays me all kinds of attentions. How can I help it . . . he's their uncle, isn't he? . . . and, anyhow, he told me all about it. It seems there is a coffee merchant who lives in Los Angeles and comes to Soledad often . . . selling his coffee, you know, to the store . . . and the day before you arrived there this Mister Eccleson wired Johnson to buy him a gold mine quick. That's all he said, except that his limit was ten thousand, and Whispering Johnson thought of *you*. It had to be a mine, no prospect hole would do, and first he thought he'd buy the Golden Bear, and then your miners came in and he heard that you were broke and that Hunnewell had thrown up his bond and lease. Well, you know the rest of that, and the minute you left town, he wired a full description of the mine. The coffee merchant bought it, sight unseen, and the next day they came out in a lovely big limousine and showed Mister Polley the mine. And, oh, he just thought it was the finest mine in the world and went into ecstasies over it, and on the way back he gave them twenty thousand in new banknotes, and Johnson and Eccleson each took half."

"I don't believe it," declared Cal. "Whoever heard of buying a mine . . . ?"

"Well, I'm telling you," she said. "You can believe what you want to. I'm mad now, so I guess I'll go. But, Cal, be sure to remember what I told you about the lake . . . you know, about my signaling and all?"

"Signaling?" he repeated, looking up at her blankly, and she jabbed a wicked spur into Stranger.

"Oh, shoot!" she exclaimed. "It's no use . . . I see you're hopeless." And she rode off down the cañon at a gallop.

Chapter Seven

A LITTLE SALE

There was no more work at the Golden Bear that day. Cal's peace of mind was as thoroughly disrupted as though Armilda had done the job with a bomb. He grabbed his field glasses and scrambled up the peak to look at the country below. The Thousand Wonders Mine was up a side cañon, a mile or more southeast of the old stage station, but he could not see the mine, nor could he see the station, which was under the brow of the hill. A drifting cloud of dust on the west side of Dry Lake marked the progress of some wagon or automobile, but except for that and chance glimpses of Armilda the country was absolutely lifeless.

He watched her dubiously, still puzzled at the mood which had prompted her madcap visit. At most times she was silent, or satisfied with few words, but this time she seemed bent upon completely overwhelming him, and she handled her news like dynamite. First she had jarred him to the depths by showing him the three cartridges and accusing him of shooting at Crump, and then on top of that she had practically admitted that she was engaged to marry the brute. Not for a minute did she deny—although she was ashamed to admit it—that Crump had sent her up on the ridge, and, after giving Cal fair warning that the Texan was on the warpath, she had blown him mile high with the big news. Whispering Johnson had sold the mine, which he had broken his back to develop, for $20,000 cash.

Here was a tale, if he believed it, to make a man doubt his destiny and question the beneficence of his Creator, for why should Whispering Johnson be given $10,000 while he, who had earned it, got $500? He had worked at the mine until his knees were weak with hunger, until he reeled at his task and fell. Yes, he had played out his hand, driving his men to their labor until they had turned at last and beaten him. He had worked and he had starved, and then Whispering Johnson had stepped in and taken the reward.

But Cal would not believe it, not until he had seen this man for himself, because Armilda had not been herself. She had been too excited, too radiant and gay, too much given to mischief and laughter. But if she turned out of the main road and rode up the Thousand Wonders trail. . . . He waited, and she took the turn! But even then she might be riding to the mine to make good her boast to him. That did not necessarily prove it was sold.

He strode back down the hill and wandered about restlessly, cooked his own meal, and grumbled as he ate, then, snatching up his glasses, he climbed the hill again and looked out over Dry Lake. Not a sign of her anywhere, and the column of dust had turned into a lumbering truck. He watched it intently, and at the fork in the road it turned and went up to the mine. It was true, then, the mine had been sold to Polley. Every word that she had told him was true.

He sat stunned at the thought, running over the absurdities of this modern *Arabian Nights* tale—the coffee merchant buying a mine before he had seen it, the mad haste and groundless ecstasy of the millionaire, and then his sudden move to the heart of the desert with his wife and his menservants and maidservant.

"I'll go down and see this bird," he declared with decision, and the next morning, early, he started. It was time for him

53

to make another trip after drinking water, so he loaded the water cans on Lemon. But when he came to the stage station, he kept on going, for there was no one camped at the spring. The water cans were light and Lemon would tag along anyway, since he and Campomoche were inseparable. In order to make a pretext for dropping in on Polley, he went up to his unsold claim. This adjoined the Thousand Wonders, being a north extension of the same vein. The idea had come to Cal that he might sell it to Polley, if he was still in the market for mines. The Thousand Wonders Mine was well worth the purchase price, for it had at one time yielded a rich pocket of gold and, through development, such as this millionaire could afford, might easily expose the main ore body. Just at this moment, of course, the Thousand Wonders was in *borrasca,* but it was on the same vein that had produced the Golden Bear, and that had been a real mine. If Cal could sell his claim for, say $20,000 more, he might make the Bear a real mine again.

The Gold Dollar claim, as Cal had named this prospect, was just over the ridge from the Thousand Wonders, and, after inspecting it carefully and picking up a few samples, he rode up on the hill and looked down. A large, striped tent house, surrounded by three smaller ones, stood on the flat just below the mine and a gang of carpenters was busily engaged, building a bunkhouse up the wash. Everything was exactly as Armilda had stated, and Cal's heart leaped with joy, for up at the mine he could see men at the windlass and there was a chance they might make a strike yet. And a strike at the Thousand Wonders would put the district on the map and make a market for his Gold Dollar claim. He withdrew unseen and, riding in on the trail, approached the camp from below.

It was built on a low bench just above the broad sand

wash that writhed like a rattlesnake between the hills, but in escaping the floods they had exposed themselves to the wind, which rushed up the cañon in savage blasts. The sides of the smaller tents bulged out like balloons at each sudden swoop of the wind, and the canvas on the tent house drummed and thundered against its framework or fell suddenly to a shuddering calm.

"Hello, there!" Cal shouted.

A woman laughed. "Come here, lit-tle darling," she entreated.

"Oh, for heaven's sake," scolded a man, "don't begin on that again. You know he won't obey you, Lura. Why don't you give him a good slap, and then maybe he'll keep still. Oh, my Lord, he'll drive me crazy."

The woman laughed again as the dog leaped at the door, but no one got up to open it.

"Hello, there!" Cal called again, and at the sound of his voice the dog went into a frenzy of mad barking. There was a sound of scurrying feet on the light wood floor, the slam of a screen door behind, and around the corner of the house a woolly dog rushed out, rearing back and barking at him spitefully. Still, no one moved, until suddenly a chair was scraped back and a man came stamping out.

"Here Buster!" he snapped, and then, back through the door: "If you don't make him stop, I'll slap him!"

"You slap him," spoke up the woman, "and you'll have me to slap. He's my dog, understand. Here, Buster!"

Buster retreated precipitately before a charge from Lemon that had an antipathy for dogs, and his barking became muffled beneath the house.

"Well, good morning," greeted Cal in the comparative silence, and the man glanced at him sharply. He was a well-built, heavy man, very red in the face, and with a bristling

55

head of iron-gray hair. Under his jowls a pair of dewlaps hung down like the pendulous cheeks of a glass blower. Cal turned against him the minute he saw him, but he tried to conceal his dislike.

"I was just coming through, and I thought I'd stop a minute and. . . ."

"What do you want?" demanded the man, and Cal's prejudice against millionaires became transformed to a positive hate. Here was a man who was his neighbor, and had just bought his mine, a man to whom he might be of service, and yet the minute he began to speak, he cut him off short with a surly question. Now there was one thing Cal needed and had intended to ask for, and that was a little salt, but he had never thought of asking for it at first— that could wait until he was ready to go. However, he was ready to go now, and at the glare in Polley's eyes he decided to make it brief.

"I want some salt," he replied, above the barking of the dog, and Polley seemed to take fresh affront.

"I don't know," he observed, "that we have any salt."

"Well, that's all right," explained Cal. "I've got everything else, but last night some cattle got hold of my salt sack and spilled it all out in the dirt."

"Is that so?" observed Polley as if he seriously doubted it. Then: "Where are you from?" It was a belated effort to make amends, but Cal only scowled at Polley forbiddingly.

"You can keep your salt," he said.

"I asked where you are from," spoke up the millionaire peremptorily, and Cal turned in his saddle to annihilate him.

"I'm from hell," he sneered, "and I'm going to hell. Where the hell are you from, Pussy?"

Then, spurring Campomoche, he cantered off up the wash with Lemon frisking gaily after him. He had not ridden long before he got a surprise.

"Hel-lo, there, Watson!" hailed a voice from the hillside, and, glancing up, he saw Peggy McCann. He was standing at the mouth of the inclined shaft where the Thousand Wonders went down on the vein and was waving his hand delightedly. "Come up!" he beckoned, and Watson rode up the trail, regardless of what Polley might think.

"Well, well"—Peggy grinned, hobbling forward to shake hands—"so here we are again, back at the mine. You hadn't been out of town two days when I gets the old job back as foreman. And this time I've got a good boss. No rushing, and dri-iving, and . . . 'Hurry up, byes!' *Whsst* . . . he's afraid to go underground! Can you beat it? I'm telling you the truth!"

He stopped and winked and cocked his ear down the shaft.

"Listen to that, now," he said, and laughed. Cal listened and heard men's rumbling voices, but not so much as the tap of a hammer. "It's the same old gang," leered Peggy. "Big Pat and the rest of 'em . . . but we've got a Britisher for a superintendent now. He's a coffee merchant, mind ye . . . and some fortuneteller told him he'd meet his death under the ground. 'Enough,' he sez, 'no undherground for me!' So he spends all his time in Los Angeles, buying machinery . . . and knocking down something arful, the scoundrel. The big boss is jist as bad. He ain't been down the shaft, ayther, so we're taking life aisy, putting in short holes, if anny, but shooting a scad of powdher. *Brromp!* she goes at the end of each shift, and the smoke is so bad we can't go down for two hours, but the boss, he thinks it's grand. What, him a mining man? He couldn't make money falling down an air shaft at sixteen dollars a foot, but to hear him talk you'd think he was Senator Clark and George

Winfield of Nevada, combined. But it's a funny thing, Cal, the way the luck breaks for these tenderfeet. You wouldn't believe it, but listen, lad . . . the ore's coming back."

"Coming back," repeated Cal, and Peggy nodded wisely as he handed him a specimen of the rock. It was the same crystalline white quartz that had occurred in the first pocket and it was shot through and through with fine gold.

"The first round of shots," declared Peggy impressively. "Jist like you said, when we quit."

"Is there much of it?" inquired Cal, and, when Peggy nodded sympathetically, he turned and rode off without a word.

Chapter Eight

"IT TAKES AN OLD CAT TO KETCH 'EM"

What the desert country was coming to with its new class of citizenry was too deep a question for Cal. First one citizen had refused him water and then another one had refused him salt, and why God Almighty had not struck them both dead was still a mystery to him. The great-hearted men who had made up the Old West were gone and almost forgotten, and now in their places there were the Barksdales and Johnsons, and Mr. Polley with his wife and dog. Polley ran a truck into town to bring out ice for his champagne, but when a stranger came by and asked for a little salt, he didn't know that he had any. And yet, why repine? The thing to do was to get in and trim the ringtails! A week went by while he was pondering upon the problem, and then he smiled again. There was a big wash boulder buried down in the creekbed that had held his thoughts from the first. It was of polished white quartz with three threads of gold running through it like fairy skeins. In its present position it was of no great value, being too hard for him to break up and mill, but differently situated it might take on a value far above its intrinsic worth. For here, although it was float, it was merely a tribute to the worked-out wealth of the Golden Bear, but at the mouth of the wash that led down from the Gold Dollar it would take on a different significance.

All gold has a source, and the placer gold of Sierra Nevada rivers led at last to the mighty mother lode, since which time it has become a habit with every good prospector to trace each piece of float to its origin. Hence, although no word or deed of Cal's even hinted at such a thing, the mere discovery of this gold ore in Gold Dollar wash would lead to one inevitable conclusion—that it had come from some hidden ledge on his claim. And if, following this conclusion, some millionaire should try to skin him by buying his claim for a song, then let the buyer beware, as the Roman traders used to say, because the price would be $20,000—cash.

Cal buried the boulder where the trail from the Thousand Wonders was dry. When Polley's men packed their water from the spring, they would pass it by every day. A white boulder like that, peeping up out of the sand, was sure to catch the eye, and unless they were blind—or so it seemed to Cal—those three lines of gold would simply jump at them. Cal waited four days, only to change his views on eyesight, and then, during a rainstorm, he uprooted the boulder and made it a stepping stone across the stream. Two days later it was gone, and, down by the station he found a prospector's camp.

"Good enough!" he nodded, and, hurrying back home, he waited for the lightning to strike. It was a long, weary wait, but at last, over the ridge, Whispering Johnson came riding down.

"Hel-lo," he bellowed, "how's the bad man from Bitter Creek?" But Cal only glanced out at him sourly. He had been reading a book titled *How to Win at Draw Poker*, and the first rule was: *Don't talk!*

The game does not require speech, the wise book went on, *except when cards are asked for.* Cal was not asking for cards.

"What's the matter?" demanded Johnson. "What are you all bowed up about? Are you sore about losing your girl? Well, never mind, kid, it takes an old cat to ketch 'em . . .

I've had my eye on Armilda for some time!"

"Yes, and she's had her eye on you, you big, fat slob," taunted Cal when his heart would behave. "You think you're a winner, don't you?"

"Never mind," hinted Johnson, "me and Armilda understand each other. It's the money that counts, these days. I may not be pretty, but I get there just the same. You just wait, that's all I can say."

"Well, I'm waiting," returned Cal. "What the hell do you want now? Come out here to collect another bill?"

"*Aw*, now." Johnson laughed, getting down off his horse and taking a drink from Watson's canteen. "You don't need to get ringy about it, Cal. A man ought to be glad to pay his honest debts . . . say, I did pretty well with that mine. Sold it to Evan Polley, the millionaire railroad man. Have you been down to see him yet?"

Cal shrugged his shoulders and started the mule again—he was still grinding ore in his *arrastra*—but whether or not he had been to see Polley was left largely to Johnson's imagination. Evan Polley was the man he had set out to lure with his boulder, and he hoped to sting him yet, but in the meanwhile he observed rule two in *How to Win at Draw Poker*, which refers to playing them close to the chest.

"He's a rich guy," conceded Johnson, "and he's sure got a pretty woman, but they say he's a tightwad in matters of business . . . has he been up to see you yet?"

"Who . . . him?" demanded Cal, and then he laughed enigmatically. Whispering Johnson was trying to string him.

"Well, you're a sociable guy!" observed Johnson sarcastically. "What makes you so gabby today? And, by the way, why don't you get out and do something, instead of camping on my water and running all my cattle away? Wayne Crump, my stock detective, reports the cattle have

61

left here, and he says you're driving them away."

"Well, whose land is this?" inquired Watson pointedly. "And don't get the idea that this water is yours. It rises on my claim, on my patented land, and it's located under a mill site to boot."

"That makes no difference!" began Johnson. And then he paused—there was other business afoot. "Now, listen, Cal, you're making me a lot of trouble, and I don't want you on my range. What'll you take to sell out and move out of the country? These claims ain't worth working, no-how!"

"Huh!" grunted Cal, and turned away from him indifferently, for in draw poker the big thing is bluff.

"I'll give you five hundred dollars," stated Johnson with finality, "and not a red cent more. And if I can't get shet of you this way, peaceably. . . ."

"Well?" prompted Cal, but Whispering Johnson preferred to leave it unsaid.

"Five hundred dollars," Johnson rumbled belligerently. "Come on, now, I've got you in the door. Ain't my brother, Dave, the sheriff of this county, and didn't I put him in his job? Well, what's the use of fighting when in twenty-four hours I can have you on your way to the pen?"

"You can't do that," replied Cal, forgetting the rules of poker, "and, if you could, I wouldn't sell."

"Well, name a price," blustered Johnson. "I don't want any trouble."

"A million dollars," jeered Cal, and Johnson gazed at him fixedly while his loose lips drew into a line.

"I'll give you five hundred for this claim, and five hundred for the one below, and that's every cent that I will give."

"The one below?" repeated Cal, and then at last he saw what Johnson was driving at. He had been leading up to this all the time.

"I suppose," he suggested, "you figure on selling it to Polley? Well, the price is twenty thousand this time."

"I figure," stormed Johnson, "on getting you off my range before I have to pinch you for cow stealing. Now . . . you've been fishing for the news and you've got a mouthful. We're on to your game, that's the size of it."

"Yes, and I'm on to your game," retorted Watson defiantly, "but you can't make me out a cow thief. My father was in this country before you ever heard of it, so I've got a better right here than you have, and, if you're looking for any trouble, I'll accommodate you right now, while there's nobody else to butt in on us."

"Don't get excited," warned Johnson as Cal took a step toward him, "don't take too much for granted, Watson. I happen to have a man up behind that ridge. . . ."

Cal glanced up quickly, and over the top of a rock he saw a tall hat that he knew. It was the brown velour sombrero of Wayne Crump, the stock detective, employed by Johnson and Barksdale.

Chapter Nine

A BARGAIN

Whispering Johnson took pains to explain, before his unhurried departure, that it was all in the nature of a joke, that no offense was intended and none was taken, and he would be glad to talk business with Cal any time. Then he mounted his big horse and rode off over the ridge. Watson stepped into his cave house. The big sombrero had disappeared, along with Whispering Johnson, but there was one place at least where Wayne Crump was dangerous, and that was behind a rock. He had a bad look in his eyes—a wild, wicked look like the gleam in a bronco horse's eyes, and Watson realized now he had been playing with a rattlesnake that was likely to fang him any time. He had shot at him from the rim rock and now Crump was out to get him.

There was no more work that day for the long-suffering Lemon, and Cal had a rifle between his knees as, from the slopes of Frémont Peak, he watched Crump and Johnson through his glasses. First they rode down to his claim, stopping long at the stage station where quite a number of prospectors were camped, and then they appeared in sight again, riding at a lope across Dry Lake until at last they arrived at Bubbling Wells. It was sundown by that time, and Cal could imagine the long evening, with Whispering Johnson bellowing coarse witticisms and Crump looking on slyly while Armilda said never a word.

But what was this that Johnson had more than hinted at,

that there was some understanding between him and Armilda? Was it possible that this girl, little more than a child, was playing those two oafs against each other? And if that was the case, where did Cal Watson come in—unless he was hopeless, as she had said? There had been a suggestion of mischief—no, almost of malice—in the way she had repeated that phrase, and now he began to wonder if it was not a veiled rebuke, perhaps even a maidenly hint to change his ways. If, as Johnson had vulgarly stated, it was only the money that counted these days, then Johnson would have been married himself, long ago, but Cal knew several ladies, unmarried and widowed, who had rejected both him and his gold.

Yet the thought would come back as he lay on his bunk in the tomb-like silence of his cave that, if he could only make a sale, and make it quick, a change would come over his life. Now he was a prospector, poor and out at the knees and elbows, but with money in the bank he could protect himself from insult and bid defiance to both storekeepers and millionaires. And if by some trick he could wrest this money from Polley, making him the laughingstock of gods and men, then even from him he would receive the grudging respect that is the due of the man who wins. Unfortunately the finding of the boulder had been ignored, and any move on his part would make things worse.

The next morning he was up at daylight, looking the country over warily from the rocky point that rose above the camp, but the only hopeful sign was an addition of two more burro men to the prospectors' camp at the station. Unless Polley had made a new strike, or was advertising his last one, it was the news of Cal's boulder that had brought them, and, although he ached to go down and find out what was in the wind, he knew it would be remembered against him. No, the only thing to do was to stay away entirely, not even go down after water. Then in a few days, if the break did not come, he could figure that he had lost again. He had set his trap, not for water hole prospectors, but for Johnson and Evan Polley, but, while Johnson had nibbled, the big bite, if it came, would be from the millionaire miner.

That day dragged wearily, with neither enemies nor friends dropping in at his lonely camp, but the following morning, although a sandstorm was raging, he saw Armilda riding against it across the lake. First a big cloud of dust would sweep down from the sand hills and envelop her completely for a minute, and then she would appear again, spurring resolutely against the wind, until at last she gained the shelter of the peak. The dust was behind her now, picked up from the sand hills that encircled the hard floor of Dry Lake, and with Stranger at a gallop she ranged off toward the west as if hunting for cattle in the draws. She looked like any cowboy in her jumper and leather chaps and her sombrero tied down over her hair, but Cal knew the horse, and he would know Armilda anywhere, although by what he could hardly say.

She disappeared up the main wash that came down from Frémont Peak, and Cal waited and watched in vain, until suddenly he heard a rock turn on the ridge just above him, and she came romping down after a cow.

"Hello, stranger!" he hailed, jumping out from his shelter and striding down the cañon to meet her.

She laughed as she brushed back her hair. "Who're you talking to, my horse or me? Say, have you seen any of my Triangle Dot cows?"

"Well, there's that one you were just running," he answered shamefacedly, "but I drove those other water bums away."

"Water bums!" she echoed, and then her lips grew tight.

"So it's true then . . . you've been driving them off!"

"That's a fact," he admitted, "but not your stuff, Armilda . . . they're welcome as the flowers in May. Get down, and tell me the news."

"No," she decided, "I had no business to come up here. But you might give me a drink of cold water."

He handed her the canteen and watched her again as she balanced on her horse and drank. She was wind-swept and dusty, but still in every line there was something that held his eye—she seemed more beautiful than ever.

"Get down," he said, holding up his hand. After a quick look, she yielded. "You're looking fine," he volunteered. "Kind of windy for chasing cows. What's the news from down below?"

"Well, I don't know," she murmured, glancing down demurely.

"How's your music?" he inquired, still watching her closely, and suddenly she looked up and flushed.

"Oh, do you care?" she asked, and, when he nodded, her eyes filled up with tears. "They don't," she stated, and struck the tears away as she sat down beneath the brush shed. But *they* was a subject that could not be discussed, and she returned to the safe ground of music. "I've learned a new song," she beamed. " 'The Night Has a Thousand Eyes'!"

"A thousand eyes?" he questioned.

"Yes . . . the stars, you know. Oh, I'm getting so I just love music. It's all so symbolical and full of poetry . . . I get tired of windmills and cows. That's all those boys talk about, at least when I'm around. Come down and I'll sing for you some time."

"Well . . . I'll do it," declared Watson impulsively. "That is," he qualified, "if I can get up to the house without

67

running into a bunch of Winchesters."

"Oh, they won't shoot you," she assured him earnestly. "That was all . . . oh, well, I can't explain it. But you might come by when the men are all away, that is, if you'd like to do it."

"Well, all right," he agreed, although rather doubtfully, now that he considered certain angles of the case, "but I don't like . . . well, what your father told me. You know, Armilda, maybe it wouldn't look quite right if I came over to see you, after that. It might look kind of like sneaking, and as if there was something to it when he told me not to speak to you again. Of course, I'm not that kind of a man, but it would give people a chance to . . . to . . . well, make trouble for you."

"Very well, then," she cut in, "you don't need to come. I just rode up here today to warn you about your mine."

"My mine?" he inquired.

She gazed at him resentfully for his apologies had hurt her pride.

"Yes, your mine," she answered. "I guess that's all you think about. But, anyhow, I wanted to tell you not to sell your Gold Dollar claim for nothing, because they've found some rich float on it somewhere. Why don't you go down there and begin to develop it?"

"Takes money," he objected, "and where can I get it . . . that is, unless you can stake me?"

He showed his teeth in a broad grin at this joke, but she was looking at the ground, drawing lines with a piece of stick.

"I would," she answered soberly, "only I'm not quite of age . . . and Father won't give me a cent."

"You would!" he cried. "Well, I begin to believe it, although it doesn't reflect much credit on your judgment. But I don't want your money . . . wouldn't even dare to take it. Your father would kill me, sure."

"No he wouldn't," she said, looking up with a quick smile. "I can keep a secret, I guess."

"Well, now, say!" he exclaimed after a moment of deep thought. "Perhaps you can help me, yet. How would you like to go in with me, strictly on the q.t., you understand, and make five or ten thousand dollars? It might come in handy if you had to leave home or . . . well, they tell me you're going to be married."

"Who told you that?" she demanded, and from the fire in her eyes Cal knew he had gone too far.

"Never mind," he said, "only I hope it isn't true."

"Never you mind!" she flared back. "I guess I can take care of myself, and I don't need any advice from anybody. But at the same time," she went on after a pause and a sigh, "I would like to make some money."

"Well, now, listen," he began, looking her straight in the eye. "Will you promise not to tell this to anybody? Because, if you do, I'll. . . ."

"I promise," she said. "What is it?"

"It's a chance," he said, "to make some easy money if you're willing to do what I say. If we succeed, you get your half. I'm trying to sell this claim that you rode up to warn me about, and I'm trying to sell it to Polley. Now . . . you go down and see him and make him want to buy it, and we'll divide up, fifty-fifty."

She looked at him again, to make sure he was in earnest, and drew some more lines in the sand.

"I don't like that Missus Polley," she said at last. "If it wasn't for her, I'd do it."

"What's the matter with her?" he complained.

"She'd spoil it," she predicted. "And, besides, I don't

69

like her . . . she isn't what Mother called a lady."

"Oh," he grunted and let it go at that. "What about Johnson?" he suggested at last, and she raised her head with a jerk.

"Was he the one," she demanded, "that was telling that stuff about me? Well, I'll do it, just to teach him a lesson. But you've got to promise me what I promised you . . . never to speak about this to anyone."

"I promise." He nodded.

But she was gazing at him curiously. "I wonder if you will? It means more, you know, to a woman. And you must promise never to ask me how I got him to buy it . . . you won't think any the less of me?" she faltered.

"Why, no," he answered, wondering. "Why should I, Armilda? Aren't you helping me out of a hole? On the contrary, I'll never forget it . . . and I promise never to ask you how you did it. The day I get the money, I'll give you your half of it. That closes the business, forever."

"I promise," she said, suddenly holding out her hand, and they shook on it.

Chapter Ten

"TURN ON THE BLOWER"

$10,000 was to be the purchase price when Whispering Johnson bought the Gold Dollar, and, when she had wrought her spell, Armilda was to give the signal by riding circles on the floor of Dry Lake. That was an old Indian sign, indicating big game in sight or the approach of some hidden enemy, and Cal was then to mount and ride into Soledad, where the big chief was lying in wait to scalp him. If Armilda had done her part, Johnson would be crazy to buy, and all Cal would have to do would be to put up such a front that Johnson would think he was robbing Cal. Anything short of that and Johnson would never buy, for he was a wolf when it came to a trade.

The signal came in three days—there had been some quick work somewhere—and Cal rode for town all grinning over the approach he had figured out to a nicety. It began with a rollicking gallop down the main street of town, where he drew up in front of the bottle house. After tying his horse and mule where Johnson would be sure to see them, he went in and ordered drinks—drinks for all. After they had clinked with him, he set out to win the hearts of the Irish. That was easy, as it turned out, for they love a good spender—and wasn't he a friend of Peggy McCann? But about the time he was getting a good start, the last of his money was gone.

"Well . . . gold then!" he swaggered, bringing out his

buckskin sack and slapping it down on the bar. "I guess old man Watson's boy knows how to find the dust. Weigh it out and give me a roll!"

"That's good gold," observed Larry, bringing out his old scales and stirring it about on the paper, "good gold. I'll give you eighteen dollars an ounce. Did you get this out of your mine?"

"Never mind where I got it," returned Watson boastfully. "I got it and I know where there's more. And I don't forget my friends . . . didn't you feed me when I was hungry, that night I came in with Peggy?"

"Well, I might've," admitted Larry with becoming humility, "but I guess you know you were welcome. What about this strike the byes have all been telling about . . . is that where you got all this gold?"

"Er . . . how's that?" inquired Cal whose wits seemed suddenly muddled. "Can't understand what you say. Well, good bye boys . . . be back soon . . . going down to see Johnson." He stumbled out the door into the street. It took him some time to get into the saddle, but, once mounted, he went down the street on the jump and reined in with a yelp at the store.

"Hello, you old slob!" he shouted at Whispering Johnson, who was standing in the doorway, watching him. "Why don't you buy a clean shirt, like I'm going to do, and set up to be a gentleman?"

"Huh! Gentleman, eh?" retorted Johnson caustically, and then he gazed at him fixedly. The news had come from Larry's Place that Cal had made a strike and was spending his gold dust like water. He said nothing, therefore, following Cal into the store and waiting on him while he bought some new clothes.

"Now I want to ask a question," began Cal importantly,

after he had bought a new hat and some shoes. "Is my credit good at this store or not?"

"It's good," returned Johnson, "if you've got the money to pay the bill. Otherwise, it ain't worth a cent."

"Oh, it ain't, eh?" sulked Watson. "Well, I guess I can't trade then. You wouldn't trust me for a pint of whiskey if I was snake-bit."

"Well, are you snake-bit?" bellowed Johnson, shoving his face into Cal's and glaring at him savagely. "You ornery son-of-a-goat, you've been buying your licker at Larry's Place, and now you come to me, asking for credit. Here, you pay for these goods, and you pay right now, or you don't take 'em out of the store."

"Well, all right," agreed Cal, fumbling drunkenly for his roll, "but, say, I want some powder and grub. I got the finest mine on the Mojave Desert. . . ."

"Yes, you have," jeered Johnson. "Here, you're three dollars short . . . is this all the money you've got? Well, gimme back that hat, then, or gimme the shoes. . . ."

"Take the shoes," said Cal. "I don't need 'em."

"No, you need a guardian more than anything else," grumbled Johnson as he put back the shoes. "Here's two dollars back . . . them shoes was five dollars."

"Well, g'bye," mumbled Cal. "Buy a drink! Buy a drink, boys!" he whooped as he bulged out onto the street. "Have another one! Turn on the blower!"

He mounted with difficulty and rode back to Larry's Place, whence he returned even drunker than before. Or, at least, so it seemed, although there were people who swore later he could always hit the ground with his hat.

"What you want?" demanded Johnson who had followed him, made more wolfish than ever by this second defection to Larry's Place. "You crazy, drunken fool, can't you read

73

that sign up there? Well, that says . . . The Keno Bar!"

"W'y . . . yes, sure," clamored Cal, tumbling down off of his horse. "Come on, boys, let's have another one!"

He started for the bar, but Johnson laid hold of him.

"Not on me!" he said, and gazed at him so sternly that Cal knew the big moment had come. "Come in here," he ordered, and Watson followed meekly until they were alone in Johnson's private office.

"Now, for cripes' sake," began Johnson, "what the devil has come over you? Are you out of your mind, or what?"

"W'y, no," returned Cal. "I'm not out of my mind. Say, did you ever hear the story . . . ?"

"No!" thundered Johnson, "and I don't want to, either. Can't you talk about anything but Watsonville?"

"I never mentioned Watsonville," defended Cal with dignity, "but say, now, you want to remember that name. I've got a mine up here, the Golden Bear, that's the richest danged gold property in the West. It hasn't been scratched, hardly, but those leasers got in there and robbed the pillars until it's kinder unsafe. It's a rich mine, I say, and you'll live to see the day when there'll be a big town up there . . . Watsonville! It'll be named after me, just like that other big camp was named after my father, Sam Watson. Say, that's a good name, ain't it? You've heard of Sam Watson? Well, I'm old man Watson's son. No, now, listen, I came down here to talk business . . . didn't you tell me to come down yourself? Well, I need some grub . . . and some powder and timbers. . . ."

"All right," spoke up Johnson, who had been biding his time, "you can have 'em . . . what've you got for security?"

"Security?" repeated Cal. "I guess I don't understand you . . . I'm not feeling very well today."

"You'll be better," predicted Johnson, "when you ain't

been drinking whiskey . . . you've been getting what Saint Patrick killed the snakes with. But here, now, I'll tell you, you've got another property . . . that Gold Dollar claim. . . ."

"Nothing doing!" announced Cal. "Absolutely!"

"No, but listen," urged Johnson.

"*You* listen!" returned Cal. "There ain't money enough in Soledad to buy one tenth of that claim!"

"There ain't?" demanded Johnson. "I'd like to know why not . . . how much do you want for your claim?"

"I want ten . . . thousand . . . dollars," said Watson solemnly. "And there ain't that much money in town. But what's ten thousand dollars? I could get twenty thousand any day if I'd just say the word to Evan Polley. But he insulted me, the ringtail. He let his little dog bark at me . . . and he refused to lend me some salt."

"You're drunk," declared Johnson, moving away in feigned disgust, but the phenomenon of drunkenness was not such a rarity as to cause special comment in Soledad.

"You will not!" shrilled Cal. "I know you, you old highbinder. You're the man that beat me out of the Thousand Wonders. That was a good mine, savvy, best mine in the country, but I was broke then and had to pay my debts. You turned around the next day and sold it for twenty thousand dollars . . . cash. 'Stung!' says I, 'but never again. Next time I deal with Polley direct!' "

"Yes, *you* deal with him!" returned Johnson contemptuously. "You seem to forget who you are. He wouldn't even talk to you. But if it was me, now, that approached him about. . . ."

Cal rose up laboriously. " 'Nother drink, boys," he muttered, making a start for the door. "Turn on the blower, the air is getting bad!"

"Where you going?" demanded Johnson with easy mastery, placing one foot against the door. "Didn't you hear me? I said I'd buy that mine."

"You did not!" contradicted Watson. "Not anything of the kind. You said you'd take it for security."

"Well, I say it now, then," replied Johnson. "I've got use for that claim. Here's my check for ten thousand dollars."

"Your check!" yelled Watson. "Who said anything about checks? I said ten . . . thousand . . . dollars. Cash! You savvy that? Ten thousand dollars. There ain't that much money in town."

"The hell they ain't," sneered Johnson, making a line for his safe.

Cal swayed on his feet and watched him. "No, they ain't," he asserted, "or I'd never have said it. That mine is worth millions, and I know it. But this petty larceny dog town . . . this dump hole of creation. . . ."

"There's your money," snapped Johnson. "Shut up!"

Chapter Eleven

ARMILDA SINGS

A word against Soledad was a word against Whispering Johnson, for he had built up the place and owned it, and, after paying off Cal Watson and making him sign the papers, he told him briefly to get out of town.

"And don't you come back," he warned him, "until you can keep a civil tongue in your head."

Cal rode out of town, laughing, after buying a last drink and a quart bottle in case of snakebite. But as soon as he struck the hills, he smashed the bottle on a rock and shuddered as he reached for his canteen.

He turned up a wash that came down from the *malpais* and slept for an hour in the warm sand. Then, after sundown, he moved camp again, for he had $10,000 in his clothes. It was nearly all new money and Cal had been suspicious, until Johnson had blurted out the truth. It was his share of the proceeds of the Thousand Wonders sale, and Polley would handle nothing but new money. Every day, when he was in the city, he sent his man to the bank to get him $100 in clean bills, and, when he had come to inspect the mine, he had brought the money with him, $20,000 in new treasury notes.

Cal roused up at daylight and counted them over again—it was exactly what Johnson had robbed him of. No, it was five hundred more, because it had cost Johnson that much to buy the mine in the first place. Well, let it go, then, as a $500 fine for attempting to defraud a drunken miner. Cal put the roll away with a smirk. Whispering Johnson might be a wolf, but *he* had been a fox, and, when the story came out, if it ever did, Johnson would be badly hacked, to say the least. It was a blow at his prestige as the big boss of the desert and might invite reprisals in kind, but Cal was in funds now and $5,000 would go far toward getting him out of jail. For Johnson was primarily a political boss, ever mindful of his influence and power, and the fact that his brother was sheriff of the county was brought up whenever he was crossed. He would threaten him, of course, as soon as he discovered the deception, but, if Cal knew Dave Johnson, there would be no spite work done merely to keep up the family prestige. For Dave was a good sheriff in his slow, quiet way and his daughters were especial friends of Armilda Barksdale, who might help him out in a pinch.

But the morning after a clean-up of $10,000 was no time for gloomy forebodings. Cal had made a dry camp and slept in the rocks, but he still had one duty to perform—he must give Armilda her money. She had done her part well, else Whispering Johnson's safe would never have contained the $10,000, and it was no more than right—and a pleasure to boot—to deliver her share to her at once. It should never be said of him, or thought for a minute, that he depreciated her services, and, if he found the coast clear, he resolved that very day to see her and put the money in her hand.

The sun was just taking the chill out of the air when Cal crept up and looked over the rim, and, although the regulation sandstorm was sweeping in from the west, he could see the ranch buildings plainly. The cowboys, Jack and John, were saddling up in the corral, the windmill man was greasing his wagon, and, as they started off on their rounds, Sol Barksdale came out and caught up his big, fat horse. As a cowman Sol Barksdale was more or less of a joke, that is among his own men, for although he rode out on the roundup and even presumed to direct it, he seldom or never rode the range. Perhaps he was afraid of the sandstorms and the solitude and the long, desolate reaches behind the rim, but day after day, while his horse grew fat and soft, Sol Barksdale lingered close to the ranch.

Some said, and they were right, that he did it to watch Armilda lest she should leave him after the manner of her mother, but the truth was he was an Easterner with no idea of the hard riding that is necessary to safeguard a brand. He did not realize the dangers of that desert range, with its prospectors and Indians and competing cowmen, and, when on the roundup his calf tally came short, he was satisfied to hire a detective. But this morning he evidently had business in town, for he rode off up the trail toward Soledad. Cal watched him uneasily, for, once up on the rim, the ranchman could take him in the rear, but Barksdale passed by, unconscious of the eyes that followed him, until he disappeared on the road to town.

They were all gone now except the man Cal hated most, and, as he lay in the wind waiting for Wayne Crump to depart, Cal's anger grew apace. He was hungry and thirsty after his dry camp in the lava, and, except for the fact that his errand was secret, he would have ridden down and out-faced the Texan. But Crump strode out at last, racking about on his high-heeled boots and, stepping up on his fine horse, went galloping away to the east. Cal turned west and, coming down through the pass, swung back and rode up to the ranch.

Armilda was practicing, going over her finger exercises as if they were the most important thing in the world, but when she heard his step on the kitchen porch, she came running out to meet him.

79

"Oh, I'm so glad!" She laughed, catching hold of his hand and dragging him willy-nilly into the house. "I've been hoping you'd come all day!"

"Well, here I am," he said, smiling dubiously at her enthusiasm, "but I'll have to make it brief. I came by to give you your money."

"O-oh! Did you get it?" she cried, and a wild look came into her eyes as he laid the pile of bills on the table. But as he spread the money out and began counting it methodically, she closed her lips and waited.

"There's your share," he said, shoving half of it over to her. "I'd better go, before somebody comes."

"No . . . wait!" she pleaded, scurrying off with the money and returning with a plate of candy. "Oh, why do you have to go?" she cried reproachfully. "They won't be back for hours. And you're starving, I just know it, so eat some of the candy while I cook you. . . ."

"No, really," he protested, "I've got to go, right now. We've pulled this off perfectly, and it would be a shame to spoil everything by. . . ."

"But they're gone," she insisted. "I know they won't be back. Don't you want to hear my music, or anything?"

Cal took a piece of fudge, and, seeing her eyes begin to fill, he strode into the big adobe room. Here by the fireplace they had often sat together while he told her of the glories of old Watsonville, and here also he had sat while she sang the old home songs that she had learned from her departed mother.

"Just one," he consented. "I've got a hunch . . . I ought to go . . . but sing 'The Night Has a Thousand Eyes'."

"Oh, it's beautiful," she sighed as she sat down at the piano, "and you don't know how much I miss someone to listen to me, after so little appreciation."

She spread out the music, and he listened expectantly as she sang the first verse of the song:

> The night has a thousand eyes,
> And the day but one;
> Yet the light of a whole day dies,
> With the setting sun.

"Is that all?" he asked, and she turned back to the beginning.

"There's another verse," she murmured. "I didn't know whether you'd like it. They . . . I only sing one verse, for them."

She ran over the introduction, fingering each phrase with loving care, and then she began the real song. Before, she had been timid and a little self-conscious, but now her voice was vibrant with emotion she could not hide, and he seemed to sense a message—to him:

> The mind has a thousand eyes,
> And the heart but one,
> Yet the light of a whole life dies,
> When love is done;
> Yet the light of a whole life dies,
> When love is done.

Cal rose from where he sat and gazed at her curiously, fingering his hat, yet unwilling to go, for, if the words were meant for him, then Armilda really loved him, but, of course, it was only a song.

"Isn't it beautiful?" she demanded, taking his hat away from him and laying it back on the table, and something rose up and choked him.

"Yes." He nodded, and the something that had choked him made him add: "And so are you, Armilda."

"Oh . . . I don't know," she said, twisting about uncomfortably but keeping her clear eyes fixed on him. "You . . . you aren't making fun of me?" she asked.

"No," he replied, and reached resolutely for his hat, "but Armilda, I've got to go."

"You've forgotten something," she pouted, putting the hat behind her. "I . . . you may not see me again."

"May not see you?" he cried.

She nodded soberly. "There's another song," she said.

"Oh, sure!" he exclaimed. "But what do you mean . . . are you thinking of leaving soon?"

"We won't talk about it," she sighed, pushing him gently away. "Do you want to hear 'The Rosary'?"

"Well, yes!" he assented, sitting down reluctantly. "But Armilda, if you're thinking of going away. . . ."

"There are two things now, that we're never going to talk about . . . and the other is . . . going away."

She went back to the piano and struck the first chord, as if dismissing the matter forever, and then her mood changed, and she sang this other song whose words might mean everything or nothing. If she loved him, they meant everything, but if not, they were only words, the words that went with the song. Nearly all songs have words that, if spoken from one to another, would mean a confession of love, but it was the way Armilda sang it, more than the words themselves, that made the song seem for him.

> The hours I spent with thee, dear heart,
> Are as a string of pearls to me;
> I count them over, every one apart,
> My rosary, my rosary.

Each hour a pearl, each pearl a prayer,
To still a heart in absence wrung;
I tell each bead unto the end,
And there a Cross is hung!
O memories that bless and burn!
O barren gain and bitter loss!
I kiss each bead and strive at last to learn
To kiss the Cross, sweetheart! To kiss the Cross.

Cal rose up impulsively and strode over toward her, but, as he passed the door, he glanced out instinctively, and there on the porch stood Crump.

Chapter Twelve

A MATTER OF BUSINESS

When a snake is enraged, he gives forth a stinking odor that sweats from his skin like poison and his glazed eyes shoot forth hate almost as deathly as the venom that slavers down from his jaws. Wayne Crump was a step advanced above the reptile, but the look in his eyes as he glared at Cal had something of the age-old hate in it. His eyes were pale blue, without a trace of the steely hardness that is supposed to go with the bad man, but they were wicked in their intensity and his thin, knife-cut lips were drawn to a cruel line. Cal stood like a statue, struck dumb with surprise, until Armilda read his eyes and stepped in front of him.

"Oh, hello, Wayne," she said, looking him over coolly, but he never moved his eyes from Watson.

"What are *you* doing here?" he demanded at last, and Cal became suddenly at ease. He was almost glad, now that the first shock was over, that Crump had surprised him with Armilda. Because if he had heard aright, there was a message in those two songs, a message from Armilda to him, and, if this lanky Texan was the cause of her tragedy, he could intervene as a friend. Whether she loved Crump or hated him, Cal did not know, but he knew all too well that Wayne Crump was the man who had come between him and Armilda. He smiled indulgently, almost pityingly, on his enemy, and then exchanged glances with Armilda. It was a glance such as passes between lovers caught unawares and the detective's eyes opened wide.

"I was just making a friendly call on Armilda," explained Cal, and stepped out onto the porch. In the house he had the advantage of being in the dark, as compared with the blazing sun, but he had never feared Wayne Crump and he did not fear him now especially as he faced him in the open. For the man who fights like a snake in the grass seldom has the daring courage of the lion, and, besides, there was Armilda, to shame the man who weakened, and Cal knew he would not be the coward. She was standing there, expectant, a half smile on her lips, and he turned and glanced at her again.

"Am I right?" he asked her, and she answered very sweetly.

"Yes, indeed. I'm glad you came."

Crump looked at her then, as black as a thundercloud, and tucked his right thumb in his belt. "Well, you git," he said, turning to scowl at Watson, "and don't you never come back. You've been warned off this ranch, and now I want you to keep off. There's your horse . . . now build a dust."

"Is this your ranch?" inquired Cal with elaborate politeness, and the cattle detective drew down his brows.

"No," he replied, "but it belongs to Mister Barksdale, and, since I'm in his employ. . . ."

"It seems to me," suggested Cal, "you're taking your job too seriously . . . that is, unless you've got some special rights?"

He glanced inquiringly at Armilda, who gazed in turn at Crump, as if leaving the answer to him.

"Well, I have!" declared Crump, raising his head up arrogantly. "Now you git . . . and stay away from here, or you're liable to git filled full of lead."

"Yes, and I'm liable not to," returned Cal grimly, but

the heart had gone out of his defiance. Armilda had said nothing, so, of course, it was true, and there was no use putting up a fight. Crump had hypnotized her somehow, won her over in spite of herself, perhaps somewhat as a snake charms a bird, but that was no reason why he should bow down or take orders from a Texican stock detective.

"Very well, Crump," he said after a silence, "I won't make any trouble under the circumstances. But you want to get over that nervous habit of yours of shooting at folks you don't like."

He stepped to Campomoche, mounted, and headed for the gate.

"*You* want to get over it!" Crump called to him vindictively. "I seen you, hiding up on that ridge."

"Oh, you did, eh?" replied Cal, "well, don't think for a minute that I was up there hiding from *you*."

"No, you were waiting to shoot me, you bushwhacking coward. I seen you . . . !"

Cal reined in his horse and looked at him again, but something told him to spur off and be gone. Why stay bandying words when Armilda stood silently and let this man speak in her place?

"Well, let it go!" he called. "Good bye, Miss Armilda . . . I'll never forget the songs."

"Come and see me again!" she called after him cordially, and he bowed and smiled back wanly. But never again would he stop at that ranch until he and Wayne Crump had had their reckoning.

He watered his animals and rode off across Dry Lake with his head bowed to meet the storm. The wind came in great blasts, like the breath of some giant who sought to blow him off his horse, but Campomoche kept on, leaning up against the wind as if it were an unseen hand. Lemon staggered along behind him, almost lifted from his feet by the fury of the pelting sand, and it was not until they gained the protection of the hills that Cal looked up from his brooding.

"Well, let him live," he said. "But what she thinks she sees in him. . . ." He shook his head somberly and spurred on.

There was quite a camp of prospectors at the old stage station and moving among them like a king was Whispering Johnson, who had come out to work on his claim. Two trucks loaded with supplies were parked by the deserted station house and an overflow of miners had moved into the adobe stables, long since left vacant by the stage company. All was bustle and excitement, with Johnson bawling out orders or telling loud stories around the campfires, but when Watson appeared, the boss of the desert gave a whoop that echoed to the peak.

"Well, well," he announced, "here comes Bitter Creek and old Lemon. Two of a kind and a hard pair to draw to. Are you just getting over that drunk?"

"You go to blazes," answered Watson glumly, and the men by the campfires roared. It was evident that Johnson had been talking. Cal watered his animals and smiled wearily at the laughter, which somehow jangled on his ears, but after a hearty meal his tense nerves relaxed and he remembered the $10,000. From his point of view, and knowing what he did about the cause of this mining excitement, he could very well afford to let the heathen rage—except that he was acting a part. Although he had sold a worthless claim, or at least an undeveloped one, for more money than he had ever had in his life, he was supposed to be a victim of Whispering Johnson's machinations, to be a man who had got drunk and lost a fortune. Every prospector in camp was secretly laughing at him for his ignorance of what they all knew—the wonderful rich boulder that had been found below his property and the value it had added to his mine—and he could see the roguish twinkle in Whispering Johnson's eye as he led up to the subject of the sale.

"Well, well," he said as they were all gathered about the campfire and the time for his coup had come, "I suppose now, Watson, you think you're pretty cute to sell me this for ten thousand?"

"Ten thousand is lots of money," conceded Watson soberly, "but, of course, I know your game . . . you figure on selling out to Polley, the way you did once before."

"I figure on keeping it!" boomed Johnson triumphantly. "Why, you poor, drunken simp, I wouldn't sell that mine for a hundred thousand dollars, cash!"

"That's what you say," returned Cal, "because you know Polley's made a strike . . . and, of course, you're on an extension of his vein. But I'm satisfied. You're welcome to the trade."

"Oh, I'm welcome, am I?" Johnson laughed, turning to wink at the crowd before he reached back into the darkness. "How's *that?*" And he slammed down the boulder. Cal gazed at it as if dumbfounded while Johnson began to cackle, and then Cal made a jump and grabbed it.

"Who the hell stole my boulder?" he demanded savagely. "I had that buried in the crick!"

"Buried!" echoed Johnson, staring about in consternation, and a silence fell on the crowd.

"Why, sure," protested Cal, "I know that boulder well. It came out of the Golden Bear."

"You . . . lie!" choked Johnson, rushing over to seize him, but Cal struck him angrily away.

"What's the matter with you?" he challenged. "Are you

trying to start something? That's my boulder and somebody stole it!"

"They did not!" cried Johnson, almost sobbing with exasperation. "It was found below your Gold Dollar claim!"

"Oho!" exclaimed Cal, and then he burst out laughing. "I thought there was something funny here, somewhere."

"Funny!" roared Johnson. "You think this is funny? Here, you gimme back that ten thousand dollars! This is a phony sale and I can prove it in court . . . you was drunk when you signed the papers!"

"Drunk?" repeated Cal. "Well, what's that got to do with it? Did I try to sell *you* the mine? No, you tried to take advantage and beat me out of a bonanza and now, by grab, you're stung. If *I* wanted to break the sale, I expect I could do it by claiming that I was drunk, but where do you get off, making a claim like that, when you know you were perfectly sober? You'd look fine, now, wouldn't you, standing up before the judge. . . ."

"There's something crooked here!" yelled Johnson. "I know it!"

"Yes, there sure is." Cal laughed. "Don't you sleep in the roundhouse? Well, what are you hollering at *me* for? Why don't you take your old claim and sell it to Polley . . . he seems to be the prize sucker around here."

"I used to be," corrected a voice from the outer darkness. "But I'm not any more, I trust."

The crowd broke away, and, as they stepped back, staring, Evan Polley strode into the firelight. He was as immaculate as ever in a shooting suit and trim puttees, but his face, if anything, was redder than ever, and it was evident he had had a drink.

"Excuse me, gentlemen," he said, "for breaking in on your controversy, but I happened to hear my name spoken disparagingly. And allow me to state further that, while I may have been a sucker, I am no longer in the market for phony mines. At the same time I *am* interested in legitimate mining . . . will you permit me to examine this boulder?"

"Why . . . certainly!" exclaimed Johnson, bending before him officiously, but Polley was addressing himself to Watson, who responded at last with a nod. What this millionaire thought, or did not think, of the boulder was a matter of indifference to him, and he rolled a scornful eye on Whispering Johnson who was kowtowing as if to a god.

"Yes, very good," pronounced Polley, after inspecting the gold and putting away his eyeglasses. "I gathered, Mister Watson, from what I heard you say, that this boulder had come from your property . . . that is, from the Golden Bear Mine."

"It came from the creekbed, below the mine," answered Cal after a surly silence.

"Yes, but how far below?" put in Whispering Johnson suspiciously. "Didn't you say you had it buried?"

"Yes, I had it buried, if it's any of your business, because it was too danged hard to crack, but all I know is it came out of the Golden Bear, because I've found some more like it in the dump"

"Just a moment!" rapped out Polley, cutting short Whispering Johnson as he began some outrageous retort. "I was speaking to Mister Watson! And since, we cannot converse here quietly, I must ask him to come to my camp. Little matter of business, Mister Watson."

Watson drew a deep breath and regarded him fixedly.

"All right," he said, "if it's business."

Chapter Thirteen

THE BEST OF EVERYTHING

The striped tent the Polleys had once occupied was now miraculously replaced by a bungalow, and, as Watson rode up, the little dog that had yapped at him barked feebly from somewhere within. Evan Polley excused himself and stepped briskly inside. A colored servant hurried out to take the horses, and the next minute another one was bowing Cal in as if he belonged to quality.

Electric lights were turned on, revealing a room luxuriously furnished. The desert seemed a hundred miles away, and to complete the illusion a liveried butler appeared, bearing a silver bucket sweating with ice water. From the top of the bucket there peeped a long, slim bottleneck, which was capped with an enormous cork, and at the signal from Polley, as Cal sank deeply into a divan, the cork blew out with a loud report.

"Won't you join me?" invited his host, and, before he could refuse, a brimming glass was set at Cal's elbow. Here was efficiency plus, and alacrity plus. The Negro servants stepped about like acrobats, for, although he seemed to ignore them, Polley's weasel-red eyes followed every move that they made.

"That will do, Willis," he said, and the Negro butler bowed.

"Yes, suh, thank you, suh," he responded, and was gone.

Cal tasted his champagne and put it back, although the

bouquet of the rare vintage tempted him. Polley tossed his off and rang for the butler, who darted in, filled his glass, and was gone again.

"Good wine, eh?" smacked Polley. "I always have the best. The best of everything . . . that is my motto. I have the finest wine that money can buy, the finest food." He took another sip and Cal gazed at him curiously—he had come here on a matter of business. "Yes," mused the millionaire, watching the bubbles mount up the stem, "I have everything that money can buy, and money, in my experience, will buy anything. The finest drink, the most beautiful works of art . . . the most beautiful women, too. Yes, money, Mister Watson, will buy anything."

"That's good," said Watson dryly. "What was this business you spoke of?" But Polley was too busy to talk business. He was talking about himself.

"Nothing succeeds like success," he went on oracularly. "I succeed in whatever I undertake. I have built great railroads, huge factories, enormous industries . . . men call me The Empire Builder. But my empires are built. I have retired now with a fortune so safeguarded that nothing can wreck it. I have an assured income of more than I can spend that comes from my stocks and bonds, but, because I have succeeded and amassed a great fortune does not change my business principles one whit. I believe in careful buying, in avoidance of all waste, and at the same time the best of everything."

He emptied his champagne glass and rang absently for Willis, who popped in again and was gone.

"You may have wondered," continued Polley, still keeping to the subject, "how I came to purchase this mine. It came about through a very curious occurrence, though similar to many others in my life. My success, Mister

Watson, is not due to technical knowledge, though I know more than many so-called experts. It is due primarily to my knowledge of men, to my ability to pick the winners. An expert in chemistry or physics or transportation can be hired . . . and I hire the best . . . but the ability to judge men is the monopoly of a few, the lucky few who are destined to succeed.

"Now . . . I am a lover, as I told you, of good things to eat and drink, and especially I love my coffee. But good coffee, as you know, is very difficult to procure, especially in this new, Western country. In Los Angeles I was delighted when, after many disappointments, Willis brought me some coffee that was perfect. Now, here is the point that I'm working up to. I had discovered a man who could make perfect coffee . . . very well. He could succeed at other things. It is this ability to succeed that I am always on the look-out for, and I sent at once for the man. He was a Mister Eccleson, a small coffee merchant who made a specialty of blends, and after a short talk I saw that he was competent.

" 'Mister Eccleson,' I said, 'you make very good coffee. Have you anything else to sell?'

" 'No, sir,' he replied, 'I make a specialty of coffees, which I put up and sell myself.'

"Now there, you see, was the secret of his success, but I had roused what I had hoped for in his mind.

" 'Was there anything in particular, sir?' he inquired respectfully, and I came to the point at once.

" 'I want to buy a gold mine,' I said. 'Do you happen to know of one for sale?'

" 'Why no, sir,' he answered, 'but I'm quite sure I could find you one. About what price would you wish to pay?'

" 'Well, twenty thousand dollars,' I stated, 'but I must have the mine at once.'

" 'Never fear, sir,' he said, and in two days' time I had purchased the Thousand Wonders Mine. I made Eccleson my superintendent, and on the first day after arrival he reported they had struck rich ore. Since then the values have increased as if by magic, and today we have made a fresh strike. Would you like to see some of the rock?"

As he followed this astounding narrative, Watson sat in a kind of trance, vaguely wondering if the wine had reached his head, but, before he could reply, Polley had rung again for Willis, who returned with the quartz, as white as shattered crystal, and across its fractured surfaces there showed colors of yellow gold that gathered in little clusters in the iron rust. Cal sat back and gazed at it, and then at this wine-flushed millionaire who bought his mines from a coffee merchant, and his heart went sick at the thought. So this was the way that empires were built and empire builders added to their gain; all the knowledge in the world was thrown into the discard, and they went ahead—and won—on bull luck.

He lost all desire to talk business with Polley, who drank continually but never was drunk, and yet he was fascinated by this glimpse behind the veil, this revelation of the mind of a millionaire. Always before he had imagined them as just the opposite of all this, men who eliminated the element of chance, and who, by doing away with luck, made their earnings more certain and the lot of the common people more onerous. But here was a man who had the money to show for it, gravely telling him to follow nothing but chance, or, to put it more exactly, to eliminate chance by backing men who had the luck to win.

"What do you think of the specimens?" inquired Polley at last, and Cal shoved them away with the back of his hand.

"They're good," he sighed, and Polley beamed on him.

"I understand," he said, "that you are the man who discovered the Thousand Wonders Mine. May I ask how much you received for it?"

"Five hundred dollars," answered Watson gloomily, "but I always knew it was good."

"Then why did you sell it?" demanded the millionaire sarcastically, and, when Cal informed him, he smiled. "Quite right," he declared, "your men had to be paid. And you sold the Gold Dollar for ten thousand?"

A flicker of triumph leaped up in Cal's eyes as he acknowledged the sale by a nod.

"Very interesting," commented Polley, taking another drink and talking, as it seemed, to himself. "What price do you put on the Golden Bear?"

"I don't put a price," answered Watson indifferently. "I intend to develop it myself."

"Quite right," approved Polley, still speaking to himself. "And you say you expect to begin the work immediately? I wonder if you'd be interested in my plans for the Thousand Wonders . . . excuse me just a moment, if you will."

He rose up with a quick decision and stepped into the next room, where Cal could hear him moving about, but, as he sat listening curiously, he was conscious of a presence and Buster stood, smelling his leg. He looked up quickly and beheld a woman so beautiful that it made his heart stop, just to look at her. She was like a classic painting of a Neapolitan flower girl idealized to portray the *ne plus ultra* of charm, but, although every feature was perfect and her dark beauty made his head whirl, there was still something for the artist to do. Her red lips that were so voluptuous had a discontented droop and her eyes a rebellious glint, and after a quick, impatient look she ignored Cal completely while she snatched the bottle of champagne from its bucket.

"The drunken brute," she muttered, and disappeared through the doorway from which she had so mysteriously entered. Cal's eyes followed her into the darkness, and he caught the glint of the bottle as she raised it and took a long drink. Then she came tiptoeing back, and slipped it into the bucket with a smile of roguish malice.

"Here, Buster!" she called, in the throaty, emotional contralto that Cal remembered so well, but the woolly dog, after smelling Cal all over, had leaped up onto a couch by the fire. There in the middle of a gay silken cushion he was coiled up, feigning sleep, and his only response to his mistress' endearments was a guilty thumping of the tail.

"He-ere, darling," she entreated, and at the suppressed laughter in her voice Buster's tail thumped harder than ever. "Oh, you little ootsie-tootsies!" she cried reproachfully, and turned to glance boldly at Watson. "Isn't he the cutest little thing? But Polley will have a fit over that pillow." She giggled mischievously, and then her face changed as she paused to listen for Polley. For the moment she was not posing, her mind was on her husband, and Cal read her vindictive hatred in a glance. "Co-ome, darling," she drawled, and thrust out her lips as she waited for Polley to appear. "Ain't you that Mister Watson that came down here to get some salt?" she inquired with a coquettish smile. "I heard him refuse you, and it made me so mad. Next time you want some salt you ask *me!*" She accompanied this invitation with so languishing a glance that Cal blushed and looked around for his hat. A little more of this and Polley would be justified in bursting in on the scene with a six-shooter.

"But, oh!" She giggled mischievously. "I'll never forget what you said to him . . . it made him just boiling for days.

GET
4 FREE BOOKS!

You can have the best Westerns delivered to your door for less than what you'd pay in a bookstore or online. Sign up for one of our book clubs today, and we'll send you **4 FREE* BOOKS**, worth $23.96, just for trying it out...**with no obligation to buy, ever!**

Authors include classic writers such as
LOUIS L'AMOUR, MAX BRAND, ZANE GREY
and more; PLUS new authors such as
COTTON SMITH, TIM CHAMPLIN, JOHNNY D. BOGGS
and others.

As a book club member you also receive the following special benefits:
- **30% OFF** all orders through our website & telecenter!
- **Exclusive access to** special discounts!
- **Convenient** home delivery **and 10 days to return any books you don't want to keep.**

There is no minimum number of books to buy,
and you may cancel membership at any time.
See back to sign up!

*Please include $2.00 for shipping and handling.

YES! ☐

Sign me up for the Leisure Western Book Club and send my FOUR FREE BOOKS! If I choose to stay in the club, I will pay only $14.00* each month, a savings of $9.96!

NAME: _____

ADDRESS: _____

_____

TELEPHONE: _____

E-MAIL: _____

☐ **I WANT TO PAY BY CREDIT CARD.**

☐ VISA   ☐ MasterCard   ☐ DISCOVER

ACCOUNT #: _____

EXPIRATION DATE: _____

SIGNATURE: _____

Send this card along with $2.00 shipping & handling to:

Leisure Western Book Club
20 Academy Street
Norwalk, CT 06850-4032

Or fax (must include credit card information!) to: 610.995.9274.
You can also sign up online at www.dorchesterpub.com.

*Plus $2.00 for shipping. Offer open to residents of the U.S. and Canada only.
Canadian residents please call 1.800.481.9191 for pricing information.
If under 18, a parent or guardian must sign. Terms, prices and conditions subject to change. Subscription subject
to acceptance. Dorchester Publishing reserves the right to reject any order or cancel any subscription.

JOIN NOW!

It was the biggest insult, he said, that had ever been offered him. But you're a real Westerner, ain't you?"

Cal blushed deeper than ever and looked at her sheepishly, and she gave him just the suggestion of a wink.

"You ought to have knocked his head off," she confided under her breath, and waited eagerly for his answer.

"Nope, he's all right," Cal mumbled at last, glancing apprehensively toward the door. But Polley was still hunting for something he could not find and the inquisition went on.

"I know a man that's not afraid to stand up to him," she said, a trifle resentfully, "and that's that handsome Wayne Crump. He's been up to see me twice . . . he's a cowboy, isn't he? And, oh, I can't resist his slow smile. It's so . . . oh, fascinating. I wish he'd call again. Why don't you come down and see me, sometime?"

"Who . . . me?" stammered Cal, but, before he could frame an answer, Polley came bustling back. He had an armful of books and blueprints and drawings, evidently a part of his mysterious plans, but at sight of Buster reposing on his cushion he dropped them on the floor with an oath.

"How many times," he demanded of his wife, "have I told you to keep that dog off of my cushion? That's *my* cushion, understand? I sleep on it myself, and I don't want it all covered with dog hair. Get off of that, Buster!" He raised his hand threateningly, but Buster only crouched lower, gazing steadfastly into the eyes of his mistress.

"Oh, poo-or Buster," she cried in honeyed accents, "won't he let the little darling sleep anywhere? But don't be afraid, Mamma Lura will take care of you. Now, Evan, you stop swearing at that dog!"

"Well, take him off my bed!" wailed Polley impotently. "For heaven's sake, Lura, what's possessed you? I believe

97

you think more of that damn', dirty dog than you do of me, your own husband!"

"Come here, Buster!" she responded, patting her knee invitingly, and like a flash he was up in her lap. "*A-ah, darl-ling,*" she murmured, giving him a hug and a kiss, and Polley turned white with rage.

"Put down that dog!" he commanded in a fury. "You put him down or I'll kill him!" He made a step forward, but she glanced up at him saucily.

"No, you won't," she said. "You don't dare to."

"What's that?" raved Polley, going quite out of his head and beginning to storm in earnest, but she only stooped over and began to cuddle Buster, laughing throatily and glancing at Watson. As for Cal, he was so astounded at this unexpected outburst that he sat like a statue and stared at her. Louder and louder became the protests, the accusations, the appeals, and all the time she sat, petting Buster and laughing deep down in her throat. But now the laugh had changed until it sounded like weeping, the low, sobbing notes of hysteria, yet all the while she crouched there, still petting the dog, still glancing mischievously at Watson.

"Well, I've got to go!" Cal spoke up at last, and the next minute was riding off down the cañon. "Ex-cuse . . . me!" he muttered. "The best of everything, eh? I don't believe I'll buy my wife."

Chapter Fourteen

THE LAST WORD

It did not call for the gift of second sight to divine the domestic life of the Polleys. He had bought her for her beauty, and she had married him for his money, and now the battle of wits was on. If she by any ruse could get him to strike her, she would be off for the divorce courts and alimony, hence, her fondling of the dog, her saucy retorts, her shameless invitations to flirt. Cal could imagine with what joy she would greet the right young man—one who would pick a quarrel with Polley and shoot him in self-defense, later marrying the widow and fortune. But such a proposition carried no appeal for him, more especially since he had seen her in action. A woman like that would burn another Troy or incite another St. Bartholomew's Eve massacre.

Cal slept late the next morning, for he had barred his door and the light could barely struggle down his chimney hole, and, when he did arise, some premonition of trouble made him strap on his pistol for the day. Campomoche and Lemon were waiting outside for their customary bait of salt and sugar, and, after watching them a while, Cal was about to step outside when he saw their ears swivel down the cañon.

He picked up his rifle and closed the door to a crack, leaving the interior of his cave fortress dark, and presently he heard a horse clacking over the rocks, while Campomoche and Lemon stood snorting. Cal slipped his roll of bills into an inside pocket and waited for the trouble to break. Some holdover from his dreams or from the turbulent day before gave him warning that this was no friend, and he was not surprised when, standing beside the door, he saw Whispering Johnson ride up. He was peering about craftily from under the shadow of his black sombrero, and Cal saw him glance up at the ridge. Then he sat in his saddle, gazing hard at the door, which Cal had set temptingly ajar.

"Hello, in there!" he hailed, not too loud, and dropped down hastily from his horse. He tiptoed through the gate built to keep out the cattle, which made up Cal's first line of defense, and a minute later the door swung in softly and Johnson stood staring into the darkness.

"Well?" inquired Cal from the edge of his bunk, and Johnson jumped and laughed noisily.

"W'y, hello, hello! Thought you was dead or something. Why don't you answer when a man hails the house?"

"Never mind," responded Watson. "What are you tiptoeing around here for? Out snooping for that ten thousand dollars?"

"Judas Priest!" responded Johnson. "You gave me a start! I guess your conscience ain't feeling just right or you wouldn't be hiding in this hole. That was a hell of a dirty trick to play on an old friend . . . planting that boulder to sell your claim."

"What are you talking about?" retorted Cal. "You're a hard man to suit. First you get me drunk and bunko me out of my mine, and the next day you want to trade back. Or maybe you just came up here to rob me?"

"Well, I didn't come here for any recriminations . . . I came to get back my money. Or, if you don't want to pay, I'll tell you what I'll do. . . ."

"I don't," returned Cal, "so you can beat it."

"Beat it, nothing," snarled Johnson. "You don't know me, boy, if you think you can put this thing through. There

100

isn't a man on the desert side that can go up against me and win out. I guess you know who's sheriff of this county and who it was put him in . . . and that ain't all, by no means. I'm a hard man to whip when I know I'm in the right, and you sold me that mine by fraud. But I'm willing to compromise . . . you give me half of the Golden Bear and I'll. . . ."

"You get nothing," broke in Cal, "so don't stand around here, talking. If you want to go to court on this Gold Dollar sale. . . ."

"That ain't the point," complained Johnson. "I *know* you jobbed me . . . you wasn't half as drunk as you pretended to be . . . but I'm willing to let bygones be bygones. If you think this Gold Dollar sale was on the level and not a fraud, why ain't you agreeable to trade back again?"

"I will," suggested Cal, "if you'll trade back the Thousand Wonders. Now, that's fair . . . you can take it or leave it."

"Yes, but . . . well, this sale involves a fraud, because I know you wasn't that drunk. You've never been drunk before."

"Did I make any kick," inquired Cal, "when you made your big clean-up on the Thousand Wonders? You bought it for five hundred and sold it to Polley for twenty thousand, and never even offered to split a nickel. Well, now, it's the other way, and I've sold you the Gold Dollar for just exactly your cut on the Thousand Wonders. That's no more than what was coming to you, and maybe next time, Johnson, you won't be so crazy to roll a drunk."

"I knowed it!" declared Johnson, backing out through the doorway, "you framed that whole business from the start!"

"And you bit, you sucker," returned Cal contemptuously. "Go on, you poor, cheap sport!"

Johnson strode out to his horse, slamming the gate after him savagely, but, when he had mounted, he turned back. "I'll tell you," he temporized, "this is my last word, understand, before I haul off and smash you like a horsefly. I'll trade you the Gold Dollar for one half the Golden Bear, and you can keep the ten thousand dollars."

"Much obliged." Cal grinned. "I'll keep it, all right. I see your detective up on the ridge."

Johnson glared up hastily, but the ridge was bare and Watson laughed after him mockingly.

"I'll . . . fix . . . you!" bellowed back Johnson as he went galloping down the cañon, and Cal knew it was war to the knife.

He had known it from the start, else he would have listened to reason, perhaps even have agreed to some compromise, but Johnson was out to get him, and at the least sign of weakness he would smash him as he had said, like a horsefly. If Johnson only knew it, the Gold Dollar claim was worth ten thousand dollars of any man's money because Polley's last strike, when the news got out, would serve to boom the whole district. Any far-seeing mining man, after looking at Polley's quartz, would be glad to take over the Gold Dollar for it was on the same vein not only of the Thousand Wonders but also of the Golden Bear.

But Johnson was no mining man. He had proved a hundred times his absolute inability to judge mineral, and the desert side of Mojave County was strewn with worthless claims, foisted off on him by prospectors for grubstakes. Yet a hundred times over, after swearing off forever, he had yielded to the lure of gold. He had kept himself poor by ill-considered ventures, often concealed from his nearest friends, only to fall again at the sight of some rich nugget in the palm of some heat-crazed burro man. Then, when his name was a byword on the desert, he had made his quick turn on the Thousand Wonders, and his pride, beaten down by a thousand humiliations, had risen and burgeoned like Jonah's gourd.

He had told it far and wide, the tale of that quick buy and

the even more astoundingly quick sale, and the story of the boulder discovered just below the Good Dollar had set his blood afire. Here was the second big chance to prove his acumen and make a name in the mining world, and helter-skelter, without looking at the property, he had bought it and paid over the hard cash. Then, when his belly was big with the pride of it, Cal Watson had knocked him flat. He had shamed and humiliated him, not only before his workmen, but in the presence of Polley and all the prospectors. Soon, as Johnson knew, the tale of the wash boulder would be told all over the desert. It would pop up to his detriment every time he talked about mining or passed on the value of some claim, and Watson knew, none better, how warily he must walk if he would escape Whispering Johnson's wrath.

But the gods had been good to him and he had taken the first trick. Who could say he would not win the game? Only now he must bestir himself and not camp in that cañon until his enemies came back and potted him. He had the money at last to open up his father's mine and prove its worth to the world, and the time to do it was before Johnson could check-mate him or Crump could hatch up some fresh treachery. For a man alone, Bitter Creek was dangerous, the very solitude an invitation to foul play, but with a gang of men at work and his teams on the road men would think twice before invading his retreat. Cal saddled up his horse and started off across Dry Lake, but his destination for once was beyond Soledad.

That was Whispering Johnson's town and his destiny beckoned him farther, to Mojave City. Soledad was but a stopping place, a way station on the journey that would take him to the cities along the coast, and, when he came back, there would be cars on the siding laden with supplies for the Golden Bear. He would deprive Johnson of his profits—after that, they would see who was boss.

Chapter Fifteen

THE HOBO TRAP

When Sam Watson followed the game, every miner was his own banker—and his own shotgun messenger as well. When Cal started for town with his whole fortune in his pocket, he carried the old man's gun. This was a sawed-off shotgun, intended to be fired from the hip, and, since the stock was as superfluous as the long, bird-killing barrels, it had been modified to a pistol grip. It was now nothing more than an oversize pistol, like the huge horse pistols of Napoléon's dragoons, and Cal carried it in a sling underneath his left arm when it was not in its holster on the saddle.

The only train that would stop to take on passengers passed through Soledad shortly after midnight, and, when it was late, as it generally was, it was more likely to pull in about daylight. Watson rode into town more like a train robber than a passenger and left his animals in the bottle house corral. The hostler would know them when he saw them in the morning, and Cal watered them and fed them for the night. Then he slipped quietly away and went over to the freight warehouse where he could wait unnoticed for the train, but the night wind was cold and, when his train was reported late, he took shelter in the lee of the warehouse. But even this was not enough, and, finding a huge box half full of straw, he crawled in and laid his shotgun beside him.

An hour or more dragged by as Cal started at vague alarms and listened for the approach of passing hobos, but no yeggs came to root him out of his warm nest. He finally cocked both barrels of his shotgun and went to sleep. It was just breaking dawn when he was aroused from his dreams by a tremendous blow on the soles of his feet, and, as he clutched for his gun, the club descended again with a smash that made him yell with pain.

"Come out of that!" commanded a voice, and Cal shot off both barrels before he knew what he was doing. At the first stinging blow he had bumped his head against the box and the second blow had completed his bewilderment. The voice from without furnished a focusing point for his rage and he fired, as one strikes instinctively. He was brought back to his right mind by a shriek of terror from without and a terrible pain in his hand. Scrambling out of the narrow box, he saw a man running away from him, heading straight for Johnson's corral. The next instant the man ran into the barbed-wire fence and went down in a tangle of strands.

"Help! Help!" he shouted, trying to struggle to his feet. "Help! I'm shot! I'm killed! I'm dying!"

Cal ran halfway to him and then stopped short—it was Bill Beagle, the town marshal, that he had shot. That cracked, agonized cry was the voice of doom for him, for Bill was an officer of the law. He was an enemy of Cal's and a friend of Whispering Johnson's, and, if he died, Johnson would see Cal hung for it. Cal turned right about and ran around behind the warehouse, chucking his gun underneath it as he passed. Then out in the open, he swung around behind the bottle house and thence with the crowd to the shooting.

Bill Beagle was still calling in a voice to chill the blood. Men were endeavoring to untangle him from the barbed wire, but all the time he fought them off and implored them to get a doctor.

"Here! What's the matter?" inquired the bull voice of Whispering Johnson, and, while the rest stood back, he jerked Beagle clear and set him down in the dirt.

"I'm shot through and through," moaned Beagle weakly. "Oh, Gawd, boys, I'm going to die. It was a damned yegg that done it . . . he was sleeping in my hobo trap, and, when I hit him on the feet, he shot me!"

Cal slunk away at that, but, although he was sick with fear, he could not leave the spot. In a minute he was back again, fighting his way through the crowd that was trying to strip Beagle of his clothing.

"No! Leave me alone!" Beagle cried, sitting bowed up in the street and clasping his stomach with both hands. "Gawd A'mighty, boys, don't stay here pestering me . . . git out and ketch that hobo!"

"We'll ketch him!" promised Johnson. "Here, you straighten out, Bill. There may be something we can do for you. Grab his feet there, Charley. He's out of his head, and let's see where he's hurt."

"I'll help!" volunteered Cal, and, unnoticed in the excitement, he leaped in and straightened Beagle out. "Now light a match," he said, and, stripping back Bill's shirt, he exposed his billowing stomach to the light. But instead of the fateful pattern that a charge of buckshot makes, there was nothing but a line of scars. "Aw, hell!" spat Cal, dropping the match in disgust, "it's nothing but the marks of the wire!"

"What?" shrilled Beagle, suddenly coming to life again, but more angry at first than pleased. "You think I don't know when I'm shot? He plugged me with a six-shooter, and I felt the bullet distinctly . . . it went right through me, there!"

He fingered a place by guess and Watson laughed

hoarsely. "You're loony," he said, "it was a shotgun."

"Well, how do you know?" demanded Beagle in a rage, and then he leaped to his feet. "Arrest that feller!" he cried. "He's the man that shot me! By the Lord, it *was* a shotgun!"

"Why, sure it was," answered Cal, "and, if it had hit you at all, it would have blowed a hole clean through you. No, you scratched your belly trying to knock down that barbed-wire fence."

"I did not!" screamed Beagle as the boys began to laugh. "I'm hurt, and badly hurt. But I'm not too far gone to take you in, Watson. I suspected this was some of your work!"

"Well, it was," admitted Cal, "although I didn't know what I was doing . . . I can't even figure it out yet. All I remember is I was sleeping in a dry-goods box when some son-of-a-goat hit me on both feet, and the next thing I knew my shotgun went off and mighty nigh crippled this hand."

He shook his right hand ruefully and in the thin morning light the crowd stood and gazed at him grimly.

"Well, you come along," spoke up Beagle at last, after he had felt with trembling hands under his shirt. "I'm weak as a cat, but I'll run you in yet. Boys, somebody bring me a drink."

They adjourned to the bar at that, and, after a general drink, Bill Beagle's injuries were more carefully looked into. Beyond the row of scratches where he had hit the barbed-wire fence, he was found to be unhurt. Unhurt, that is, physically, for his feelings were so badly lacerated that he swelled and blew like a Gila monster.

"What was you doing in that there box?" he demanded of Watson, after a second and third drink had restored his courage. "Didn't you know I put that out there to ketch hobos?"

"No, I didn't," answered Cal, "but I wouldn't put it past

107

you. Hasn't a hobo got a right to live?"

"He's a vagrant," declared Beagle, "without visible means of support, and his sleeping there proves it conclusively. And now I'll just show you who's marshal in this town. You're arrested and charged with vagrancy."

"All right," challenged Watson, "you can arrest me, if you want to, but you do it and I'll sue you for false imprisonment. I was over at that station waiting for Number Nine to come in, and that gave me a right to be there, and, if you think I'm broke, just cast your eyes on that . . . is that visible means of support?"

He drew out his roll of bills and brandished them in Beagle's face, at which the marshal drew sullenly away, but, as he was heading toward the bar, Whispering Johnson reached out and grabbed him, talking rapidly into his ear. That was enough for Cal—he knew what was coming and made a break for the door. Before they could stop him, he was up at the corral and had the saddle thrown onto Campomoche.

"Just tell them that you saw me, boys," he chanted as he rode out the gate and hit the trail for home.

Chapter Sixteen

A MAN'S HOUSE IS HIS CASTLE

There was no doubt in Watson's mind as to what was coming next, when he fled from The Keno bar—in another minute he would have been arrested and searched and his roll taken away from him by force. Once Whispering Johnson got his hands on that bank roll, its value would be reduced to an expectancy. Perhaps, after loud and tedious litigation, Cal might recover it from the minions of the law, but that was not the way that he had learned to play the game. Cal had lost his chance to develop the Golden Bear by fleeing from the clutches of the law, but his heart was blithe and gay, and, as he rode up the trail, he laughed and spat despitefully at Soledad.

There was a town in which he had always had trouble, no matter how circumspectly he walked, but who would imagine that merely sleeping in a dry-goods box would bring down this avalanche upon him? If No. 9 had not been late, or if he had chosen another box, or if Beagle had not hit quite so hard—but why hold a *post-mortem?* He was still in the open and his roll was still on his hip. They would be mounting in hot haste and a measured pursuit, for his enemies would not press him too hard. What they wanted was his money, and Bill Beagle for one had learned to respect his gun.

Cal pounded up through the pass and down the long slope and across Dry Lake for home, but, as he circled his camp, he saw that someone had been there, for his gate was left open to the cows. Looking back across the flat, he saw three horsemen in the distance, riding in from Bubbling Wells. So, giving up the idea of hiding his money in his cave house, he turned back to the Thousand Wonders Mine. In a case like this what he needed was a friend, and, outside of Armilda, the only friend he could count on was the big Irishman, Peggy McCann. Peggy's leg had a hollow in the middle of it that would conceal several rolls such as his.

Peggy was standing as usual at the mouth of the inclined shaft, where he performed two men's work at the windlass, and the moment he sighted Cal, he began to signal him violently at the same time retiring to the tool house.

"Have you heard the news?" he demanded, his eyes bulging with excitement. "We've struck Golden Bear ore on the foot wall!"

"Yes, I've heard it," responded Cal. "Say, Peggy, how's that leg of yours . . . do the rats get into it at night?"

"Divil a bit they do." Peggy laughed. "Don't I wear it in me sleep? No, me leg feels that natural that, when I git up at night, I forgit all about its being arf. Manny's the tumble I had before I learned me lesson, and now I wear it with me to bed."

"Good enough," pronounced Cal, fetching out his roll of bills. "Put that in it, and no questions asked."

"No questions asked, he says." Peggy grinned, unstrapping his limb and slipping the bills inside. "And now Watson, me bye, you'd better beat it to the house, because the big boss himself is out looking for ye."

He hobbled back to his windlass, chuckling softly to himself. Cal took the hint to absent himself at once, the better to throw off suspicion. Polley, the big boss, was, indeed, out looking for him, having seen him ride past the house.

110

"Mister Watson," he said, "I owe you an apology . . . won't you stop over and join me at dinner? Because really we never got to the business that I spoke of, on account of that . . . er . . . unfortunate incident."

"Why, sure," answered Cal, "if you'll just call it breakfast and tell the Duke of Senegambia to get a move on. I left town this morning just ahead of a town marshal, and I see he's coming after me with a posse."

Polley laughed good-naturedly—taking the story for a joke—and soon his servants were hopping about like jumping jacks, but when he discovered that his guest was in earnest, his indignation knew no bounds.

"What's that?" he exploded. "They attempted to arrest you? They charged you with being a vagrant? I should begin a suit at once for one hundred thousand dollars for damage to my good name and reputation! Why, a man's good name is such a priceless thing that a hundred thousand dollars is nothing. I recovered two hundred thousand and a public retraction from a newspaper that scurrilously attacked me. They published a cartoon, reflecting upon my private character, and in two days I had brought them to their knees. I engaged three of the most expensive criminal lawyers in New York and told them to proceed, regardless of expense, and, when they looked up the law, those same defamatory newspapermen came rushing to tender their apologies. They had discovered that a man has certain rights in the courts that are commonly ignored and trampled upon. And since that time no paper in the United States has dared to question my good name."

"Well, that's grand," admitted Cal, "but what are you going to do when a man tells you his brother is the sheriff . . . and when he tells you further that in twenty-four hours he can have you on the way to the pen?"

"Did he tell you that?" stormed Polley. "He's a low-bred fellow. I never did like that Whispering Johnson."

"Yes, and more than that," said Cal. "Unless I'm badly mistaken he's coming with that posse to arrest me."

"The scoundrel!" cried Polley. "We'll soon bring him to terms. Mister Watson, will you do me a favor? I've taken quite a fancy to you, and it would give me great pleasure to tender you the services of my attorneys. They are hired by the year, so it will be no expense, but I declare this is one of the most despicable tricks that has ever come to my knowledge."

"Never mind." Cal laughed. "I've got my money hid, and that's what Johnson is after. It's nothing but a bluff. But if worse comes to worst. . . ."

"I'll defend you," snapped Polley, "never fear."

The clatter of hoofs outside the house roused him up with all the fury of a watchdog, and, as they looked out the door, Whispering Johnson came up, closely followed by Beagle and Wayne Crump.

"Just a moment!" warned Polley, carefully latching the screen door. "I forbid you to enter this house."

"We want you, Watson," said Johnson, crooking his finger. "Come out now and don't make any trouble."

"You remain here," directed Polley, thrusting Watson behind him. "Mister Johnson, you are on my private grounds . . . don't forget that a man's house is his castle!"

"Well, I don't know about that," answered Johnson judicially. "But no matter, we've come here to get Watson."

"Have you a warrant for his arrest?" inquired Polley sharply. "What is the charge against the gentleman?"

"Well . . . no charge as yet," hedged Johnson. "He's wanted for resisting an officer."

"Mister Johnson," began Polley, shaking his finger at him impressively, "let me give you a word of warning. You may be related to the sheriff of this county, but that gives you no immunity under the law. You are responsible for your actions, and, being a man of some wealth, you can be sued for heavy damages. Now I want to warn you right now not to enter my house without a search warrant, as the law requires. If you do, I will have you punished if it costs me a million dollars. Furthermore, I wish to inform you that Mister Watson is my friend and I am firmly convinced of his innocence. If you overstep your authority by arresting him without a warrant . . . unless you have seen him in the commission of some crime . . . I will direct my attorneys to defend him to the utmost and also to bring suit for false imprisonment. Now . . . what are you going to do?"

"I'm not going to do anything," answered Whispering Johnson grimly, and rode off without a word.

Chapter Seventeen

THE GREAT SECRET OF SUCCESS

"The great secret of my success," observed Evan Polley affably as he rang for another drink, "lies in the fact that I stand up for my rights. The United States is nominally a republic, but most of its citizens are enslaved. Every officer on his beat is a king in little, every sheriff is a law unto himself, every shyster is engaged in infringing upon men's liberties. To succeed you must stand up for your rights."

"I will," said Cal, "when I get to be a millionaire. Until then I'll just have to fight him."

"Well said." Polley nodded. "You have a keen sense of proportion, and that is the great thing in business. Would you mind telling me a little more about your past life?"

He listened attentively as Cal ran through his history, and then he nodded again.

"Good!" he pronounced, and sat pondering the matter. "I think we can do business," he said. "You remember, Mister Watson, the rather unusual circumstances under which I bought the Thousand Wonders Mine. I purchased it not so much because I wanted a gold mine as to demonstrate my theory of life. 'Nothing succeeds like success' has always been my motto, and Mister Eccleson has proved it conclusively. This man, I understand, has never been underground in his life on account of some fortuneteller's prophecy, and yet, despite his ignorance of the first principle of mining, he has led me to a very rich mine.

"Now, here is the point I have been gradually working up to . . . I believe that you also are a winner. You have the rugged qualities that make for success, and, besides, you are a mining man. Although it was Mister Eccleson who helped me purchase the Thousand Wonders, it was you, Mister Watson, who discovered it, and it was only the fact that you felt obligated to pay your workmen that induced you to part with it at all. Have you any other claims which you could honestly recommend to me, and, if so, at what prices do you hold them?"

"Well," began Cal, and then he stopped, for he feared to commit himself rashly. "I own the Golden Bear Mine," he said at last, "but I intend to work that myself."

"Very good," replied Polley making a hurried note of the name. "How long have you owned this mine? You say that your father was the original discoverer? What success did he have with the property? Very promising, indeed . . . the mine has produced a million. There again is an interesting sidelight. It has been my observation that success is often transmissible, handed down from father to son, and the fact that your father made a success of the property is another point in its favor with me. And now, Mister Watson, I told you once before that money, in my experience, will buy anything.

"You may not know it, but there is a price, nevertheless, at which you will sell this mine. At present it is worth nothing, except potentially, and it will require considerable capital to develop it. There is also to be borne in mind the occurrences that may follow in their wake. You must bear in mind, furthermore, that any cash sale represents one hundred percent clear profit, whereas, although the mine might be held at a million dollars, the actual net product, after the expense of working it is deducted, would not exceed one tenth of that amount.

"I am always, as I told you, a very careful buyer, but at the same time I try to be fair. There is one thing more . . . put out of your mind entirely the fact that I am a millionaire. The mine as it stands is worth no more to me than it is to Whispering Johnson . . . and I shall refer your offer to an expert. Now . . . name your bottom price, for cash."

Cal rubbed his nose and regarded him speculatively, revolving the different elements in his mind, and he was satisfied with them all, except the expert. A mining expert, in his opinion, was at best a rank imposter, when he did not turn out a plain crook, and the mines that were recommended without some kind of a secret commission were very rare, indeed. Leaving out the expert, the problem reduced itself to what the Golden Bear was really worth. A million, he had always said, but so far it had done no more than pay him day's wages at the *arrastra*. No, it was not worth a million in clean cash money, and he doubted if his five thousand would so prove it. Besides, there was a difference, as Polley had said, between its value as a mine and the net profit.

"I'll take a hundred thousand dollars," he said at last, and Polley wrote the price down gravely.

"Very well," he replied, "that seems a reasonable price if the mine is all that you have stated. Now there is one thing more that I would like to ask of you, and, if you agree, we will draw up the option. I want you to vacate the property for thirty days while my expert is making his examination, and, if at the end of the time he reports favorably on the mine, the Golden Bear is as good as sold. But there is one thing I must insist upon, there must be no collusion, direct or indirect, between you and the expert I employ. I shall engage a man of the highest professional standing and demand an impartial report, but if I find that you have so much as inquired his name and address, the deal will be off right there."

"Fair enough," agreed Cal, "but look at the other side of it. The average mining expert isn't even a mining man. He's a hot-air merchant who writes phony reports. Now, if my mine is turned down, I want a chance for a comeback, and especially if he isn't a practical man. It's a common practice with these birds to write out a big report, hemming and hawing but turning the mine down, and then they'll slip around to the man that's selling it and let him look at it first. If he comes through with ten percent, they'll change their recommendation. Otherwise the property gets a black eye."

"What you say," said Polley, "is no news to me. That is just what I am trying to avoid. You may not be aware of it, but I am making a study of mining . . . you must come in some time and inspect my library . . . and, as for mining experts, there was seldom a day when one failed to call me up at the hotel. I am prejudiced in advance in favor of your mine and would like to buy it on my hunch, but, since reading the works of the most eminent engineers, I find them all agreed on this . . . that every mine should be examined and sampled exhaustively before ever an offer is made. I am violating that principle in the case of the Golden Bear because I have picked you, my boy, for a winner, and now let's have a drink and we'll draw up the option . . . here's to our continued success."

They toasted the half-made sale and several lesser events, some past and others to come, and, when Cal left the house, he was walking on air and humming a roundelay. But who would not sing and go rollicking down the cañon after such a run of good luck? The millionaire he had flouted and told to go to hell had turned the other cheek

117

like a Christian, and the powers of evil as personified by Johnson had been routed and driven away in disgrace.

All the world was so delightfully topsy-turvy that Cal doubted if he was perfectly sober, but except for a slight flush and a singing in his ears he was none the worse for the rounds of champagne. This tentative sale of his mine had been timed to a nicety to solve his troubles with Johnson, for now that he was under contract to vacate the premises, he could drop out of sight with good grace. Things were getting a little feverish for a quiet young man who objected to being smashed like a horsefly, and a trip out through Death Valley would serve to shake off any pursuit on the part of zealots like Crump. There were those, he knew, to whom the news of his good fortune would be like gall and wormwood, but Polley had agreed to safeguard his mine and Peggy would take care of his roll.

The sun was hanging low when Cal rode up Bitter Creek and stopped to gaze again at the Golden Bear. It bulked big against the skyline, its ancient gallows frame dismantled, its huge dump sprawling off down the hill, but in the golden glow of sunset the gallows frame was transfigured, and he saw a modern hoist in its place and an engine house and tool shop grouped closely about it. There were cabins and cook house below, and above it all the spirit of old Sam Watson looked down in benediction.

Chapter Eighteen

THE DEAD MAN'S HAND

There was something that went to the head like wine about being picked for a winner by Polley. Polley was a winner himself. Polley had not, while deep in his cups, tried to flatter him by indiscriminate praise. He had questioned him closely, taking nothing for granted, and ended by practically buying his mine. As an earnest of his good faith he had put up $500 to bind his option on the mine, and with a buyer like Polley—a man who was close, and proud of it—that was practically equivalent to a buy. And, miracle of miracles, after all that Cal had said to him, he had insisted upon being his friend.

The sycophants like Whispering Johnson, who had kowtowed and groveled to him, had been turned away from his door in scorn, while the insulting young prospector who had referred him to the antipodes had been invited to his house and made much of. Cal remembered the grapy tang of that sparkling champagne with a passing sigh of regret, but, as he rode up to his cave house, other thoughts rushed upon him, for the gate was swinging open. A J Prod cow had her head in his kitchen and his salt sack was spilled on the ground, and high up on his door, like a black hand warning, five playing cards were fastened by a knife. It was only a jack-knife, such as cowboys use for cutting the earmarks on calves, and the cards were just an ordinary hand—a pair of jacks and a pair of eights, with a three spot down in the corner.

Cal stepped down off of his horse, and, after he had rousted out the J Prod cow, he examined the hand carefully. As he stood in contemplation some memory came back to him, something to do with jacks and eights. He had heard a phrase somewhere about jacks and eights—yes, the phrase was: "Jacks and eights win!" But why should some enemy, with probably a superior knowledge of poker, pin a winning hand on his door? The very knife, although it was only a work knife, somehow gave it a sinister import, and, as Watson examined it, noting the cow hairs between the blades, the answer came over him like a flash. Jacks and eights was the dead man's hand, so shunned by certain players of poker.

The story of the dead man's hand was a tradition among gamblers, each ascribing a different origin, but the old desert rats claimed that the hand that had won the name had been held by a gambler at Bodie. At a time when men played poker with a pistol between their knees, he was sitting in a game with three professionals, one of whom showed a poorer hand and claimed the pot.

"Jacks and eights win!" announced the gambler, showing the fateful hand, and he was shot as he was raking in the pot. When the smoke had cleared away, they found him still sitting there, the stakes clutched in a stiffening hand, and the other hand, as it lopped down before him, still held fast the dead man's hand. He had won the pot, but he had lost his life, and many a hand since has been thrown into the discard by some man who would not dally with death.

Cal tore the cards down and threw them into the stove, but the knife he put in his pocket. Then he looked for tracks and found too many of them to tell the story he sought. Three men had ridden down and stopped at his cabin—Whispering Johnson and Bill Beagle and Crump—but the cattle had been in and trampled out the footprints of the man who had stuck up the cards. Which man of the three was the one who had done it? Probably Crump, for it was a cowboy's knife. It was a small knife with two blades, both kept razor sharp to cut through the gristle of calves' ears and the red cow hair in the hinge made it all the more positive, besides the dried blood on the handle.

But why should Crump waste a perfectly good jackknife in stabbing this hand on Cal's door? It was Whispering Johnson who had led the raid, and the message, from him, would be plain; it was more, in fact, than Johnson had said with his own lips, which made it all the more strange. Cal had won the stakes in their game over the mines, but in payment he would lose his life.

That was Johnson's old bluff, either by threat or innuendo, but somehow this did not seem like him. Whispering Johnson was not a man who indulged in *double entendre*—his meanings and mental processes were plain. No, the message was plain, no matter whom it came from, but the knife and the method were Crump's.

Wayne Crump was a man whose facial contour followed the fox—a sloping forehead and deep-set eyes—and his small, sharp nose and mysterious smile spoke of a nature at once inquisitive and sly. He was a man who sat silently, studying out plans and devices that his companions were not privileged to know. Yes, Crump was the man to think up such a thing. But why the message—from *him?* What stake had Cal won in the feud between them that would justify the figure of the hand? There was only one stake—the heart of Armilda. Could it be that Cal had won it?

He sat down in the gathering dusk and let his mind turn back to Armilda and his visit to Bubbling Wells. She had welcomed him like a lover, her songs had been of love, and at the end she had invited him to return. After all Crump's threats, after he had claimed the right to speak for her and to warn Cal never to return, Armilda had smiled after him as sweetly as ever and called out: "Come and see me again!"

Could it be that, following his departure, Armilda and Crump had quarreled and Armilda had put him in his place? And yet what was more reasonable, considering his arrogance and his high-handed way of speaking for her? Armilda was not a girl to submit to dictation—Sol Barksdale, her own father, was afraid of her—and now, unknown to them, she had $5,000 with which to assert her independence.

Cal smiled triumphantly as he thought of that great roll that he had laid on the table before her. She was playing a deep game with these two overbearing tyrants, knowing well she could quit them overnight. To be able so to quit them was the reason, beyond a doubt, why she had consented to approach Whispering Johnson and prepare the way for their coup, and she had told Cal distinctly, while they were discussing the arrangement, that her father wouldn't give her a cent.

A sudden impulse came to Cal to ride down and see her, to make sure where he stood in her regard, and not, as once before, stay away until too late and then have her tell him he was hopeless. He knew in his heart that, if Crump had not interrupted them, Armilda would have acknowledged her love, or, barring that, a comradeship in spirit that was different only in name. But at the same time something warned him that, if he went to Bubbling Wells, he would be lucky to come away with his life.

After a restless night, Cal was up at dawn, looking out across gleaming Dry Lake. The first rays of the sun warmed the air layers unevenly, causing the mesquite trees to loom up and spread. They rose like mountains and stretched out in a broad mesa that reached out long fingers to the hills, then the top air layers floated away, and the mesquite trees shrank back to their place. In the hollow of the lake a pool of water began to quiver—the daily mirage had begun.

Cal sat on the ridge and looked out across Dry Lake, and it brought up strange memories in his mind. He remembered the time when he had limped across that flat and Barksdale had denied him a drink. He dismissed the thought impatiently, but another took its place—he saw Wayne Crump, spinning his rope. Then followed such a series of unpleasant memories that he turned and looked away north.

If Polley was right, men succeeded by playing their luck, by following wherever it led, and nothing but bad luck had ever come to him when he headed for Bubbling Wells. He had had a run of bad luck, there was no use denying it, and now in a day it had changed. From a fugitive in the morning he had become a successful mining man, picked by Polley himself to win. His feet were set on the highroad to fortune, but that road led away from Bubbling Wells. It led away from Crump and Beagle and Johnson—and away from Armilda, too. There his troubles had begun and there they would begin again, if he went down to claim his answer now. But if he left them behind and followed on after his star, he might live to win her yet.

He turned away reluctantly, for something told him that she needed him, but his feet were on the highroad to success.

Chapter Nineteen

IN DEATH VALLEY SINK

The road to Death Valley led up broad and windy valleys, past lonely windmills on the shores of dead lakes, and lying by the tanks or grazing far out on the flats were bands of JB cattle. It was Whispering Johnson's range, for he owned the windmills and his cowboys pushed back outside stock, but it was Barksdale's range, too, and, as he rode past the tanks, Cal saw J Prod and Triangle Dot cows as well. The Triangle Dots were Armilda's, inherited from her mother and built up from a few pet cows, but something was wrong now for few of the cows had calves and those few were young.

Cal thought again of the mysterious band of cattle thieves that was reputed to be running off stock, and he wondered with a shrug if Barksdale's alleged stock detective ever rode this far from the ranch. It was a fine, large country for cow thieves to operate in while Crump stayed at Bubbling Wells.

He was like the lazy man who owned a 1,000-acre farm with only one tree that threw a shade—you always knew where to find him. The windmill man drove from one tank to another, putting in valves and looking after the pumps, and the cowboys were supposed to cover the water holes, but Barksdale and Crump, the two most interested parties, stuck around the home ranch like twin Arguses. They were back there now, perhaps watching the road for Cal or riding to Black Cañon and beyond, but, although Wayne Crump had posted the warning hand on Watson's door, he would not follow on his trail. That called for courage and a certain desert hardihood, besides a knowledge of landmarks and springs. Although Crump was sometimes gone for several days at a time, Cal doubted if he was riding the range. He always headed east, up Black Cañon and then on, but never with a pack horse and his bed, and the man who caught those cow thieves would have to camp on their trail and pack a greasy-sack outfit himself.

Past the second dry lake beyond the Bitter Water the road swung from north to west, winding up toward a pass in the hills, and soon in the distance great dumps of rock appeared, standing out white against the gray of the range. Houses and gallows frames showed up, half hidden behind the waste, and a mill, boarded up and still. As Cal rode through the camp, only a single house showed signs of life—a woman with her flock by the door. For a camp may wax and wane until the last mine is closed and the chipmunks move in and take the town, but there is always one man who clings to his dream—and a woman must stay with her man.

But over the divide beyond this desolate and abandoned camp there was the rumble and thunder of heavy stamps. A great mill up on the mountainside was spewing out tailings like a river; the whole top of the mountain was gone, and the man who tipped the car down the long slope of the dump looked like a pinpoint against the sky. It was a big mine, the Yellow Sandstorm, one that had turned out $20,000,000 and was still grinding ponderously on. In the cañon below a swarming town had sprung up as if it sucked life and richness from the hill. There they stood, the two camps, and the one was dead and desolate while the other was in its heyday, for gold, as they say, is where you find it.

A long ride the next day took Watson to Searles Lake, where beach mark after beach mark on the gray hills all about indicated the shores of what was once an inland sea. When the glaciers of the Sierras were grinding the granite to powder and their meltings were washing it away, the potash in the feldspar was taken up in solution and deposited in this third great lake. It was held in solution still, beneath a floor of crystallized salt as solid as the ice of the Great Lakes, and great pumps sucked it up and sent it through boilers and vats until it gave up its treasure at last. Here another town had sprung up on the desert, this time sucking its life from the lake.

The surface of the great sink was gleaming like snow when Cal, still riding north, crossed its floor. The ground all about was frozen solid with salt and soda that crunched beneath boots like rotten ice. His big canteen was filled now and there was grain on his pack, for the rich grama grass of the south country was gone. Here, so far from the sea, the rain seldom came, and, when it did fall, it was poisoned on the flats. A rank odor, like dead fish, rose up from the earth that was impregnated with borax and different salts. As he gazed out across the marshes, Cal thought of the men who had lost their lives in this place. The glare of the sun was reflected from each crystal, making his eyes ache and throb with its brilliance, and Campomoche raised his head and snarled uneasily, for he knew that Death Valley was ahead.

A day's journey to the east and they would be into it, and into it at its worst, but Cal was working north, to make a last stop at Ballarat before he ventured into the valley beyond. No pursuers had appeared on the long road behind him, although automobiles had gone plunging past, but now he was going where no automobile could travel and men traveled either on horseback or afoot. If Crump or some hireling came in over the trail, he would know with whom he had to reckon. If no one came, then he could lose himself completely and come out on the other side of the world. For the east side of Death Valley was a world unto itself, cut off from California and the mountains on its west side by a fissure like the gash of a knife. North and south for 200 miles Death Valley divided the country with its waste of sand and marsh and poisoned flats and to cross it, if one could, was like passing down into oblivion and coming out of the Great Silence a new man.

That was what Cal wanted, to shake off all his enemies and with them the clinging burs of his ill luck, to disappear for thirty days, and then come in on them from nowhere and take up his new life—and succeed. Crump would think he had fled, intimidated by his warning, stampeded by the dead man's hand, but when he came back, Crump would know, and they would all know, that he was there to stand up for his rights. Polley had taught him a lesson by the way he had handled Johnson and turned away the minions of the law, for Evan Polley had no more legal rights than he had—all he knew was how to stand up for them. Cal had always regarded the officers as potential enemies, although they represented the law, but Polley had shown him that the officers were his servants and the law was in existence to protect *him*.

In the country where he was going there was no law, more than what a man made for himself. When men were found dead there, the coroner refused to view the body, the sheriff rarely answered a call, and the best way, all around, was the way the desert men lived, each one a law unto himself. It was a quiet and peaceable country, where men attended to their own business and did not ask any leading questions, and yet a country where a stranger was gladly welcomed if he came with good intent. Cal had been as far as Ballarat—once a roaring mining camp, now a collection of empty houses on the flat. When he camped in the old saloon, the population turned out to greet him—six men who held claims in the hills..

These rose up in mighty ramparts to the east of the town, hills that once had been rich with gold, and beyond them towered the Panamints, now white with snow, barring the way to Death Valley. A chill and bitter wind was sweeping down on the old town, rattling the signboards and making the doors bang and creak, but there was plenty of wood in wind-blown and dismantled houses whose owners would never come back. Cal made himself at home, and, after he had eaten, the news-hungry company came back. They gathered about his fire in the big saloon stove, where rock specimens were exhibited along the entire bar. Far into the night they sat there telling stories of the good old days, long ago. The son of old Sam Watson was more than welcome, and he camped for more than a week.

But now the time was come when he must begin the great circle that would bring him back at last to Bitter Creek, and, since one of the prospectors was going up to Panamint, he rode after him to that city among the peaks. Away back in the 1870s a stage road from Los Angeles had been built to this world-famous silver camp. Now it stood like the rest of them, one more abandoned city, hidden away among the crags of the Panamints. There was the brick mill in the cañon, the aërial tramway to the summit, the huge store and empty cabins and saloon, but one prospector and the wild burros that brayed discordantly were the sole inhabitants of the town.

Beyond there was nothing—an Indian trail up over the ridge and then Death Valley and the silence. Cal lingered, reluctant to brave the valley alone and yet determined to push his way through, until at last the old prospector followed after him to the summit and pointed out the way to Bennett's Well. It was so far below that the cliffs and slides seemed endless, and the long, boulder-strewn slopes beyond, but at the bottom of it all, on the edge of the poisoned marshes, was the water hole that had saved many a life. All the other water was bad. This land, which in geological times had been awash with turbulent floods, was dried away to nothingness and of all that ancient sea nothing was left but the poisonous salts.

With the prospector's last warnings still ringing in his ears, Cal led off down the perilous trail, and, although the sun was blazing hot, his feet sank deeply in snow, unmelted since the last big storm. It was winter on these high crags and the wind along the summit soughed and thundered among the tall pines, but as hour after hour he broke his way down the trail, he felt the winter wane. The sweat gathered under his hatband and began to trickle down his face; Campomoche and Lemon were in a lather. When they rounded a point and came out of the deep cañon, the ground was suddenly free from snow. It was dry already and green grass was springing up, and that evening, when he camped at a deserted ranch, he found all the fruit trees in bloom.

A mile below, the ranch creek sank from sight, and with the water went the willow trees and spring. The cañon opened out and the bushes that looked so green snapped off like glass at a touch. A puff of wind came up from below, bone-dry and smelling of alkali, and Cal knew he was nearing the abyss. At every turn of the boulder-strewn cañon he craned his neck to look out, but the walls were getting higher, the channel more tortuous, the wash more like a concrete floor. The air grew cold and dank in the sunless passageway. His animals snorted and started at the echoes. Then suddenly they snapped out into the dazzling sunshine and Death Valley spread out before them like a map. But it was a map hard to read, for the old prospector's directions did not fit into this chaos of peaks, and the trail, striking the open, split up and almost vanished, for the packed ground would barely hold a track.

One trail went down the wash, which broadened out into forty washes, torn and guttered and piled full of rocks. Another climbed the bank past an Indian monument, circling around the point to the north. The third trail circled south, but Cal turned away from it—the prospector had said to go north. North and east the trail led, around the shoulders of countless ridges, losing itself completely at every dip into a wash. But for the piles of rocks that the Indians had set up, any search for the point of egress would have been hopeless.

On every sloping point the trail itself would split, banding the hillside like ribbons of white dust. Although the formation had changed to clay, it was broken by great blowouts of lava that were strewn along the mesa for miles. Cal rode on steadily, dismounting to walk up the hills or to seek out the vanishing trail, but at last the inevitable happened. It disappeared completely and he stood in Death Valley—lost.

Yet no man is lost as long as he knows where he came from, or where he is trying to go. Cal kept on across the boulder-strewn patches, crossing wash after wash until Campomoche became outraged and balked. He was a big, Roman-nosed horse with a mind of his own, and, when Cal began to waver and turn back on his trail, Campomoche knew he was lost. Campomoche knew further that the boulders were getting thicker and thicker and the sharp rocks were hurting his hoofs and that the only thing to do, from a horse's point of view, was to turn around and go back to the ranch. So he set his hoofs stubbornly and refused to mount a cut bank, and, after thinking it over, Cal stopped. He was getting a little heated, and talking to himself, which is always a bad sign on the desert. While Campomoche stood, snapping his teeth and jerking his head indignantly, Cal sat down and looked over the land.

The trail that he had lost had followed along the base of a range of chalky-white hills. Somewhere along its course, the old prospector had told him, there was a tank of water in a gulch. But his canteen was still full and in the cool winter weather his animals would not give out from thirst. The thing to do was to get out of the rocks and then try again for Bennett's Well. He struck off down the wash, and Campomoche followed willingly, until at last the rough boulders were left behind, but still they kept on for the prospector had shown Cal where the old borax road came in from the south.

Once on this road he would have something to follow and his animals would make better time. By following it north, he would come to the well where the lost Bennett party had made its camp of death. He could even go on up to Furnace Creek Ranch if he missed this first water hole. Although it would take him another day, he was sure to find water in the end. So he plodded along down the broad, sandy wash that seemed to extend to infinitude, and, just as he was beginning to doubt his own sanity, he cut the Death Valley Road.

It was a broad trail through the brush, without a wagon track on it, but stamped boldly in the dust—and heading north like himself—was a shod horse's track, almost fresh. In that waste of barren rocks and windswept sands it was like meeting a friend on the road. Campomoche, desert-wise, noted the track and where it headed, and turned north of his own accord. Cal mounted and they traveled faster, scuffling along over the ground in a kind of walking trot. As the ground became lower and mesquite trees appeared, Cal knew they were approaching Bennett's Well. Here some seep of fresh water, flowing underground from the snow peaks, had forced itself up through the sand. The twenty-mule borax teams had made it their camping place, for there was wood and water and feed.

Cal knew that he was safe now, for the sun was still well up and the wild burro tracks would lead to the well, but the horse track that he had followed suddenly quit the road and turned off into the brush. They were now on damp land, powdered over with drifting sand from which bunches of coarse grass sprang up. The tracks of the wild burros were here mixed with those of cattle that had been browsing on the sacaton and salt grass. Lemon reached up in passing and nipped the tips of the mesquite twigs that were rich with long, feathery leaves, and, seeing the mesquite beans beneath the trees, Cal wondered if some cattleman had not come here to winter his herd. It had never occurred to him that he would find cattle in such a country, but here were their tracks and the man on the shod pony was undoubtedly the cowboy in charge.

But what a country to run cows in—the man must needs be desperate to venture so far from his kind, and by what trail had he come to find this cattleman's paradise and to drive in his gaunt herd? On both sides of the broad sink the mountains loomed like walls, their black ramparts cutting off the evening sun, and only from the south, or the far Nevada side, was it possible to trail a herd in. The Indians, if there were any, might know of these rich marshes where the grass would feed hundreds of head, but an Indian pony had not made that horse track in the road—it was a white man's horse, and a good one. There was something mysterious, and a little sinister, about that track which had disappeared into the brush.

Campomoche stopped short and pointed his ears to the right, snorting and staring out among the trees. Cal reached for his gun as he saw a brush corral, hidden away in a thicket of mesquite. He rode in on it slowly, glancing nervously about for something he could not name. As he looked over the bars, he saw a bunch of J Prod cows, each one with a new-branded calf. The answer was plain and he reined his horse away. He had stumbled on a rustlers' camp.

Chapter Twenty

ANOTHER NOTION

Every land has its etiquette, its unwritten law of conduct, devised to meet the needs of the times. The first rule in the cow country was to mind your own business and not be too damned inquisitive. Watson was no longer a cowboy, but he had learned his lesson well, and he reined his horse away in a flash. That corral full of cattle might cause him a lot of trouble if he dallied too long at the bars, more particularly if the horseman who had disappeared in the brush happened to be hidden thereabouts with a rifle. Here was a tremendous *faux pas,* like surprising a pair of lovers or discovering the boss tapping his own till. Cal rode away without looking back, or showing the least sign of haste.

Whether they watched him now or read his tracks later, the rustlers would know what it meant—he had just ridden over to see what was there, and then had proceeded on his way. He was no hired detective, no officer of the law, sent out here to spy on their doings, but only a chance wayfarer, riding briefly off the trail to see what was in their pen. To be sure he had discovered where Barksdale's cows were going, and probably Johnson's, too, but neither of those men was such a dear friend of his as to make that cause him any worry. If the rustlers stole them blind, it was all the same to him—only the trouble was the rustlers did not know that. They might come across his tracks and, believing the worst, follow after him and shoot him on sight.

A short distance down the road Cal came to Bennett's Well, where he watered his thirsty animals, but a new dread was upon him, greater than the dread of the desert, and he kept on riding north. The sun was behind the peaks when, a few miles up the road, he came upon an Indian camp. But as the dogs all came out at him and the Indians hid, he judged he was not wanted and rode past. It was a wild and desolate land, one of desperate uses and savage in every aspect, and the friendship of these Shoshones was a doubtful blessing anyway, since they were shameless beggars, at best. Their camp was beneath the mesquite trees on the edge of the salt marshes that here were many miles in extent. Above the tall grass Cal could see the heads of their burros, although not a cow was in sight.

The darkness was gathering when, tired and limping, he came to Tule Hole. Cal passed a cheerless night out on the grassy flat, while his animals ate their fill. After the heat of the day the iron cold of the desert seemed to strike to his very bones, but he went without a fire, rather than tempt any prowlers who might be searching for his camp.

Before daylight he was up, boiling a cup of coffee and throwing the pack on his mule, and, as dawn painted the weird landscape in fantastic colors, he mounted and spurred away. Something about that mysterious horseman and the disappearing Indians had given him a bad case of nerves, but when the warm sun came up, he quit looking back, for the valley was now level as a floor.

The marshes, the thickets, the great expanse of stinking waters, were now no more than a dream, and he jogged along across a flat of rubbery softness toward the Nevada side of the sink. The old borax road, now broken and neglected, led straight across the vast sink, and ahead in the distance the Funeral Range loomed up as black and frowning as the

Panamints. Then the spongy ground was passed and they crossed a miry slough, where the flood waters flowed in from the north, and, plunging out of its quicksands, they found a foothold on solid salt, like frozen waves of the sea.

From the corduroy bridge that had once spanned the slough, the road cut through the salt crests for miles. Campomoche shied as it sounded hollowly beneath his hoofs and deep holes opened up on either side. Here was salt enough to supply the whole world, if it could ever be put to use, but the day was past when even borax was worth the hauling, and the twenty-mule teams were a dream.

Salt and marshes were succeeded by piebald hills, white with borax, running parallel with the slough on the east. By noon they came in sight of the tall palms of Furnace Creek Ranch, where the borax company still kept a man. Even taller than the palms were the two stacks of alfalfa that rose beside the green fields, and for two days Cal rested while Campomoche and Lemon were up to their ears in sweet hay. The dread valley was crossed and their way was now easy, for the railroad lay behind the Funeral Range.

For the next week Cal drifted from desert town to desert town until he brought up at Shoshone, on the railroad. Now his circle was almost completed, for Nevada was behind him and Death Valley off to the west. The Armagosa River that flowed through the town found its end in the sink he had crossed. There were salt-grass meadows along the Armagosa, and prospectors camped among the trees, but if anyone suspected that Cal had come through Death Valley, he was much too polite to mention it. Here again was the studied silence, the careful avoidance of leading questions, the friendly welcome at each camp. Cal in his turn refrained from asking any questions about the cow thieves who had their hold out in the sink. It gave him, if anything, a

136

laughing sensation to think of Barksdale's and Johnson's unexplained loss, but at the same time he planned on his homeward journey to keep a sharp look-out for tracks. If cattle were being driven from Barksdale's range, he knew they must water on the way—either at Granite Well or Saratoga Spring—before they began the long drive into the sink.

No one bade him good bye when he rode out of Shoshone and took the long trail for home, but lest some secret enemy should follow him in the night, he camped away from the springs. Unless the cowboy in Death Valley was new to the desert, he must have seen Cal's tracks at his corral, and, by cross-questioning the Indians, he must have learned further that his visitor had a lemon-colored mule. Now a mule the color of Lemon was like the *pajaro amarillo*, a very rare bird to find. It was too much to hope that his identity was not known. Hence Cal's business was to see the cowboy first. He would know that big horse track if he saw it in Hades, for it had guided him to water when he was lost, but the man who rode the horse might not share Cal's friendly feelings—might be ready to shoot on sight.

Cal rode for two days without seeing a sign of any unusual movement of stock. But on the morning of the third, shortly after he had sighted Frémont Peak, he found where the herd had passed. It was still none of his business, but by this time his intellectual curiosity was rapidly getting the better of his judgment, for unless this band of rustlers had discovered some new water holes, they could never travel by the route they had come. The leader of the gang was either an Indian or he had one in his employ, for they had gone through a country where few white men ever ventured—the sandy wastes south of Death Valley. Even after heavy storms, cattle range far in search of uncropped grass, not drifting sands, and rocks down which water can run, but there were no potholes in those hills, nor yet water, so far as known, and wise men kept to the trail. But Watson had come too far to get lost now and he backtracked the cow trail west.

Where they went he already knew, for he had seen them in Death Valley. It was where they came from that interested him now. Not twenty miles ahead, across the rolling sand hills, he could see the summit of Black Mountain, and just beyond that lay Dry Lake and Bubbling Wells, with Frémont Peak off to the north. It was the heart of the J Prod range, and yet here was a broad trail showing where cattle had been gathered and driven off. Cal backtracked them for ten miles, his mind on many things besides rustlers and hidden hold outs in the hills, for now his thirty days were up and Evan Polley would give him the answer that might make or break him for life.

If Polley bought the Golden Bear, paying $100,000 in cash, a new world of opportunity would open up, but if he turned the property down, Cal would have his battle to fight all over again with the odds in favor of his enemies. Yet, if he could check up on these cattle and incidentally on Wayne Crump, it might help him to get rid of one enemy, for it was apparent that Crump was no detective at all, to let these cattle be driven off in one bunch. All the calves that the prospectors and Indians combined might kill in the course of a year would not equal the total of this one loss, and, if it ever came to a showdown and Cal could prove his case, Crump might be hunting for a job. And then, with Barksdale placated or at least quieted down, the friendly calls on Armilda could be renewed—and with $100,000 and a friend like Polley his reception might be different from the last.

His reveries were interrupted by a snort from Lemon, trotting behind him. Cal could see in the distance a trailing streak of dust down the pass. He hazed Lemon behind the ridge without an instant's delay, for that was no place to meditate, and then, with his glasses, he crept back to the summit and dropped down behind a bush. What he saw was three men, driving a bunch of cattle before them and heading straight for him across the flats. From the way one man rode he knew he was an Indian—the other man was Crump. A suspicion long dormant suddenly sprang to full life—Wayne Crump was a rustler himself! While he took the pay of Barksdale, and of Barksdale and Johnson, he was engaged in running off their stock and his position as stock detective was only a blind to cover up his nefarious work. That explained the wild look in those sly and cunning eyes that smiled to cover up a great fear, and it explained as well those mysterious disappearances, when Crump rode up Black Cañon alone. He had come over the range to join his confederates and direct them while they ran off Barksdale's stock.

Cal crouched behind the sand hill and watched them intently as they hurried the cows toward his hiding place, but just out of the hills Crump turned back and left them, and the herd swung off to the north. Except for their dust, which the wind snatched up and waved like a banner above them, the Indian and cowboy were lost, but Cal watched them out of sight—and Wayne Crump, too—before he ventured to build a dust of his own. Then he rode on after Crump who had disappeared up the pass down which the cattle had come. It was Cal's shortest way home, now that he had come so far south; otherwise, he would have taken to the hills.

He had learned all he wanted to about the unsuspecting

Crump. A trained detective could not have handled the case better, but enough was enough, and he had other affairs on hand, affairs that would brook no delay. When the time was ripe and he had Crump where he wanted him, he would cut the ground from under him with one word. Now he was more interested in Evan Polley and his answer regarding the Golden Bear. Having paid $500 down, Polley's intentions were obvious, but many things can happen in thirty days, and, before anything else happened to break up the trade, the best thing to do was to be prompt.

If it was luck that made or marred, then now was the time to strike, for never in his life had Cal felt luckier, and the way he had checked up on Crump without even being seen was little short of miraculous. It was a large country to ride over, and the chances of meeting this herd were about one in 100,000,000, yet he had hit it to a nicety, and all he wanted now was to make an equally clean getaway.

Crump was over an hour ahead of him and he was not encumbered with a pack animal, but even then Cal was careful not to travel too fast, for he was not seeking a meeting with him now. That would only lead to trouble, and perhaps to a shooting, if Crump found that the game was up. As Cal entered a narrow cañon, he pulled his horse to a walk, keeping an eye to the front.

It was past noon now and his animals, being thirsty, were impatient to reach the water hole ahead, but Wiggletail Spring was the very place where Crump was likely to stop. Cal remembered where it was, and so did Campomoche, in a little cove just off the trail, but it had been a long time since he had ridden that way, and they were upon it before he knew it. Around a curve they swung and there in the little open was Wayne Crump, and a bunch of cows!

140

He had just driven them in from the other way and halted them at the water to rest. Oblivious of Cal's presence, he was busily engaged in wrestling down a maverick calf. As for Cal, he sat irresolute, unwilling to turn back yet reluctant to make his presence known. It was only when Crump ran to a brand fire he had built that he perceived his hated enemy. He had taken the running iron red hot from the coals before he noticed what the cattle had all been staring at, and so strong is force of habit that he hurried to his maverick before the iron could cool. Cal started his horse ahead and reined in to watch him, vaguely wondering what brand he would run, but, now that he had a visitor, Crump burned a big J Prod and rubbed his smoking iron in the dirt. Then, still ignoring him, he felt for his jackknife to put the finishing touches on the ears.

So far the play acting had been all that could be asked for and Cal looked on, almost convinced. If Sol Barksdale had been present, he would have commended his detective for so zealously branding up his stock. So far the bluff was good. But Crump had misplaced his jackknife, and, as he searched for it, Cal Watson smiled.

"Lost your jackknife?" he inquired. "Here, maybe this is it!" And he threw a small knife into the dust. Crump snatched it up impatiently and had it almost opened before he saw what it was—the knife was the one that had been stabbed through the dead man's hand, and Cal had caught him in a trap.

"Damn your knife!" he cried, throwing it angrily away from him and rising up waspishly to his feet. "What are you doing here, anyway?" he demanded.

"Oh, rambling 'round . . . rambling 'round," answered Watson vaguely. "You never know when you'll meet a friend."

"No, or a god-damned cow thief!" came back Wayne Crump spitefully, and then he stood, twitching his lip. He had been taken off his guard and caught in the very act of tying down an unbranded maverick, and the fact that he had burned a big J Prod on its hip only added in a way to his humiliation. Cal simply sat and looked at him, a humorous twinkle in his eye, and Crump knew that the prospector was wise. But was this all that his hated enemy knew? Perhaps this was more than an accident. Having come in from the east, it was almost a certainty that he had witnessed the driving off of the herd. Yes, and then followed on, to trap him in the act.

"You get out of here!" he ordered, hooking his thumb into his belt just above his long-barreled revolver. "I've got a damned good notion to arrest you!"

"Never spoil a good notion," returned Watson hectoringly, and Crump seemed to sense what he meant. They were man to man now, in that desolate cañon, and Cal had called for a showdown.

"I don't want any trouble," Crump answered impatiently, and Cal looked him over insultingly.

"Yes . . . you arrest *me?* You've got a notion to do it, eh? Well, you've got another notion that beats that all to hell. You don't dare to arrest me . . . you cow thief!"

Cal reined his horse away and sat poised in his saddle, awaiting the response to his challenge, but fear and his own guilt had weakened Crump's nerve.

"I don't want any trouble," he muttered sullenly, and Cal rode off and left him.

Chapter Twenty-One

ADULARIA

If it was luck that won fortunes and decided the fate of empires, Cal felt qualified to go up against anything—he had taken every trick in his game with Crump and left him looking like a two-spot. And the first rule in gambling is to follow your luck, cashing in when the cards turn against you. Bright and early the next morning Cal rode down to the Thousand Wonders, almost regretting that he had agreed to sell his mine, but one look at the set countenance of Polley convinced him that the luck had turned. Polley was friendly and set out the drinks, but his cordiality was forced and, after the first awkward silence, Cal asked him point-blank whether he had decided to buy the Golden Bear.

"Well . . . no," responded Polley, "I regret very much. . . ."

"Never mind the regrets," cut in Watson shortly. "What's the matter with the proposition, anyway?"

"No ore in sight," answered Polley, equally brusque. "Here's the report of my consulting engineer."

Watson snatched it away from him and read the first few paragraphs with lips that curled scornfully apart.

"Bunk!" he pronounced. "What windjammer wrote this? He never went down the shaft."

"He is a man," replied Polley stiffly, "of international fame, both as a mining engineer and a manager of large enterprises. We must accept his decision as final."

"Listen to this . . . ," raved Cal, squaring his elbows to read the document, but Polley cut him short.

"No one regrets more than I do," he stated with finality, "that my engineer has reported adversely. But I make it a principle, when I am employing an expert, never to override his technical judgment. Mister Hunnewell's name. . . ."

"What's that? Hunnewell!" cried Cal, and then he flapped his hands and handed the alleged report back. "You don't mean to say," he went on in measured accents, "that you consider Everett J. Hunnewell an expert? Well, by all the gods and little fishes, if this don't naturally . . . beat . . . hell!" He drew a long breath and sighed despairingly, at which Polley's red face became mottled.

"Mister Watson," he barked, "if you intend any reflection upon my ability to engage a competent expert. . . ."

"Oh, not at all." Cal smiled. "I was just going to say that I know Mister Hunnewell . . . slightly."

"And don't you consider him," inquired Polley with some asperity, "perfectly competent to report on your mine? I am aware that in our agreement it was definitely understood that you had the privilege of going behind the returns. . . ."

"Yes, and I claim it!" announced Cal. "No guy with a plug hat and a Prince Albert coat is going to say that my mine is n.g.! This Everett J. Hunnewell never went down the shaft, and I'll bring a man out here to prove it. You don't have to buy the mine unless you want to . . . I've got money enough to open it up myself, but I know it's rich, and my father, Sam Watson, always said it had only been scratched. I guess he ought to know . . . he took out a million dollars when the freight cost two hundred a ton . . . and, if he could do it then, why can't I do it now? I'll just show you, Mister Polley, who's the expert."

144

He rose up confidently and was reaching for his hat when a change came over his host.

"Just a moment!" Polley insisted, ringing for the bell for the drinks. "You may be right, Mister Watson. I confess that I was tempted to follow my hunch and buy your property anyway. Mister Hunnewell, I will admit, did not spend a great while exploring the lower workings of your mine. He said it was decidedly unsafe. But if you can show me a *favorable* report from an equally distinguished expert. . . ."

"I'll do it!" Watson grinned, and they drank on it.

Cal already had in mind the distinguished engineer whose services he would frugally engage, and three days afterward, in a Los Angeles hotel, he found him—sobering up. It was Everett J. Hunnewell, and at sight of Cal he ducked down under the sheets.

"You mining expert asshole!" began Cal, calling him the worst name he could think of, "do you know what I'm going to do to you now? I'm going to break your damned back by pulling the crooks out of it, if you don't come through with that money you stole. It's all right to write reports and turn down the Golden Bear . . . that's what we expect of you experts . . . but you owe me four hundred dollars on that Thousand Wonders deal, and here's where I collect it . . . by hand."

He took off his coat and made a grab through the sheets, and then Hunnewell began to beg. It was the morning after for him—Polley's money was all spent, and he did not have the price of a drink.

"Well, that's all right," said Watson. "I didn't expect you to have a cent . . . I'm going to take it out of your hide. You went off and left me to starve and the miners beat hell out of me. I'll do as much for you!"

He grabbed again and the big promoter screamed, for

God had cursed him by making him a coward. In size he was a monster of corpulent flesh, and in a deal his nerve was cold-chilled, but man to man he was a blubbering baby, as Cal knew very well from the start. But here was the expert who was going to eat his own words or suffer the just punishment for his crimes.

"Oh, don't strike me!" pleaded Hunnewell. "Perhaps I can refund it to you later."

"*You* refund it!" Cal laughed. "You never refund anything . . . you'd slip out of my hands like an eel. No, you bilked me on the Thousand Wonders, and I let the matter pass. Now, by grab, you come back on the Bear! What kind of a jellyfish do you take me for, anyway . . . don't you think I can fight for my rights?"

"Just let me explain," cried Hunnewell eagerly. "Now, listen, Cal, this can all be rectified. I am personally acquainted with Evan Polley, and I'm sure I can persuade him to reconsider. My report was quite favorable, until just at the end I mentioned the lack of ore. I can report to him now that the return from later assays indicate an unexpected richness. Now, just kindly release me . . . no occasion to resort to violence . . . and we will fix the matter right up. But Watson, as a favor, as a great personal favor, won't you advance me five dollars for the drinks?"

"Not a cent!" pronounced Cal, still regarding him sternly. "And there's no use talking about Polley. If you'd recommended it in the first place, the Golden Bear would be sold, but now it's everlastingly too late. Polley is off of it for life, and what good did it do you? Didn't he pay you the same price, anyway? Well, why couldn't you pretend to be decent for once, and write out an honest report?"

"I . . . I inquired for you everywhere," protested Hunnewell feebly, "but I'm willing to make amends."

"Amends nothing!" stormed Watson. "The deal is off, I tell you. Old Polley has refused to buy. Now, it's up to me to get some bull-shoving report and hunt up another buyer."

"Oh . . . oh, let me write that report!" babbled Hunnewell frantically. "I'm broke, Cal, absolutely broke. I owe money everywhere and the proprietor of the hotel has just given me notice to vacate. I'll tell you what I'll do . . . for five hundred dollars. . . ."

"You nervy son-of-a-bitch!" exclaimed Cal. "You want to charge me money. . . ."

"No, but listen!" clamored Hunnewell. "Give me one hundred dollars and let the rest of it go for my debt. I've sought you repeatedly when I was in funds and. . . ."

"You have not," stated Cal. "I'll give you fifty."

"Well, fifty then. But, Cal, give me five of it now. I'm dying, positively dying, for a drink."

"Buy a bottle," advised Cal, laying a dollar on the table. "And I want that report tonight."

He got it, nicely typed by the hotel stenographer who had fallen for Hunnewell's wiles, and the promoter stood by purring while Cal read it over coldly, grimly noting the complete change of front.

"*Hmm* . . . what's this here?" he asked, scowling at the technical jargon of it. "Where do you get this line of talk?"

The principal vein, while containing much crystalline and crypty-crystalline quartz of a highly metalliferous character, carries, especially near the hanging wall, much iron and manganese-stained quartz, with the former calcite gangue largely replaced, particle by particle, by silica. It also contains some adularia with brecciated rock more or less banded. Pannings made on the ground showed native gold in paying quantities, but an assay of the adularia. . . .

"What is this adularia?"

"Well, I can't say," confessed Hunnewell by no means abashed. "I lifted the whole paragraph from a prospectus. But here's what counts . . . the recommendations at the end. That ought to sell any man's mine!"

"Yes," grumbled Cal, "wonder you didn't write it in the first place, when there was a chance to make a sale. Well, here's your forty-nine dollars."

He counted out the money and put the report in his pocket.

"Well, what're you going to do now?" he asked Hunnewell.

"*Ahem!* Ha!" Hunnewell smirked, smoothing the bills out lovingly, "this will finance a little deal I have on. Polley, you know, has taken quite a fancy to me and recommended me to several wealthy friends. He says that I am destined to succeed."

"What . . . *you* are!" cried Cal, suddenly cut to the quick. "Well, guess again, Hunnewell. Do you know what I'm going to do with this bull-shoving report? I'm going to show it to Evan Polley."

Chapter Twenty-Two

FAIR WARNING

There was a siren, in a story, who could steal any woman's husband by certain words that she murmured in his ear, and, when a jealous wife finally discovered the Circe's charm, it was: "I admire your taste in neckties!"

Cal wondered as he rode back to interview Polley if he also was not doing something similar. It was not so bad to be classed with Eccleson, the coffee merchant, because he was an honest tradesman, but when Polley had told Hunnewell that *he* was destined to succeed, he lost one ardent friend and admirer. The best Cal could say for him after that was that the champagne had finally got to him and destroyed his boasted knowledge of men, either that, or he had inherited his fortune from his father and had never really picked potential winners.

Hunnewell was a natural-born crook and a drunkard to boot, and the combination is fatal. Any crook will tell you that if you step up to his cell grating and ask: "My good man, what brought you to this place?"

"Booze!" he will answer—although more likely to get rid of you than to state any world-old truth. Still it is a fact that a crook must remain sober if he expects to succeed at his graft, and the only Hall of Fame that Hunnewell would ever qualify for was the one where they register your fingerprints.

Knowing this fact for a certainty, Cal was forced to consider its obvious bearing on himself. For if Polley's estimate of men was as fallible as all that, of what value was his prediction of Cal's success? He had stated, over the wineglass, that Cal was a born winner and destined to a great success, but in the light of recent events Cal's estimate of his chances had suffered a revision downward. He still believed he would succeed, but no longer through any hocus-pocus or magic formula of Polley's. From now on it was his intention to play a lone hand and let Hunnewell follow the gonfalon.

Polley was a man of moods, as Watson had discovered in his previous interviews with the millionaire, and this time he was feeling expansive. He welcomed Cal most cordially and for a moment Cal almost weakened in his stern resolution to show up Everett J. Hunnewell. But he had laid a straight line, and he intended to hew to it, let the chips fall where they would. So, assuming a cheery smile, he passed over his report and asked Polley what he thought of that. Polley read page after page, first in puzzlement and chagrin, and then with a new-born enthusiasm, but when, at the end, he found Hunnewell's signature, he whirled on Cal with a snarl.

"What's the joke?" he demanded. "Nothing funny about this . . . in cursed poor taste, it seems to me! Don't you know, Mister Watson, you could be prosecuted for this? Who signed Hunnewell's name to this report?"

"Hunnewell did," answered Cal, looking him straight in the eye. "Didn't I tell you that man was a crook?"

"I don't believe it," returned Polley, laying the report down deliberately. "I don't believe he signed it."

"He signed it, and he wrote it," declared Watson defiantly. "I can show you the original manuscript."

"Yes . . . but Hunnewell!" protested Polley, passing his hand over his forehead. "Can it be the man is dishonest? Why, I'd wager my life . . . but well, well, never mind, no man is quite infallible." He put on his glasses to glance over the original manuscript, and, as he read it through, Cal could see his jaws turn red like the wattles of an apoplectic turkey cock. "What is your object," he barked, "in bringing this to me? Do you expect me to buy your mine now?"

"No!" thundered back Cal. "I just wanted you to know what I think of these wind-jamming experts."

"Very well," bowed Polley, "you have had your wish. I wish you a very good buy."

"Same to you," returned Cal, getting blithely to his feet and making a break for the door, but Polley had not vented his spleen.

"Just a moment!" he snapped. "You have forgotten your report. And, by the way, how did you get him to write it?"

"Found him drunk and dead broke . . . told him he'd killed my deal with you. He offered to write this for some sucker."

"Oh." Polley smiled, slightly mollified by the implied compliment. "Then this was written for somebody else?"

"That's the idea," acknowledged Cal. "He nearly dropped dead when I told him I'd show it to you."

"Just wait!" Polley nodded. "I haven't finished with Mister Hunnewell. I shall wire my attorneys to prosecute."

"Go after him," encouraged Cal. "And next time you hire an expert be sure you get a good one."

With this parting advice he strode out and mounted his horse and was nearly back to camp when he met Sol Barksdale, riding down the cañon from his mine. If Polley had been in one mood, Sol Barksdale was in the other, and, as he confronted Watson, his Puritan chin stuck out as solid and blue as basalt.

"Watson," he rasped, "I have been up to see you and to warn you to leave this country. I have positive information

151

that you are stealing my cattle and driving them off into Nevada."

"From Crump, eh?" sneered Cal. "Well, he ought to know. Did he tell you about our meeting, over in the hills?"

"He informed me," replied Barksdale, "that you are the head of this gang of outlaws that have been stealing my cattle for months. I am a man of few words. If you do not leave at once, I shall swear out a warrant against you."

"Well, swear it out," challenged Cal, "and, when we get into court, I'll show your Crump up. And while we're handing out advice, let me give you a little . . . you'd better do some riding, Barksdale. Don't think because a man happens to call himself a detective that he won't stand a little watching."

"What do you mean?" demanded Barksdale, his intolerant eyes gleaming, but Watson had said enough.

"I mean just that," he said, "and I am speaking as a friend, because I have never stolen any of your cattle. I am not a cowman . . . don't even carry a rope . . . and, besides, I'm making money at mining. Why should I be engaged in this petty-larceny cow stealing when I've still got the Golden Bear?"

"You are a swindler, sir!" declared Barksdale with unnecessary vehemence. "Mister Johnson is willing to swear that you cheated him. And a man who will salt claims in order to sell them is not above stealing my cattle."

"Maybe Crump has stolen a few cows himself . . . he came from Texas, you know . . . and in any case you're taking a whole lot for granted when you come here and call me a thief. My good name is just as valuable as yours is, Barksdale, and I intend from now on to protect it. Don't you call me a thief unless you can prove it in the courts! Do you think you can prove it now?"

"No!" snarled Barksdale. "If I could, I'd have you arrested and sent to the penitentiary. I've come up here to warn you, and, if you're caught later on, you need look for no mercy from me."

He drew down his lips and spurred out awkwardly among the rocks, and Cal let him pass in silence. If it were not for Armilda and what might come from it, he would have told Sol Barksdale what he thought of him. The memory of that day when Barksdale had refused him water came back and made his head whirl. He remembered his sore feet, his aching body and parched lips—and Peggy, limping along behind—and a man-size hate rose up in his breast against this soured, vindictive Easterner. But he was Armilda's father and Cal gave him the trail, gazing after him until he rounded the next point. Then he remembered Wayne Crump and took to the high ground, for he had a hunch about Crump.

How easy it was to see his lying tongue in his new set of accusations. He had declared Cal the thief, the real leader of the gang that was driving cattle off into Nevada. Any countercharges would now look like spite work, although they would be the truth. But such ingenious lying always fails in the end. Sooner or later Crump would get tangled in his own rope, doubly dangerous, for then he was likely to shoot. That was the fear in Cal's heart as he rode for the ridge—he was afraid Crump was hiding there, to shoot him.

Chapter Twenty-Three

WHEELS WITHIN WHEELS

There was something decidedly ominous in these repeated accusations charging Watson with stealing J Prod cows. The most he had ever done was to rock them away from his cabin when they came down to Bitter Creek for water, yet ever since that time it had been dinned into his ears that he was in danger of arrest as a cow thief. Whispering Johnson had threatened him openly, warning him off of the range. Armilda seemed to have heard all about it. Now came Barksdale with another accusation and another last warning to move. Yet the water was his and he could, if he wanted to, fence it in and make the J Prods move. But a cowman is like an Indian—he claims all the land as far as he can see as his own particular and God-given domain.

It had been Cal's intention to hire some timber men and start work on the Golden Bear, but this encounter with Sol Barksdale served once more to divert his purpose and send him up on the peak to his look-out. The cowmen had all confessed that they had no case against him, had conceded that he was innocent before the law, and yet they hovered about his cabin like a band of Indians until his nerves were getting raw. He was up before daylight, watching the ridges like a scared rabbit before he dared to venture out of his hole. Once in the open he had a haunting sense of some presence that lurked among the rocks. Up on the ridge it was no better, for there were ridges above that, and on the second day Cal climbed up to the very top to look at the country below.

With his glasses he could see the ranch at Bubbling Wells and the cowboys riding off on their rounds. But if Armilda was there, she rode no circles on the lakebed to invite him to make another call. Perhaps she, too, believed Crump's lying stories and considered Cal unworthy of further thought, or, more likely, she was waiting until he summoned up the nerve to accept her previous invitation. "Come and see me again!" she had called after him as he had left, but he had never headed that way. Bubbling Wells was anathema for him. Even seen through the glasses, it conveyed an evil effect, as of some thicket where wood demons dwelt. The white-walled house seemed a trap set to catch him, surrounded by its black clumps of mesquite. And yet, up there on the peak with the whole world before him, he kept his glasses on the ranch. There dwelt his dearest friend and his two most hated enemies; his world, for the moment, was there.

Crump rode out first of all, galloping off across the flat toward the mouth of Black Cañon Pass, but once in the hills Cal saw him turn off north, circling toward the Thousand Wonders Mine. Polley's limousine was missing, so he must have gone to town. Cal wondered what mischief was afoot, until at last he saw a pony leave the house and gallop off. Mrs. Polley was going out for her ride. Like needles afloat in a basin of water, the two specks threaded the cañons and approached, and then, drawn together as if magnetized, they met and came to rest. Cal put down his glasses and swore softly to himself. Here, again, like attracted like.

The woman adventuress sought out the male adventurer, and he in turn sought her. If Evan Polley ever got an inkling of the truth, his turkey-gobbler apoplexy would return. The stroke might be fatal and leave her a widow, that consummation she so devoutly desired. If he survived, she would be a widow of a different kind, for had he not bought her at a price? "The best of everything!" That had been his motto, and this would detract from her worth. It could hardly be claimed, in the face of this affair, that he had bought the best of womankind. An appeal to the courts might result in his favor, thus ending their long *duel de sexe,* but Cal was not engaged in carrying gossip. He put up his glasses and came away. What a country this had come to, and what people had moved into it! There was only one who was worth a second thought, and she, cursed spite, was ensnared by this same serpent who seemed to hold women with his eye. Cal threw on the packs and hit the road for Klondike, to get away from it all.

Klondike was the town that lay beneath the hill where the Yellowstone Sandstorm pounded out its gold, but it was not written that he should reach his destination that day, for halfway up the road he met Wiggins. First a racing streak of dust showed yellow against the hills, and then a stripped machine that writhed and leaped. Finally there was a flash of teeth from the passing automobile and a cloud of dirt as he stopped. It was the same little man who had given him the ride into Soledad and saved him from Bill Beagle and the calaboose—the man who could have Cal's shirt any time.

"What are you doing with that mine?" inquired Wiggins, after they had passed the news of the day. "You know . . . the Golden Bear. Like to come up and look at it sometime. I wonder," he went on, fumbling absently in his pocket, "if I ever gave you my card." He drew out his pocketbook and handed over a professional card that made Cal's eyes protrude.

"Hell's bells," he exclaimed, "are you S. Parker Wiggins, the man that found the Yellow Sandstorm ore? I thought your face looked kind of familiar!"

"That's my name," admitted Wiggins, "for professional purposes. I generally go by the name of Sam. Have to come back, once in a while, to see how things look. Yes, most people associate me with the Sandstorm."

"I guess yes!" assented Cal, gazing down on him admiringly. S. Parker Wiggins was the last of some eight or ten alleged experts who had been called in to examine the Yellow Sandstorm, and, after the rest had failed to find the values, he had proved it a mountain of gold. Low grade, to be sure, but free milling and easy to handle. Since then it had been a small mint. Hence S. Parker Wiggins had become a name to conjure with, although he had subsequently turned down several good properties. In fact, it was a saying among old-style practical miners that he had turned down every good mine in the West. But here he was, a quiet little man, riding around in a jack-rabbit flivver. Cal dropped down from his horse to shake hands again, and Wiggins regarded him quizzically.

"I've been keeping track of you, young man," he said at last, "ever since I picked you up that night. I wonder if we can't do a little business?"

"Sure thing," agreed Cal. "Just tell me what you want, and I'll go right out and get it. No joking . . . I'm your friend for life!"

"That's very flattering," said Wiggins, "but the business I had in mind ought to make a little money for us both. How would you like to sell the Golden Bear?"

"Just tried it," answered Cal, "and that same son-of-a-bitching Hunnewell bobbed up and ditched me again. But I put the bee on him this time."

Wiggins chuckled indulgently as Cal gave him the whole story, including the writing of the second report, but as the narrative ran on, he raised his hand at a sudden thought, although he held his peace to the end. What S. Parker Wiggins thought had to be important if he mentioned it at all—and even then he was willing to wait before doing so.

He was a standing rebuke to those loud-mouthed and fussy persons who interrupt and browbeat and dominate. He was like the precious parrot that, while he could not speak a word, nevertheless kept up a devil of a thinking.

"I wonder . . . ," he began, then stopped to think again. "What do you hold your mine at?" he asked.

"A hundred thousand dollars," answered Watson promptly, but Wiggins shook his head.

"Too cheap," he said. "If you sell it at all, you can just as well get two-fifty."

"That's agreeable." Cal grinned. "How much will your cut be? Don't be bashful . . . I'm your friend, you know."

"Very flattering," murmured Wiggins. "If we put this deal through, the cut will be fifty-fifty."

"Good enough," agreed Cal. "And now let's get down to business. Who's going to buy our mine?"

"That's my part of it," said Wiggins. "All you have to do is to hold out for two hundred and fifty thousand dollars. No matter what I do, no matter what I say, the price is two-fifty . . . cash."

"I get you," agreed Cal. "But is that all I do? I'm game to climb spider webs, if necessary."

"Not necessary," returned Wiggins with the quiet smile that made his face so attractive. "Your task is infinitely more difficult. You must stay at the mine and trust me absolutely, no matter if I don't come for a month. I will do all the work . . . the planning and everything, and bring the man up to your mine. Your job is to stay put and keep your hand out of it, and remember that the price is two-fifty."

"Sounds easy," conceded Cal, "but give me your system. I sold a mine once myself."

"So I heard," observed Wiggins with a shade of sarcasm, "but this deal is absolutely on the square. No salting, understand, no professional strong-arm work. We are dealing with high-grade men. Put out of your mind all thought of men like Hunnewell . . . they are the panhandlers of an honorable profession. There are two kinds of mining experts, or consulting engineers as we reputable men prefer to be called . . . the beginners, who boost everything, and men like myself who make more money by turning them down. Now, I am telling you this in confidence and against my better judgment, but I want you to understand. It will help you to wait when you think that I've forgotten you or have given up the whole matter.

"You have doubtless heard men say, and particularly the miners, that I never found but one good mine in my life, and that since Yellow Sandstorm I've been afraid to take a chance, and, therefore, I turn them all down. They've probably told you that capitalists keep on employing a consulting expert, no matter how many mines he turns down, but that, if he recommends a bad one, they never forget it, since it has cost them several million dollars. Now, I do not deny that there is something in this, though not just exactly as stated. Mining magnates do make a practice of employing engineers who have a reputation for turning down mines, but in most cases the engineer makes an adverse report in order to keep down the price. What the engineer knows and reports to his employer is something different from what he publishes to the world, and the result as you can see is a lucrative practice, which compensates in a way for the deception. In any case, it is more reputable than the antics of men like Hunnewell who represent the dregs of the profession. There is this side to it, also . . . that when we do recommend a mine . . . well, it's extremely likely to sell."

He favored Cal with a shrewd and fleeting smile that made him open his eyes.

"I see." Cal nodded. "This is going to be one of those times."

"Very likely," responded Wiggins. "Very likely."

Chapter Twenty-four

THE COW THIEF

Great thoughts lie deeply and there is not one man in a million who understands what is going on around him. Cal had spent his whole life in a mining community where he had learned the common scorn of mining experts. He had heard and always believed that they were charlatans *par excellence,* and had proved it by the mines they had turned down. The Yellow Sandstorm, the United Verde, the Copper Queen— all had been condemned by mining experts of the first rank, and yet they stood today as producers without a peer, three of the really great mines in the West. But here came along a man that no one would look at twice—a little, dried-up man with a shy smile—who in a burst of sudden confidence, although against his better judgment, gave him a peep behind the veil. They turned the mines down so that they could be bought cheaply, and each failure was in reality a success.

Cal rode home in a daze, pondering cynically on the saying that the man who knows most, knows nothing. He is simply aware of his ignorance. But there are degrees, even of ignorance, and between Polley and Wiggins he began to feel that he was cutting his teeth. The diet of solid food that had been fed to him lately was weaning him from being a child. When he had been a child, he had thought as a child, but now, darkly as through a glass, he began to perceive the truth. He began to wonder vaguely whether there was any royal road to success, for he had tried Polley's system and failed. Yes, and Polley had failed, and failed abjectly, when he picked Everett J. Hunnewell for a winner. Unless Watson's hunch was wrong, the millionaire's absence from home was not unconnected with a suit against Hunnewell.

So much for Polley—the man who followed his luck and won out by picking the winners. Enter S. Parker Wiggins. Cal could not but feel a pang that so nice a little man should be capable of what was practically a fraud. It was his intention to sell his services to some high-grade investor and engage his interest in the Golden Bear and then, right or wrong, deliberately recommend the mine and accept a conspirator's share in the proceeds. But Cal's skirts were clean, for this most considerate of conspirators had agreed to do the dirty work. All Cal had to do was to keep his face straight and offer his mine for $250,000—cash. Nothing could be simpler and yet the son of old Sam Watson felt a premonitory pricking of conscience. The Golden Bear was worth $250,000 of any multi-millionaire's money, but it was a shame to sell it by fraud. There was a big mine in Colorado that had sold for $8,000,000 by an ingenious method of salting the samples, yet the English syndicate that bought it had made a profit. But when the chloride of gold was injected through the sample sacks, it involved a moral and legal fraud. Cal had entered wholeheartedly into the trimming of Whispering Johnson, for there he was stabbing back at a thief, but this capitalist that Wiggins would bring to buy a legacy would be innocent of any intent to defraud. Cal had a feeling that, if his father were there, he would not consent to the deal.

But Cal's gloomy thoughts were swept away like a mist when Wiggins appeared with his capitalist in tow. It was none other than Evan Polley, the apostle of success, the man who stood alone against the world. $250,000 of his un-

161

earned increment would be duck soup for California Watson. They came riding up the cañon, for the road was washed out, on the morning of the second day, and Cal saw them from afar from his look-out on the peak where he lay, watching for friend or enemy. That boxed-in cañon was no place for a man who had Johnson and Wayne Crump on his trail, but he came down gladly to welcome his neighbor, although this was Polley's first visit. Such phrases as neighbor and friend and partner were seldom on his materialistic tongue, and even now he was strictly business.

"Mister Watson," he began, "allow me to introduce Mister Wiggins, whose name you may have heard before . . . S. Parker Wiggins, you know."

"Oh," acknowledged Cal, and nodded shortly, "glad to meet you, Mister Wiggins."

"I have engaged Mister Wiggins," went on Polley a little pompously, "to make an inspection of your mine. You have no objections, I trust?"

"Well . . . no," replied Cal. "Always glad to have visitors . . . but what's the idea, Mister Polley?"

"The idea?" repeated Polley, apparently very much astonished. "Why, to report on it, of course. I take it your mine is for sale?"

"Well, yes," answered Cal, "but that's just the point. These adverse reports don't help."

"Adverse!" Polley glowered. "I don't understand you at all, sir."

"I'll explain, then," said Cal. "Mister Wiggins has the name of turning down every mine he examines. That may be fine for you, but a few more of these reports and I can't sell my mine at all."

"What, what?" blustered Polley. "Are you going to let this absurd prejudice deprive you of the sale of your mine? I am satisfied now that my former mining expert was not competent to make a report, but Mister Wiggins, as you know, is the most distinguished consulting engineer to be found in the West today."

"Fine and dandy," retorted Cal, "and, if I thought it would do any good, I'd have him down the shaft in no time, but that son-of-a-bitch, Hunnewell, has given my mine one black eye. . . ."

"Oh, nonsense!" exclaimed Polley. "My time is valuable, Mister Watson, and I can't stand here arguing all day. Will you allow my consulting expert to examine your mine?"

"I will," answered Cal, "only now, Mister Polley, the price is two hundred and fifty thousand dollars."

"What?" shouted Polley, turning turkey-cock red and raising his hands in protest. "I could have bought it for a hundred thousand dollars!"

"But you didn't do it," returned Cal. "You listened to a bum expert, and now, by grab, you bring another one who was never known to recommend a mine. He made a ten-strike on the Yellow Sandstorm . . . and that let him out . . . I might as well ask you a million."

"Well . . . call if two-fifty and let him examine the mine! We can talk the price over later."

"There won't be any talking," answered Watson grimly. "My price is two-fifty . . . cash."

"Shall we draw up a little option?" inquired Wiggins pleasantly, and the curtain went down on Act One.

Act Two began with Wiggins's examination of the mine, which he sampled with the greatest care. When he departed to work out his report, Cal waited for Act Three and the end.

Whether the play would turn out another farce comedy, or a crook play where the toff got trimmed, now depended upon the stage director, the able S. Parker Wiggins, but the acting up to date had been so realistic and convincing Cal wondered if it was not the real thing. Wiggins had taken a chance and gone into every drift that was not blocked with falling rock, and from the look in his eye Cal had derived the impression that he had come upon something good. Then he had followed the outcrop for several miles until he had connected it up definitely with the Thousand Wonders. He had measured the hot water that gushed out at the contact and that, flowing down, became Bitter Creek. He had examined with special interest the few pillars of the original ore that were left in the caved-in chambers, and then he had sampled and measured the old dump, besides taking some pannings of the rock. All the while his face was grave and set, as if he locked a great secret in his breast.

Then followed the long wait, with no thumping behind the scenes to give hope that the curtain would soon rise. This option, like the former one, was good for thirty days and Cal fretted as he watched the trail. Now, as before, he watched for friends or enemies, for the J Prod cowboys were riding the hills. Although they sometimes passed near, they always avoided Bitter Creek, and the cave house was as lonely as a tomb. A fever of unrest kept him continually on the move, and sometimes he even ventured down the shaft, but the rattle of dropping pebbles gave warning of falling ground and he dared not venture too far. Then the loneliness crept in and his old hunch came back—he sensed a hidden presence among the rocks.

The end came one day at dawn, beginning with a shot below his house, and he grabbed up his rifle and peered out. It was just good daylight, that time of all times for treachery, ambush, and sudden death. Yet, so tense were his nerves, that he slipped off down the cañon where he could hear the frightened bawling of a calf. Something evil was afoot, he could feel it in the air, and he ducked as he heard another shot. Above him, on both sides, the jagged cañon wall seemed to menace him, but no head appeared above the rim. He crouched lower and crept on, gliding from boulder to boulder, craning his head to see who had shot. He had hidden long enough, now he wanted to see his enemy—and he found him stooping over a dead calf.

His slouched Texas hat proclaimed him a cowboy at the same time that it covered up his face, and his shoulders rose and fell as with nervous haste he set about skinning the calf. Cal gazed at him, fascinated, still trying to make him out and to guess his motives for such an act. At last the cowboy looked up. He was no more than a boy, with a weak, tough face, and at sight of Cal he broke and ran. Up over the rocks he went like a frightened rabbit until he topped the ridge, and was gone.

Cal glanced about and listened, then, deceived by the silence, he walked down and looked at the calf. It was a red J Prod yearling, shot cleanly between the eyes, partly butchered and with the brand half cut out. A bloody knife, which the cowboy had dropped, lay reeking in the sand. Cal stooped down and picked it up. There was something about it that seemed strangely familiar, and yet—he started and grabbed for his pistol.

"Put 'em up!" said a voice, and over the top of a rock he saw Crump's tall hat and a gun.

Watson jumped like a wolf that has stepped into a steel trap, but he put up his hands with a jerk. Something told him that Wayne Crump was hoping he would not—that he would resist and get shot in the trap. But Cal put them up high, and, even above the fear that was clutching at his throat, he felt a mad rage at being fooled. He had walked into this booby trap as guilelessly as a child, even picking up the bloody knife. Now he knew why the knife looked so familiar—it was the one he had given back to Crump! The same cowboy knife that had been stabbed through the dead man's hand and stuck into his cabin door. He had played with a rattlesnake and it had snapped back and bit him. Now he would be lucky to escape with his life.

"You dog-goned smart Aleck!" hissed the detective provocatively. "I caught you with the goods, eh, this time?"

"That's right," agreed Cal, still holding them high. "Pretty smooth, I'll have to admit."

"You're a cowardly damned jasper," observed Crump, after a minute of strained silence. "I thought you were on the shoot."

"Nope," returned Cal. "You've got me in the door. I know better than to resist an officer."

"Oh, Bill!" hailed Crump, still crouching behind his rock.

After a short wait, Bill Beagle came scrambling down to them with his rifle held ready to shoot.

"Well, you caught him, eh?" He laughed, stopping to look Cal over. "I knowed he was the culprit all the time."

Cal took this fling without making any retort—Bill Beagle had killed Kid Benson. The reward had read DEAD OR ALIVE, and Bill had confessed in his cups that he never took any chances with a prisoner.

"That devil tried to murder me," he hinted to Crump. "You want to watch him like a hawk . . . he's dangerous!"

"I'm watching him," said Crump. "You go down there, off to one side, and reach over and git his pistol."

"You're welcome to it," spoke up Cal. "I'm caught and I know it. You won't have any trouble with me."

"You keep them hands up!" yelled Beagle, suddenly

jumping back and signaling Crump to shoot. "By Gawd, he'd like to shoot me!"

"Naw, he's all right," said Crump, still watching Cal expectantly. "He's too damned scairt to do anything."

"That's all right, boys," said Cal. "Go ahead and have your joke. But I've surrendered . . . and I'm not going to run."

"Aw, hell, Bill!" exclaimed Crump, striding impatiently down the hill and snatching away Cal's gun. "Quit your fooling . . . can't you see he's harmless?"

A sudden gleam came into Cal's eye, but his face was like a mask. He knew what they were trying to do. If they could get him to resist or tempt him to flee, there would be a grave in Bitter Creek wash. Crump stood gazing at him scornfully, his evil eyes alight with a smile of cunning triumph.

"Here's his knife," he said to Beagle, picking up the bloody jackknife. "We'll call that Exhibit B."

"Caught red-handed!" Beagle cackled, wagging his head at Watson. "This is good for twenty years, at the least. And your previous record won't do you no good. I knowed all the time you was a criminal at heart, even before you tried to hold up the stage, but that night down at Soledad, when you tried to murder me with that shotgun, convinced the whole country that you was desperate. You been warned time and ag'in to git out of the country, and now you'll have to take your medicine."

"All right," answered Cal. "Just take me to jail. I'm not asking favors of any man."

"You go up to the house, Bill," directed Crump abruptly, "and bring down his pack mule and horse. We've got to take that yearling in, too."

"No, you go," objected Beagle, trying to give him the

wink, but Crump had his reasons for being obdurate.

"Now, lookee here," he said to Cal when Bill was out of sight. "We want that ten thousand dollars. We've got you dead to rights, but. . . ."

"I haven't got it . . . here," temporized Watson.

Crump glanced up the cañon and came a little nearer.

"Where is it?" he asked ingratiatingly. Cal looked at him again and in a flash he understood why Crump had not shot him at the start—he was after the $10,000.

"We can talk that over," he suggested, "after I've come up for trial. Are you going to appear against me?"

"I am," declared Crump, "and more than that, my man, I'm going to send you to the pen. Any yap that thinks he can put one over on me has got another guess coming, that's all. At the same time, if you'll tell me where you've got the stuff hid. . . ."

"I can't tell you," parried Cal. "I'd have to show you. Does Beagle come in on this?"

"No," grumbled Crump. "Can't you draw me a map? I can't get rid of the hick."

"He's trying to kill me," stated Cal, looking him straight in the eye. "Are you going to protect me, or not?"

"Well, come through," commanded Crump. "D'ye think I'm out here for my health? Dig up what you've got and we'll talk."

Cal drove down into his pocket and handed him over his roll, which amounted to nearly $500, and Crump tucked it away in his shirt. A new look had come into his eyes.

"That old walloper is crazy to kill you," he confided under his breath. "But I'll protect you . . . for ten thousand dollars. How's that, now?" he demanded in the silence that followed, but Watson shook his head.

"No," he said. "I'm not making any promises. But if I

168

get killed, that ten thousand is gone."

"Never mind," menaced Crump. "I don't need any promises. You'll come through with the ten thousand, all right. And you'll do it before the trial or I'll turn in a bunch of testimony that will send you to the penitentiary for life. If you dig, I may forget a part of it."

"All right," assented Cal, "I'll think the matter over. But don't let that old scoundrel ride behind me."

Bill Beagle came spurring along down the cañon, dragging the reluctant Lemon behind him, and after a careful examination of what would be Exhibit A, they lashed the dead yearling on the pack. Then at Beagle's insistence they tied Cal's hands to the horn and his feet beneath Campomoche's belly. With Beagle leading his horse behind, they rode off across Dry Lake to Bubbling Wells. Cal kept his mouth shut, for Bill Beagle was feeling ugly and Crump was far from being his friend, but, when they drew up at the ranch house gate, he made a stand for his rights.

"Cut my feet loose," he said. "I'm getting weak, riding this way. You don't need to treat me like an Indian."

"Aw, to hell with you!" blustered Crump. "You're lucky to be alive. You stay tied till we git to the railroad."

He spurred in at the gate, rushing Campomoche ahead of him, and reined in before the Barksdales' with a flourish.

"Well, here's your cow thief, Mister Barksdale," he announced triumphantly. "I told you I'd spotted the right man. Here's the yearling he was working on . . . Bill and I heard him shoot, and I nailed him in the act of skinning it."

He stripped off the canvas and exposed Exhibit A, and, while Barksdale examined it, Armilda stepped back and flashed an inquiring glance at Cal.

"There's where he shot it," went on Crump, pointing out the hole in the forehead, "and look here what he was doing to your brand. That's a J Prod, all right, but a minute later and he'd've had all the evidence destroyed. Right then was where I threw down on him with my Winchester. Do you think that will convict him in the courts?"

"It certainly will," answered Barksdale, speaking with painful directness and glaring at Watson indignantly. "He need expect no mercy from me. I'll accompany you to Soledad and swear out the warrant myself. What do you think of *that,* Armilda?"

He turned upon her accusingly, and Armilda hung her head.

"I don't know what to think," she said.

She went over and fingered the slashed brand ruefully, and then she turned to her father.

"Aren't you going to use the meat?" she asked. "All they need to take in is the skin."

"Yes, skin it," ordered Barksdale as he went off to saddle his horse. "That slashed brand is evidence enough."

Beagle glanced at Crump doubtfully, for the carcass told the story in a way that a hide could not, but Crump knew his boss and he knew that in such matters it was useless to combat his will. He was thrifty and the meat would not keep.

"I'll bring a tub," suggested Armilda helpfully, and she was halfway to the house before Crump could get over laughing.

"This ain't a rabbit," he called after her. "Bring a rope and the butcher knife!" And while they watched him, he skinned the calf swiftly.

Cal looked on with the rest, shifting his weight in the saddle and trying to catch Armilda's eye, but she ignored his presence.

"Say, cut that rope," he complained as Crump straightened up. "You don't need to hog-tie me like this."

"What'd I tell you?" demanded Crump, handing the bloody knife back to Armilda. "You stay tied till we reach the railroad!"

Armilda made a quick slash at the rope that bound Cal's hands and another across the one that bound his feet.

"You ought to be ashamed!" she said to Crump, and marched off into the house.

Chapter Twenty-five

WIGGINS

The prisoner in the case had nothing to think about as he rode his led horse toward Soledad, for either Armilda was his friend and secret ally, or she had thrown him over completely. His feet were lashed again beneath the belly of Campomoche and his legs ached miserably from the strain, but now that the danger of imminent death was removed, his mind began to recover from the shock. With Barksdale along he knew his life was safe, although the old man spoke never a word. They all rode in silence, for the excitement had left them weak, and each had his regrets and hopes, but Cal Watson had the keenest, for he had been caught like a fool—and Armilda had cut him loose. It had passed for a joke, and Crump had bound his hands tighter, shouting back rough witticisms at the house, but, perhaps, with her it had been a sign, in place of words, to show him she was still his friend. Yet her solicitude about the meat had seemed a little forced to one who knew her as Cal did. Unless he was mistaken, her mind had been on other things than the saving of a little range meat. It had seemed, as he watched her, that she was wrestling with some problem and that this was the outcome of her thoughts. Armilda was deep, she had a certain steel-trap quickness that enabled her to read men at a glance, and with this quickness she had the power to take a situation in hand and mold it to suit her will. Something would come of this, he felt sure, unless, for his sins, the calm-eyed Armilda had forsaken him.

The word of Cal's capture seemed to have preceded them to Soledad. As the cavalcade approached town, a flight of horsemen came whipping toward them, with Whispering Johnson in the lead.

"Well, well!" he brayed, whirling his horse in a half circle and reining in to gloat at the prisoner. "It sure takes an old cat to ketch 'em! How'd you do it, Bill? Like you caught Kid Benson? Well, well, so you got him at last?"

"Right in the door!" boasted Beagle, disregarding Crump's scowl. "I knowed he was the culprit all the time. Stands to reason he had some object, living out by that watering place, and we caught him, by grab, in the act."

"We heard him shoot," explained Crump, "and, when I come over the hill, there he was, down butchering the beef. But it was a J Prod calf that he killed."

"I'll swear out the warrant," said Barksdale reassuringly. "One brand is as good as another."

"But I thought . . . ," began Johnson, then stopped abruptly, for Cal had glanced up at him inquiringly. "Well, all right," he said; "only I always thought . . . well, no matter, let's get him into town. We can flag the four-ten if the judge will get a move on, and I'll wire Dave to put him in solitary."

He rode in behind Cal and jumped Campomoche into a gallop, and so they pounded along into town. It was rough on the prisoner, with his feet tied Indian fashion, but now suddenly he had become a nonentity. No one spoke to him directly. Even Johnson ignored him except to look over and laugh. The result of his examination before old Judge Brown seemed to be taken for granted by everyone. It was a mere formality, to be rushed through perfunctorily in order to catch the four-ten, and at Mojave City the sheriff would be waiting to throw him into solitary confinement. Cal clung to the horn the last mile of his ride, and, when they cut off his bonds, he fell from the saddle for his legs were numb to the hips.

"Give him a drink," suggested a kindly voice as the crowd gathered around him, and Cal looked up to recognize Wiggins. There was something about Wiggins that he had always liked immensely, and he knew now that it was his smile. The others were all scowling or staring curiously, but Wiggins had the smile of an angel. "Try this," he went on, producing a bottle, and Cal took a drink and shuddered. "Have some water?" inquired Wiggins, passing over his canteen. "How long since he's eaten?" he asked.

"Oh, this morning . . . I guess," answered Crump indifferently. "Believe I could do a little eating myself."

"You'll have to hurry!" bellowed Johnson, then, beginning to take shame at the way they had manhandled their prisoner, he added: "Well, you've got time, I guess."

"I'll pay for his meal," spoke up Wiggins quietly. "I've met this boy, out at his mine."

"Have to go to the county jail, if you want to meet him now!" called out Johnson as they passed into the dining room, but his joke did not draw any big laugh. S. Parker Wiggins was known wherever mines and mining men existed, and his name commanded a certain respect, but the man himself was greater than the name that he retained for professional purposes. Without seeming to oppose anybody, he stated his wishes in such a way that a veritable boor could hardly refuse him, and, if any boor did, there were men who knew Wiggins who said he was chain lightning in a fight. But no one opposed him, for what he asked was reasonable, and after paying for the meal he went out.

Cal ate in gloomy silence, for he was aching from head

to foot, and Bill Beagle sat across from him, watching. He was gnashing his food as well, but there was a six-shooter by his plate and every movement seemed to excite fresh suspicion. As Cal met Bill's evil eyes, he was reminded of a gorilla that he had seen once, glaring through the bars.

The examination before Judge Brown was as brief as it could be made and still stand the test of law. After Crump had stated that he had caught Cal in the act, he was held on the charge of grand larceny. He was then remanded into the custody of the sheriff, to be held until the grand jury met. When the four-ten came through, Watson was taken aboard by Beagle and shackled to a seat in the smoker. Then the train rushed on its way, across the arid desert and up over the mountain pass beyond, and shortly after dark they arrived in Mojave City and were met by Dave Johnson, the sheriff. Down the long, depot street they were driven to the county jail, which was in the basement of the big brick courthouse. Cal stumbled into a cell and dropped down on the narrow bunk without asking whether it was the solitary or the jag cell. All he knew was the bunk looked good to him, and the next minute he was sleeping like the dead.

He was still asleep when late the following morning someone knocked on his cell door with a huge key.

"Here's a visitor to see you!" called a voice from without, and, as he looked through the grating, he saw Johnson. Not Whispering Johnson, but his more amiable brother, for Cal found Dave had placed him in the bridal chamber. The women's cell was not occupied, and, when that was the case, Dave kept it for any white man that was decent.

" 'Morning, Cal." He nodded. "Get a good night's sleep? They's a gentleman in the office wants to see you."

Dave was a big man but quiet, with a slow, farmer's

smile and a face full of rugged good nature. As Cal rose up and began a hasty wash, Dave unlocked the door of his cell.

"I guess you won't run away," he said, and went back to his office.

The county jail at Mojave City was primitive in a way, and yet it served its purpose. First was the sheriff's big office, with a row of chairs for visitors, and a huge safe built into the wall, then, past the bedroom, where the jailer and chance deputies slept, was the one broad door to the cell room. Past it there was the women's cell, and a dog hole for the drunks, and beyond that the bull pen for general prisoners. Off on the side, in absolute darkness, were the cavern and crypts of the solitary cells. Here, if Whispering Johnson had had his way, Cal Watson would now be incarcerated, but Dave had known Cal for several years, and he did not take dictation from anybody.

Cal came out at last, and Dave opened the big door with one of the huge keys that he rattled on his chain.

"Meet Mister McKinney," he said. "He's down here to get you out on bail."

A tall, lanky man with a mass of iron-gray hair came forward and shook hands impressively.

"Mister Watson?" he inquired. "I have been retained by one of your friends to attend to the granting of bail."

"What friend?" blurted out Cal, but the lawyer coughed deprecatingly and glanced across at the sheriff.

"He preferred," he said, "not to appear in the case. But since he has put up cash bail in the amount of ten thousand dollars, you may safely take my word that he's your friend. I've seen the judge and the matter is all arranged. That's all, isn't it, Dave? Well, good bye."

He started out the door, but Cal did not follow.

"Can I go?" he asked, turning to Johnson.

"Sure thing." The sheriff grinned. "No use sticking around here . . . the grand jury don't convene for a month."

Cal looked at him again and passed a hand across his brow, but caution was seared deeply into his brain. Just the morning before he had jumped out of bed and gone off down the cañon on the run, and the next thing he knew he was holding a bloody jackknife and looking down the muzzle of a Winchester. All that long day Bill Beagle had been trying to get him to run. It was burned into his brain—not to run whatever happened!

"No, I'll stay," he decided, but before he could speak the words, McKinney came back and beckoned him.

"It was Wiggins," he whispered, speaking behind his hand. "He's outside around the corner, waiting for you!"

Sam Wiggins was not only waiting. He had a high-powered automobile up to the curb ready to take off. As Cal stepped in, he opened up to the legal limit and drove out of town, heading north. He listened a trifle absently to Cal's protestations and thanks, only responding with his shy smile.

"That's all right," he said. "Please don't take this too seriously . . . it is largely a matter of business. We are partners, in a way, in a certain venture, and that is why I put up the cash. Ten thousand isn't much, compared to the stakes we are playing for, and the sale is as good as made. Now the thing to do is to get you back to Polley before he can change his mind."

"He's ready to sign, eh?" exulted Cal. "Well, that suits me down to the ground. If I can just grab some money to hire a few expensive lawyers, I'll get out of this jackpot yet. How'd you come to get down here so soon?"

"Why, you didn't see me, but I came down on the same train . . . stepped off on the opposite side . . . and now, if you don't mind making a breakfast on canned goods, I'm going to rush you back to Polley. There's a certain influence against us."

"Well, burn up the road, then," said Cal, "because you know Polley! Who is it that's blocking the deal?"

"Well . . . nobody," hesitated Wiggins, "only I have the feeling that Missus Polley isn't quite friendly. Not from anything she's said, but there's something about her manner. . . ."

"She's a bad one." Cal nodded. "I know her."

"Know her well?" inquired Wiggins, looking over with sudden interest. "I may have to ask you to handle her."

"Well enough," grumbled Cal, "to stay away from her. But where does she come in on the deal?"

"A wife," observed Wiggins, as if speaking from sad experience, "always exerts a certain influence over her husband, whether they are happily married or not. Next to whiskey and jealous competitors I have had more trouble with women than with all other elements combined. A woman is rarely qualified to advise her husband wisely, even if she understands the pros and cons of a mining trade, but it is the exception rather than the rule when they do not interfere, and especially if they're the least bit opposed. I knew a woman once who, by refusing to sign a deed, knocked her husband out of a million-dollar sale, and he's a ruined man today. The only reason she ever gave was that they tried to make her sign before she'd finished looking at the papers. And yet, if you play up to them too much, they immediately become suspicious and jump just as far the other way."

"What did she do," persisted Cal, "that makes you think she's against you? Did Polley consult her about the sale?"

"Not in the least," returned Wiggins. "He knows his

own mind. She was listening outside the door."

"Aw, she's lonely," burst out Cal. "All these women get that way, living out here where nothing ever happens. But I don't see where it makes any difference to her if he buys all the mines in the country."

"Nor I," agreed Wiggins, "and I hope I'm all wrong. But it was very unfortunate that they arrested you when they did, because yesterday he was crazy to buy. I was just leaving his camp to go up and get you when I saw the officers in the distance, and a young man I met gave me the information that you had just been arrested for cattle stealing."

"What kind of a young man?" inquired Watson eagerly. "Was he a cowboy with a big slouch hat? Well, that's the very guy I'm looking for. He killed that calf himself, and, if I can ever catch him . . . which way did he ride from there?"

"Why, off to the east . . . I thought he was working for Johnson."

"He was," returned Cal, "but I'll trail him all right . . . he's in the cow-stealing business with Crump."

"See this deal through first," advised Wiggins sagely. Although he was fretting to take up the trail, Cal reluctantly agreed to wait. Except for Wiggins and his cash bail, he would still be in prison, and, as Wiggins had frankly stated, his object in putting up bail was to consummate the sale immediately. Years of handling such ticklish affairs had given him an insight into the way men's minds behave, and he knew that the buying impulse is like a rush of blood to the head, sure to be followed by a period of sober thought. He knew that at all such times the least word, said or unsaid, might break the prepossession to buy, and that, even when the pen was poised over the dotted line, the possibility of failure still remained. And Polley of all men was the hardest to handle because his moods were as variable as the winds. He also had a wife who was pretty enough to make mischief and a cellar full of champagne to boot.

They went boiling up over the summit and thundering down the other side of the range, but, before they reached Soledad, they saw Polley's big limousine, boring its way down the desert road. He was going to Mojave City—or perhaps to Los Angeles, for distance meant nothing in his machine. When he saw Wiggins, he stopped reluctantly, which was sign enough of his mood.

"Mister Wiggins," he called, without waiting for Wiggins to speak, "I'm not fully decided about that mine. I find that, up to date, the Thousand Wonders Mine has cost me forty thousand dollars without a single dollar coming back. Now, of course, I know. . . ."

"Oh, that's all right, Mister Polley," returned Wiggins cordially, "I didn't want to influence your judgment, but if you don't want to buy the mine. . . ."

"I don't say that!" hedged Polley with a quick glance at Cal. "What I say is . . . I'm not quite decided. Is Mister Watson leaving, or. . . ."

"Mister Watson," spoke up Cal, "has got to do something quick, so if you want to buy that mine, I wish you'd kindly say so, and, if you don't, let's tear up the option."

"The option," returned Polley tartly, "is a legal instrument, and I'm going to have it recorded. It would be too bad if this arrest has made a quick answer imperative, because in that case it would only be no, but the option, as you know, was for thirty days, and I don't wish to do anything hastily."

"What I was going to say," put in Wiggins, "was that Mister Watson is now a free agent, being released on bail pending his trial, but if, by any chance, he should happen to be convicted, he could not give title to the mine. The state would then be his legal guardian."

"I see." Polley nodded. "I see. Well . . . I'll be back in two days . . . come down and see me, then. That's all. Mister Watson, good day."

He whipped off down the road, sucking a cloud of dust behind him, and Wiggins shook his head.

"This is bad," he said, "very bad. Now, who the devil put that flea in his ear . . . about the cost of the Thousand Wonders up to date?"

"His wife," guessed Cal. "You go over and talk reason to her while I talk reason to this cow thief. I've got to buy me another gun, because they're holding my others for evidence, but you put me down at Soledad, where I can pick up my horse and mule and. . . ."

"You can get your outfit together and make all your preparations to go," said Wiggins, "but I want you to promise me you won't start off on any trip until this matter of the sale is attended to. I know it's a temptation to ride after this accomplice before he disappears entirely, but he seemed in no hurry when I stopped to chat, and I'll wager he's still back in those hills. Besides, in my opinion, you need money to employ lawyers more than you do any witness in the world. This case has been framed and a skillful cross-examiner can make your accusers sweat blood, but, if you come to trial broke, or with an incompetent lawyer, they're more than likely to convict. Now I've got to keep out of this affair with Polley . . . I simply appear as his expert . . . so I'm going to disappear and leave the business in your hands on the chance you can push it through. Just use your own judgment, and, when Polley comes back, my advice is to be there and meet him."

"I'll stay," promised Cal, "if I go to the pen for it, because I never run out on a friend, but at the same time I've got to

181

start before we have another sandstorm or I'll lose that cow thief's tracks."

"I've got an idea," suggested Wiggins as they thundered along the road. "You're a man of considerable finesse. What I mean is . . . you act a part without seeming to be conscious of it, a very rare thing in this world. Now, the information that we seek in this particular case happens to be in the possession of a woman . . . you know who I mean, Missus Polley . . . and it has occurred to me that a visit from you might give some promise of success. If the lady is lonely, in the absence of her husband. . . ."

"She won't be," observed Cal dryly, "don't you worry. But if I can slip in between the visits of a certain cowboy. . . ."

"You don't mean it!" exclaimed Wiggins in surprise.

"Oh, I don't, hey?" said Cal grimly. "Well, you're right then, maybe I don't. Maybe his intentions, as they say, are honorable. But that gives me an idea . . . and, by grab, it's the right one, knowing the gentleman as I do for a crook. What percent would you be willing to pay?"

"Percent of what?" inquired Wiggins, although from the pained look in his eye it was evident he had guessed the worst.

"Percent of the sum total, the cash payment for our mine, provided she gets Polley to buy it."

"Well . . . ten percent," answered Wiggins grudgingly, "but that is very poor policy, Watson. The moment you begin to pay these blackmailing demands, you lay yourself open to everything. Now, why can't you go down and have a pleasant talk with her and find out, first of all, if she's behind this, and then, if she is, find out what's her motive in the case and what she expects to gain by it. If she threatens to block the deal, you might mention incidentally

182

your knowledge of the visits of this cowboy."

"You don't savvy," broke in Cal. "This cowboy that she's running with is Crump, the detective that arrested me, and, knowing them both, what I think they're trying to do is to make a big touch and then a getaway. Now . . . we can't hush her up, because Crump will be behind it, and she's a spiteful little hellcat herself. There's this consolation . . . if Crump should skip out with her . . . he's the only witness against me!"

"Make it twenty, then," conceded Wiggins, "but only if you're driven to it. I tell you this crookedness is dangerous. You've got to play the game straight or they'll rend you to fragments . . . and Polley isn't our only buyer. Now, you tell Missus Polley that you're anxious to make a sale, and find out how she stands with her husband. Then, if you have to, you offer her ten percent . . . twenty if you must . . . for her influence in putting over the deal. This is business, pure and simple, and, if she goes to talking blackmail, you turn right around and leave her. If you don't, you'll live to regret it."

"Damn that Crump!" burst out Cal. "He's put her up to this devilment. But you wait . . . I'll put a torch under him."

Chapter Twenty-Six

THE STOAT

Some men have a genius for lightning calculation and others for lifting pig iron, and, wherever they go, they find calculations to perform or heavy things to be lifted. Place a weasel in any field and he will find a hole to plunge into, and come up with his jaws red with blood. Wayne Crump had a genius for stratagems and spoils, and he had found room for it even on the desert. But to those who could read signs, he had the mark of Cain on his brow and, for women, the Judas kiss. He made love, but with a purpose, and beneath his quiet smile there was the slyness of the serpent and the stoat. In his heart he loved nothing but money.

Cal looked back ruefully to the day of his arrest, when Crump had taken his roll and asked for more. He saw that, even in his hates, the Texan was willing to forget for gold. He had demanded Cal's $10,000 and promised to get it yet, or send him to the penitentiary for life, but Cal had other plans. As he rode back to Bitter Creek, he brooded over schemes for revenge. Short of shooting him dead, there was nothing that Crump could do in the way of further reprisals. Having read his heart's secret, Cal was fully satisfied the Texan would not resort to murder, or at least not until he had located the $10,000. Armilda had half of it and Peggy McCann the rest, and Cal was stripped down to his guns.

There had been surprise, and some chagrin, when he had bobbed up again at Soledad and purchased a new carbine and pistol, but, although Bill Beagle glowered and Whispering Johnson looked glum, they dared not refuse him the guns. Cal rode away quickly, returning black looks for black looks, and after dark that night he pulled in to his cabin, which had been looted and left open to the cows. This little attention he attributed to Bill Beagle, when he had gone back to get his horse, but, having confidence in a hereafter for men of Bill's stripe, Cal left him to the mercies of a just God. The man he was gunning for was Wayne Crump, the arch-conspirator, and the cowboy who had butchered that calf. The next morning he rode off early down the cañon to pick up his trail for the pursuit. Polley could wait, and Wiggins would have to, until he had run down this renegade cow thief.

The trail led up over the ridge and down the next cañon above Bitter Creek, where the cowpuncher had tied his horse. At the first sight of his tracks Cal knew for a certainty what he had suspected from the start. The boy who had killed the calf had left those same horse tracks in Death Valley—he was the man Cal had trailed to the corral—and, if nothing better offered, Cal could take the trip again and pick him up in the sink. But, since that time, Watson had seen those tracks again—this was the cowboy he had seen riding with the Indian. He had worn the same slouch hat that Wiggins had described, for such things loom up big through a glass, and, unless Cal was mistaken, the kid was hiding out in the hills, or even gathering another cut of stock. But a promise is a promise, and, before he could take the trail, Cal was scheduled for an interview with Missus Polley.

She was attired in a riding habit of such daring design that Cal hesitated to ride up to the corral, but she for some reason seemed rather glad to see him, although she was obviously setting out to meet Crump. Her horse was all saddled, but she stood waiting for Cal's arrival, and Buster rushed out to welcome him.

"Good morning," she hailed. "Mister Polley hasn't got back yet. Did you come down to see him about the mine?"

"Why, yes," answered Watson bluffly, "but I guess it doesn't matter. Getting ready to go out for a ride?"

"I was," she confessed, "but it was just because I'm lonely. Won't you come in . . . and we'll have a cool drink!"

"Never refuse a lady," observed Cal, smiling gallantly, and she returned his smile mischievously.

"That's just the way *he* talks," she said. "Do you ever see Wayne Crump?"

"Why, yes," he said, "we had a long ride together only a couple of days ago."

"Well, where *is* he?" She pouted as she led the way into the bungalow. "I haven't seen him for days and days."

"Down at the ranch," suggested Cal, easing himself into a big chair and accepting the glass of champagne. "How's every little thing around here?"

"Well, if you mean me," she sulked, "I'm just feeling rotten. Why don't you come down and see me once in a while?"

" 'Fraid Crump will take a shot at me," he answered boldly and she went off into paroxysm of giggles.

"I just love you Western men," she said at last. "Do you know what he said to me one time? There was an awful wind that day, and, oh, I just hate it, so I said . . . 'Does the wind blow this way all the time?'

" 'W'y, no,' he said, 'sometimes it blows the other way!' And I just simply thought I would *die!*"

"Oh, he's a funny cuss," returned Cal, smiling weakly at the joke. "How do you like it out here on the desert?"

"I just hate it!" she answered, and the sulky pout came back while her eyes took on an instant angry glow. "He just keeps me out here from spite!"

"Who, your husband?" inquired Cal innocently.

She stamped her foot petulantly. "He never takes me anywhere . . . and he won't let me have a machine! He's afraid some man will run away with me."

"I bet ye," responded Cal while gazing at her so frankly that she blushed and wriggled in her chair. "I wonder," asked Cal, "when Mister Polley will be back. Did he say, when he started for town?"

"No!" she answered, swiftly changing her mood. "He never tells me anything. But I know very well what you're trying to do, and you'll have to see me first."

"Well, here's looking at you," jested Cal, lifting the glass in salute, but she thrust out her lip and smiled pityingly.

"You can't fool me," she stated. "I'm wiser than I look. Two years on Broadway, and, if that don't wise a girl up, I'd like to know what does. I used to be with the Follies."

"Well, you *are* wise, then," agreed Cal, although he had his reservations. "What did you want me to see you about? I'll do 'most anything to accommodate a lady."

"I want you to come through," she spat out vindictively, "with fifty percent of the proceeds. Otherwise, you don't sell your mine."

"What gave you the idea that I wanted to sell my mine? And fifty percent is some cut."

"Yes, and two hundred and fifty thousand is some price, I'm telling you, for that hole that you call a mine. But I'm tired of sitting by here and seeing other people trim him of hundreds of thousands of dollars . . . if you want to sell your mine, you split fifty-fifty, or I'll fight the deal to a finish. He never gives me a cent that I can call my own, and now I'm just going to *get* it."

"Fine and dandy"—Cal smiled—"but not from me. I might consider ten percent, if you'd get behind the project and help to boost the sale, but fifty percent is too big to be honest . . . I'm afraid we can't make a trade."

"Well, twenty-five," she offered, after biting her lips in silence. "I've never done anything like this before. But he said. . . ."

"Who . . . Crump?" he interpolated, and, before she knew it, she had nodded her head in assent.

"I thought this was his work," he went on coolly, as she stamped her foot in rage at her break, "but you can tell him the limit is too high. Ten percent I can stand, if you deliver the goods, but I'm not going to pay any blackmail."

"Deliver the goods?" she asked, now visibly subdued by his knowledge of her understanding with Crump. "What is it you want me to do?"

"Well, quit knocking the deal, for one thing. But that won't help much now. He's just about off the trade. Ten percent of two hundred and fifty thousand is quite a little sum for just letting the deal go through. Couldn't you jolly him along some and get him to feeling good-natured . . . we can't do business with a grouch."

"I just hate him!" she burst out, snatching Buster into her arms and then slapping him and putting him down. "He's so stuck on himself!" she wailed. "Oh, I just can't do it, I can't be pleasant to him . . . I hate him, that's all, I hate him!"

"Sure," agreed Cal, "I know how you feel. But what about the twenty-five thousand?"

"Well, I'll do it!" she decided. "You come back in a week. But I don't care . . . I just hate him, that's all."

There was a man-size hate within the poured-in riding

habit that encased the emotional Lura Polley. Evan Polley had bought her, and he thought he had paid for her, but Watson could see that he would pay again, and pay heavily, before the purchase price was in. The striped tent that Polley had set up when he first brought his wife to the desert was faintly suggestive of a sultan's harem, and this woman, beautiful as a flower but steeped in discontent, had made the picture complete. But there are some women, and often beautiful ones, whose allure is never so compelling as on the first time they practice their wiles. After that it declines until, their box of tricks used up, men avoid them like Scylla and Charybdis. Cal had been carried off his feet the first time he had met her by Lura Polley's exotic charm, but now he saw her as a spoiled woman, as shallow and spiteful as she was beautiful.

With a grim curse for Wayne Crump, who would also pay through the nose, he mounted and rode off up to Polley's mine.

The pay streak in the Thousand Wonders had pinched again, although the main vein still widened out. This, among other things, had probably influenced the temperamental Polley in his decision not to buy the Golden Bear. Yet something that Wiggins had said had set Cal to thinking. He wondered if all was well underground—for Pat Duffy and his gang were high-graders from Grass Valley when it came to robbing the boss. Not a man had quit to go to Soledad on a drunk since they had hired out to work for Polley, and that in itself was grounds enough for suspicion that they had found rich pickings somewhere. Wiggins had gone down the hole, but what he found there was known to no one but Polley—and it might even be it was *not* known to Polley, for Wiggins gave nothing away. He had been hired to examine the Golden Bear, which he had done most conscientiously, but he had not been retained to report on the Thousand Wonders, hence his close-mouthed silence on its wonders.

An expensive hoist had been installed at the shaft head in place of the old-fashioned windlass, and Peggy McCann, who had once wound the windlass, was now a full-fledged foreman. He was standing at the collar, watching for Cal to leave the house, and, when he saw him, he came hobbling down the path.

"W'y, hello, Watson, me bye!" he cackled gleefully. "Where the divil have you been, all the time? There was a man come through yesterday that said you'd been pinched, but I can see he didn't know what he was talking about."

"Yes, he did," replied Cal. "They arrested me, all right, but a friend got me out on bail. Have to tap you for that money, to hire me a lawyer. How much of it is there left?"

"How much?" repeated Peggy, drawing his eyebrows down fiercely. "There's jist as much as you give me!"

"Good enough!" pronounced Cal. "I thought the rats might have got in there and. . . ."

"I wear it to bed!" Peggy grinned.

He limped over to his cabin under the edge of the hill and began to unstrap his leg, but, as Cal told his story, he frowned.

"That's bad, me bye, ba-ad! They'll convict ye undoubtedly. Why don't you jump your bail and beat it? Old Mexico is a fine country . . . go down to the Cananeas and tell 'em you're a friend of Peggy McCann."

"Nope," said Cal, "I haven't got through with them yet. In fact, I haven't got started. Just give me the roll, so I can hire a good lawyer, and I'll take a fall out of them yet."

"You will not," returned Peggy. "Don't I know that Whispering Johnson? Look what he's done to Larry

Kilgallon! There's the squarest man that ever handled a dollar and he can't hardly get his mail. And Larry's smart, mind ye, he wasn't born yesterday, but what can ye do against a gang?"

"Never mind," answered Cal. "Larry's still doing business. So shake out that rat's nest and let's see how much is missing . . . these pack rats are hell on the trade. Maybe that thousand-dollar bill has been packed down to Larry's Place and a hundred dollars left in its place."

"There it is!" Peggy nodded, laying the bill down impressively.

"Thanks," said Cal, stowing his bankroll away. And then: "But what's this here, Mister McCann?"

He had picked up a chunk of ore that had fallen out of the hollow and regarded honest Peggy intently. The ore, and he knew it, was solid native silver—and Peggy was looking wild.

"What . . . that?" he shrilled, grabbing it away from Cal and turning it over dumbly. "Well, dommed if I know what it is!"

"I'll tell you, then," said Watson, "it's native silver . . . and I see it's in Thousand Wonders quartz."

"Ah, go 'way with ye, ye divil!" burst out Peggy in mock despair. "And was it you that was tarking about pack rats? Sure, it's nothing but some ore from the old Silver King, the richest mine in the world in its day. Take your money now and go and don't be asking questions of a man that's done ye a favor. It's small thanks I git, after all I've done for ye. . . ."

"Aw, forget it!" broke in Watson. "Who's doing any talking? Sure it's Silver King ore, and I never even saw it . . . do you think I'd throw down a friend? But on the level, Peggy, is this what you boys are high-grading? I know you're up to something!"

"Well, it is, then," said Peggy, and sighed resignedly as he fixed his stern eyes on Watson.

"The reason I know," explained Cal, "is that Pat Duffy and his gang haven't been in on a drunk for a month. It stands to reason the pickings are good."

"They are that," declared McCann, "but I'm having the divil's own time trying to kape the scoundrels from blabbin'. Drunk, ye say? They're drunk without whiskey, jist from comtimplating the money we've made. The news will break, sooner or later, but we're sneaking the stuff out as fast as the truck man can work. We pack it on our backs, away out on the desert, and he picks it up going to town. And five dollars a pound is the least that we get for it . . . that shows how good it is. But spaking of Eccleson, do you know what he done? He's the man that discovered this silver!"

Peggy paused to laugh and strap on his wooden leg, and Cal murmured the proper disbelief.

"Was I telling ye," went on McCann, "about this prophecy or something, and the super being afraid to go underground? Well, believe it or not, he's a fool for luck, and he's never been down the hole. Wan day he come running up with some book he'd been reading and directs me to start a cross-cut. So at it we went, right out through the country rock, and at forty feet we tapped the new vein! She runs alongside the main lead, as pretty as ye plaze, and the silver ore is there in big lenses. But silver! Out here? It's never been dreamed of . . . so we figured it was meant for ourselves. What! Muck out that ore and send it to the top for this millionaire to buy a new autymobile? Nahthin' doin', sez I, and the byes was all with me. We've been shipping it out for a month."

"Did this mining expert, Wiggins, happen to see any of

that ore?" asked Cal after a long, thoughtful pause, and the huge Irishman shook with laughter.

"Naht a sliver," he said. "Pat looked after that. Will you catch a weasel asleep?"

Cal picked up the rock and examined it closely while McCann sat back and leered.

"So you're a mining man, eh?" Peggy inquired scathingly. "Ever see anything like that before?"

"I believe I have, but I don't know where."

"On your Gold Dollar claim, which ye sold to Whispering Johnson! You white-handed byes make me tired!"

"No!" exclaimed Cal, jumping up from his chair. "Whereabout did you find the ore?"

"Right next to that big dyke that goes clean to the peak . . . we found it in a hole that you'd shot!"

"And never mucked it out? I remember the very spot! I just did it for assessment work."

"Ah, now, listen, me bye, t'row away all them books and learn to muck out clean, like a man. How many times have I told ye that them theories are ruinin' ye? Go to work underground and learn minin'!"

"I don't need to," said Cal. "I let you people do that . . . and then I muck out after you. Have you got any more of this ore?"

"Well, I may have," observed Peggy, "but it's not for a man that'll go arf without mucking out his hole. You're a good bye, Watson, but a dommed poor miner. You couldn't work for me a day."

Chapter Twenty-Seven

ANOTHER MAN'S COW

They say over in Ireland that God loves the Irish, and now and again, as far west as the Mojave, the evidence points that way. The native sons would have to rustle to keep up with the run of luck that was attendant upon Pat Duffy and his gang, but, although Cal was sorely tempted, he rode off east without following up Peggy McCann's tip. In fifty years of mining and prospecting through the district, from Klondike to Bitter Creek and beyond, no man had ever reported a showing of silver, although float had now and then been found. But until very recently silver had not been worth the mining, any more than lead and zinc, and the impatient prospectors cast these specimens aside without giving them a second thought. They were in a gold country, so why trifle with silver—and Cal had been as bad as the rest.

He remembered with a pang that he had found evidences of silver in the hole on the Gold Dollar claim, but it had taken the Irish to follow along after him and muck out after his shot. What a yell would go up from Whispering Johnson when he found that his despised claim was rich, and how he would twit Cal over salting his best claim in order to sell it for $10,000! If the ore came in at depth, as it had in the Thousand Wonders, the Gold Dollar was worth a small fortune, and something must be done to cut off Johnson from his treasure and leave him braying like a wild ass of the desert. What a revenge it would be if Cal could circumvent him and buy back his claim before word leaked out. But now he must ride off, bearing his secret with him, and trail down Wayne Crump's pet cow thief. It was that or go to prison.

Cal felt vaguely resentful as he considered the last trick that an unkind fate had played him. All the skeins of his life seemed to be tangled up and mixed as if by a mischievous sprite. Things were happening too fast, one on top of the other, and one day he was in jail and the next day rushing home, and the third day starting off again. He was always a lap, or two laps, behind when it came to catching up with his destiny, and what might save his life or change the run of luck always came in a day or two late. Now he had in his hand a secret that was priceless if he could use it without delay. And fate compelled him to run down a cow thief in 1,000 square miles of rock and sand. Yet any day, any hour, some of Duffy's crowd might get drunk and give the whole thing away.

Campomoche snapped his teeth at the constant jabbing of the spurs and rolled a vicious eye at the quirt, but Watson had found the trail of the Texan and he was following it on the lope. The boy cow thief was his, unless a sandstorm came up and wiped out the clean line of tracks. Now that Campomoche knew what was in the wind, he followed the trail by himself. More than once in his day he had galloped after wild cattle or trailed lost horses from range to range, and what a man can see a horse can see, too, if he has the wit to look. Campomoche was desert-wise, if he did resent the pace, and, once on the trail, he was a sleuth.

They cut through the clay hills and came out at Wiggletail Spring just as the sun was sinking low in the west, but the cowboy had fled, his campfire was cold, and his horse tracks led off to the east. That morning he had been there, resting up for the plunge, and now he was out on the desert. What trail he would follow to cross the rolling sand hills Cal Watson could not even guess, but he knew that where he went Campomoche and Lemon could follow, and he had water cans stored in his kyacks. This boy rode alone on a single big horse—the desert might swallow him up, but Cal could water his animals and follow his own trail back if he became lost. He camped at the spring, and before daylight was on his way, for the wind had been blowing all night.

The rocks on the great desert are seldom if ever smooth, except in the bed of some wash where the wind has full sweep and they are made sharp by the sand blasts that roll in on them day after day. The sand hills, that pile up like rollers in a huge surf after a driving gale, move about so restlessly that no landmark can exist unless it rises above their tide. In winter they move south, as the prevailing north winds sweep down through the draw to Death Valley, and in the spring they start back again as the hot southeast wind returns for a month at a time. It was winter yet, and the sand was driving south when Cal came out into the open.

Each moving wave of sand had a delicate feather edge, a plume of scudding dust and biting flint, and the tracks of the Texan's horse were filling up at the bottom, although a line of holes were still there. They led on across the flat, weaving about to avoid the sand hills, but leading north, as the cattle had gone. Sighting ahead as he followed, Cal could see the low gap toward which the boy was making his way, and, when the tracks grew dim, he pressed on toward the hills, hoping to pick them up in the pass. Hours and hours he toiled on, jostled and buffeted by the wind, bowing his head to avoid the lash of the sharp sand, and, when he rode up the black lava buttes, he found a track not two hours old. It came in from the west, around the brow of the hill, and he knew that the boy had become lost.

From the top of the divide Cal looked out over a waste of sand that extended to the far horizon, and across it in yellow waves the clouds of dust drifted ceaselessly, blotting out the dreary landscape as they passed. From the hills it was like a murky sea that seethed and boiled up toward the pass, but somewhere in that inferno there were a man and a horse, fighting their way against the storm. A day and a night they had been wandering through the sand before they had found their way to the pass, and the horse tracks still led on, barely dimmed by the blasts that rushed up through the notch in the hills.

Cal gazed, long and anxious, before he rode down the trail, and at last he made out his man. That column of thicker dust, rising high at every swirl, marked the place where his horse was walking; the strange thing was, he was coming toward them. As Cal moved down out of the gap, the violence of the wind abated. It no longer whipped tears into his eyes, and on the edge of the sand Cal stopped and gazed at the object beneath the pillar of dust. The horse he could see, but the man was not riding—perhaps he was not even there. His eyes swept the waste beyond, gauging the size of each column of dust, and at last he located what he sought. It was a lesser cloud of sand, rising up in erratic puffs, dying down and rising up again crazily. The man was off and rambling, and his horse, more sober-minded, was starting on the long trail back. Cal rode down rapidly, picking the horse up in passing, and toiled on till he came to the Texan. The slouch hat was missing, his hair was blowing wildly, and he was running from hill to hill.

"Where'd you ketch that horse?" he yelled, rushing toward it in a fury, and, as he jerked at the cruel bit, the horse flew back. The cowboy looked about for a rock to hurl, panting frantically as he tried to curse, and then he fell face down in the sand after Cal stepped off his horse and struck him down from behind, at the same time taking away his gun. Then, turning him over, he poured water in his face and handed him the sloshing canteen.

"*A-ah!*" he sighed, after he had taken a big drink, and then he looked up into Cal's face. "What . . . you?" he yelled, and leaped up to start to run again, but Cal tripped him and brought him to earth. Then he dragged him into the lee of a winnowing sand hill and gave him another drink.

"You're running wild," he said. "Key down and keep your shirt on. Sure it's me. Did you think I was dead?"

"I've been out of my head," murmured the Texan feebly. "How'd you come to ketch my horse?"

"I saw him rambling," answered Cal. "He's got more sense than you have. Where'd you think you were trying to go?"

"W'y, back to my camp," defended the man. "But the wind blew out the trail. I ain't been in these parts very long."

"Didn't I see you," questioned Cal, "down in Death Valley sink? You were driving some J Prod cows."

"You might've," he admitted, "but I never seen you, up to that time you came down the crick. How come you're out here, when them fellers arrested you? Didn't Wayne take you to jail?"

"He might've," mimicked Cal, "but you don't know me, kid. I came out here on purpose to get you."

"Well, I surrender," sobbed the boy, suddenly bursting

out crying. "I'm scairt of this hyer desert . . . it ain't natural! And if you hadn't come, I'd 'a' died, sure as hell. My horse done pitched me off and run away!"

"Don't say a word against that horse," advised Watson grimly, and gave it a drink out of the crown of his hat. Then he opened a can of water and gave them a drink all around, winding up with a big drink himself.

"Well, we'll go," he said, heaving his man up into the saddle and turning his horse toward home.

Traveling with the wind, they drifted through the pass until at last they made Wiggletail Spring. With the storm howling past them and throwing sand in their teeth, there was no chance for any further remarks, and not until supper had been cooked and devoured did Cal revert to the subject of the calf.

"Now, listen, kid," he said, "I know all about you and just what you've been doing with these cows. I was over in Death Valley and left my mule tracks by your corral. I saw you go through here with that Indian. But that was your business, as far as I was concerned . . . until you capped me in on that calf-killing game. Now it's *my* business, see, and I guess you understand I didn't come out here for pleasure. I can take you into town and turn you over to the sheriff, and that will let me out, right there. But if you cut out this sniveling and tell me what you know, I may change my mind . . . understand?"

He sat gazing at the boy, who had broken down completely and every line in his face was weak, and yet, with the weakness, there was a tough look, too—the combination had made him a criminal. The slack, willful lips had a vicious, cruel pout, and his eyes were little and furtive, but the tears that welled out of them and his narrow, pinched face told of a weakness that was more than youth. He was the type of the boy accomplice in crime—a weak boy, easily led—and, unless Cal was mistaken, the hand that had led him astray was that of the masterful Wayne Crump.

"What's your name?" he demanded.

After glancing up sullenly, the boy answered with a sniff: "Lester Wood."

"All right, Lester," went on Cal, "now just tell me all you know about this man that calls himself Crump. What was his name when you knew him back in Texas?"

The slack lips of the boy cow thief drew into a defiant line. "I don't snitch on my pals."

"Oh, he's your pal, eh?" jeered Watson. "Well, you sure picked a dandy . . . how much did he pay you for killing that calf?"

"I didn't kill it!" declared the boy, and leaped hastily to his feet as Cal reached over for his quirt. "Oh, don't whip me, mister!" he quavered abjectly, but Cal caught him as he broke for the brush.

"You limber-necked little walloper!" he hissed as he brought him back. "Didn't I see you right there, butchering it?"

"Yes, but *he* killed it!" wailed the boy. "All I done was to take his jackknife and make-believe butcher it. And when I seen you, I run!"

"Well, don't run again," advised Watson, "or I'll burn you up with this quirt. Now, come through, kid . . . I've got no time for fooling. What was Crump's name when he was back in Texas?"

"It was Hackett," sniffled the kid, "Wayne Hackett. You won't tell him I told you, will you?"

"I won't tell him anything, if I get what I'm looking for. What was it he did back in Texas?"

"He . . . we stole some cows, down in Valverde County,

and drove 'em across the line into Mexico."

"And then what?" asked Cal, and, as the boy rambled on, he sensed that he was covering up something.

"Yes, but before that?" interrupted Cal. "I want the whole record. Give me the whole thing, kid, and I'll turn you loose."

"Plumb loose?" questioned the boy. "Because he'll kill me, if he knows it. He helped rob a train in Oklahoma."

"I thought so!" exulted Cal. "Now one thing more . . . has he ever been sent to the pen?"

"He served two years at Huntsville," admitted the boy reluctantly, "but he said it was all a mistake. Something about another man's cow."

"I knew it." Cal nodded. "He's a natural-born cow thief. That's all, kid . . . I'll get the rest from Texas."

Chapter Twenty-Eight

PHANTASMAGORIA

It is *always* a mistake, if you take the word of the man who is caught stealing another man's cow. When the pardoning governor of South Carolina made inquiries at the state prison, he found only one man that was guilty—the rest were all there by mistake. Well, it was all a mistake as far as Cal Watson was concerned, but there would be no occasion for troubling the governor. A tactful request for the Bertillon record and a photograph of Wayne Hackett, the cow thief, and Wayne Crump, the alleged detective, would be No. 1323, while California Watson walked out of court free. For Wayne Crump was the only witness against him and his testimony would be thrown out of court. But Cal would let him testify before he sprang his surprise.

The trial would not take place for a month or more. The men who opposed him were desperate, and, if Cal began by discrediting Whispering Johnson's star witness, he might get another one. But the game had gone so far that its last few plays were slated, and Cal could see the fall of the cards as they went down, one after the other, until he made his grand slam at the end. Let the district attorney rave and bring on all his witnesses, let him lay his hand down and smile, and then with this last card Cal could destroy his whole case and put the star witness in jail. There would be no comeback, as far as Crump was concerned, for he was himself a fugitive from the law. A mere word to Dave

Johnson, a mention of the reward, and Crump would be started for Texas.

The sandstorm was still sifting its grit down Cal's neck and his eyes were red from the wind, but, as he rode back after starting the boy off for Nevada, he felt like the king of the world. It had taken half a day to put young Lester Wood on the trail, but Cal did not begrudge the time. The little cow thief had lost his nerve, and, besides, he might need him, so he had directed him to a rancher that he knew. $100 and some food and a canteen were not too much to pay for such a witness, and along with the rest Cal had given him some good advice about the effect of evil associates. Not that it would make much difference, for the boy was on his way, but the point was to avoid men like Hackett. For after all that he had done for him, Lester Wood's sole reward had been a quirting from the hand of Crump.

Out on Dry Lake below, the wind was still blowing great guns, throwing the dirt 1,000 feet high, but riding down Black Cañon Cal escaped its full fury, and he hummed a little song to himself:

I'm a wild, woolly wolf from Bitter Creek
And this is my night to howl.

That was his war song, when he was winning, and right then he felt lucky, for he held all the cards in the deck. The shadow of state prison no longer hung over him; he had Wayne Crump on the hip. As soon as he got the time, he could consider ways and means of making a big clean-up on silver. Peggy McCann's game was a good one, but it could not last, and no harm would come to him if Cal slipped in and euchred Johnson out of his Gold Dollar claim. This strike in Polley's mine put a new face on the conspiracy to sell him the Golden Bear.

Not until he had investigated, and traced the vein that carried the silver, would Cal consent to the sale of his heritage, but, of course, Polley, if he chose, could insist upon his rights and his option had two weeks to run. If Cal showed his hand too soon, by trying to get back the Gold Dollar, the canny millionaire might smell a rat and buy. On the other hand, if he waited for the option to expire, the Irish might get drunk and spill everything. Then what a scramble there would be to get in on the new strike, the ground would be staked to the peak, and the Bitter Creek silver district would be the talk of the mining world.

But the danger was slight of Polley's wanting to buy, for he was carrying a morning-after grouch, and any efforts of Mrs. Polley would have slight hope of success, unless she learned to change her ways. The good ship *Matrimony* was headed for the rocks, as far as the Polleys were concerned, and any sudden change of front would only excite his suspicion if she continued to nurse her hate. Any sincere repentance, sufficient to break his low mood, would mean putting aside her dog, and half of her time, during Cal's last visit, she had been kissing and cuddling Buster.

Cal had told her the story of his horse, Campomoche, and how he had won his name, and then, half to tease her, he had warned her against lizards, the bane of desert cats. When a horse eats a *campomoche* along with his sacaton grass, he goes into a decline and dies—unless, like Campomoche, he has a mule lover like Lemon to imbue him with the will to live. If a diet of lizards will kill cats, what might it not do to a delicate dog like Buster! Cal had told it to her to give her something to worry about besides her own foolish self, for Buster was death on lizards, but, if anyone could gauge the processes of her hummingbird mind, Lura Polley would never succeed as a conspirator. For she thought more of Buster than she did of her husband, Wayne Crump, and the ten percent combined.

At the mouth of Black Cañon, Cal paused to squint at the sun and decide whether to turn north or south. To the north lay home, or what passed for a home with him, and perhaps a merry evening with Polley, but duty called him south, to array lawyers and detectives and put them on the blood trail of Crump. The time had come at last when he must fight the devil with fire, for Crump had shown himself ruthless, but the long ride after Crump's accomplice had tried Cal's animals until now they were gaunt and fretful.

Above that inferno of dust the sun hung, red and murky, swinging low toward the western hills, and with each mighty gust the dirt leaped from the sand hills and scudded across the lake floor like a wall. It was the third day of the wind and the morrow might be fair. . . .

Suddenly Cal heard a clacking of rocks. He whirled in his saddle, for someone was smashing through the brush, coming down off the north hill after some cows, but when they hit the flat, they were enveloped in such a cloud that Cal could hardly see them for the dust. Some bold and hardy rider was chasing a bunch of wild cattle, turning and twisting to cut off their escape.

As the horse came to a stand and the dust was swept away, Cal saw that it was Armilda's Stranger. Then the cattle broke again, and Stranger galloped to head them off. They turned back again, and he was prancing before them. Finally the mad procession went dashing up the draw again, leaving Cal to scratch his head. What new devilment was this in that most ill-omened of desert places. Had Armilda loaned some cowboy her pet horse? Or, if not, and this slashing rider was Armilda on a rampage, whose cattle was she driving off? Surely not her own, for she—and suddenly he was sure it was she—had turned these away from home, and, if they were her father's, or Johnson's, what then? She came out of the draw again, whipping savagely after a red yearling, and, as it turned, she shook her rope and charged. Cal drew down behind a knoll and watched her in amazement. She missed, and rode in again. Then with a sudden, graceful flip she snapped her loop over the calf's head, and Stranger sat back on the rope. Down she dropped with her tie strings, and, as the calf was jerked into a somersault, she ran in and knelt on its neck. There was a struggle as she noosed its hoofs and drew them together, and Cal crouched out of sight and swore. Had Crump gone so far that he had corrupted even Armilda—and was she branding this yearling for him?

The muffled *pop* of a pistol dismissed that question forever—Armilda had killed the calf. Already Cal could see her casting loose the rope. She tied Stranger to a bush and went back. Then, down in the dirt, she began butchering the calf, and Watson ripped out an oath. Was this the Armilda that he had known at Bubbling Wells, the girl who loved music and poetry? Here she was out in a sandstorm skinning the hide off of a calf, her delicate hands fouled with blood. But why? His brain reeled as he sat back and tried to think of any reason except the one he feared. She could not be doing this for Crump! But why, then, kill a calf? Why was she out in this sandstorm, if not because it was a good time to work unseen? He crouched down grimly and waited.

For half an hour—an hour—she worked there in the sand wash, stooping over the carcass of the calf, and then he saw her digging, covering up something, and at dusk she mounted Stranger and rode away. Cal had rushed in once to inspect the body of a calf and been caught with the bloody knife in his hand. Now he waited until dark, and, when he began to dig, his pistol lay at his side. She had buried the hide deep, but he was there to learn the story that brand and earmarks would tell, although why he should wish to prove Armilda a cow thief was still somewhat obscure in his mind. It was all a part of the phantasmagoria of wind and dust and night, and, if the girl he had loved had fallen so low, he might as well know the truth. To kill and butcher a calf merely for the beef it would yield and bury the damning evidence in the sand! He shuddered as his hand encountered a protruding hoof, but here was no hide, only the meat.

Once more Watson's brain whirled as he laid hold of a leg and yanked the fresh-skinned carcass from its resting place. Armilda had buried the meat and gone away with the hide! He sat back on his heels and considered. Here was a mystery within a mystery, the world was topsy-turvy. Hides were being carried away behind saddles and fresh meat left buried in holes.

He looked about him quickly, then pushed the body back and smoothed the dirt over the hole. This was something he could not fathom. It went against all reason, but so it had been when Crump had set his booby trap and lured him to the dead calf on Bitter Creek. Then, as now, his brain had spun; he had looked on astounded as the cowboy had begun skinning the calf. But when Crump had risen up and thrown down on him with a Winchester, the reason had been all too plain.

Cal stepped upon his horse and rode off through the storm, and suddenly he was afraid of the night.

Chapter Twenty-Nine

BUSTER'S LIZARD

The sandstorm had ceased and Dry Lake lay smiling, its phantom water dimpling peacefully in the sink. A week had passed and Cal had been to town and back, but still the storm had roared in his ears. Now all was peaceful to the eye, but as he looked across the lake, he saw Black Cañon and remembered Armilda. Cal had seen her in Mojave City with Dave Johnson's daughters, daintily gowned and carrying herself laughingly, but his heart had failed him, and he turned back before she saw him for he feared to meet her now. She was buying pretty things with the $5,000 they had wrung from vulgar Whispering Johnson. But would she be so gay if she knew that Wayne Crump was a cow thief and an ex-convict to boot? Would she dress herself so daintily to please his fickle eye if she knew he had a rendezvous with Lura Polley? Now she was visiting with Dave Johnson's daughters when she knew that their father would soon hail him into court a prisoner.

Yet, although his heart was sore, Cal could not turn against her. Sometimes love performs its miracles with a man like Crump, and, although Cal had written for Wayne Crump's record, he had done it in such a way that no sheriff would come rushing in from Texas. There would be a reward for Wayne Hackett, and even the most guarded inquiry might set the Texas sleuths on his trail. But here was the curious thing—when Crump had come to Soledad, posing as a cattle detective from Texas, he had inquired for a cow thief named Hackett. A man with nerve like that could get by almost anywhere. Love is one thing and friendship another, and he did not intend, out of misguided devotion, to let Armilda's lover railroad *him*. Cal would get the information and hold it as a club, and, if Crump forced his hand, he would strike.

The grand jury had convened and indicted Watson for grand larceny. Whispering Johnson and his gang were confident, but Wiggins had spoken well when he had said that a good lawyer could break down any case that was framed. Crump was telling a lie and he was acting a lie, and Cal had engaged Abe McKinney to defend him. When McKinney unlimbered his long forefinger, he would make the alleged detective look sick. There was the matter of the money that he had extorted from Cal as payment for protecting him from Beagle. A few pointed inquiries about his past life in Texas would make him squirm like a worm on a hook. Moreover, if Mrs. Polley had been nice to her husband, there might even be money to hire more legal talent. The last word from Wiggins was that Polley was ripe. It is the little things that count in putting over a big sale, and the day was beauteously calm. All nature seemed at peace, and Mr. Polley received Watson with open arms. Willis set up the drinks, Mrs. Polley looked in, smiling, and Buster was for once out of the way. But as the talk worked around to the merits of the Golden Bear, they heard an excited yapping up the gulch. Mrs. Polley rose up anxiously, then controlled herself by an effort and beamed a trifle fatuously at her husband. She was thinking of her ten percent.

"What's that devilish dog up to?" burst out Polley impatiently, and, at a glance from Cal, Mrs. Polley slipped out quietly and the apostle of success went on. He was talking at the moment about the Thousand Wonders Mine, which had developed a lean streak of ore, and, as he fingered the rich quartz that Willis had brought in, Cal saw that Wiggins had spoken the truth. Mr. Polley was ready to buy.

"There is something about gold," he observed, smiling pensively, "that gives it a strange fascination . . . I mean the virgin gold. It has always been a fad or fancy with me never to handle a soiled or used banknote. I accept nothing but brand new money. But how much more fascinating is the native gold you have dug from the earth yourself. A treasury note is merely a promise to pay, but gold is the foundation of finance. When I have mined a few more tons, I am going to set up a mill . . . by Jove, I'll order it now! Here! Willis, Willis, bring me that memorandum that Mister Eccleson submitted to me yesterday! Yes, and then, Mister Watson, when I have milled all the ore, I'm going to have the gold cast into a bar. Or a slug, such as they used in the days of 'Forty-Nine . . . some of those beautiful fifty-dollar gold pieces!"

"That would be fun," agreed Cal. "When the Golden Bear was going big, the old man used to cash his gold in ingots, and every time. . . ."

"What's that? What's that?" broke in Polley irritably. "Oh, damn that confounded dog! Mister Watson, you can't imagine . . . why, that's Lura, screaming! Something terrible must have happened. I only hope he's killed!"

He rushed out the back door, closely followed by Watson, who was muttering under his breath.

"What's the matter? What's the matter?" demanded Polley irascibly. "Why, Lura, I thought you were hurt!"

"No, it's Buster!" she wailed. "He et a lizard! Oh, my darling, do you think he'll die?"

"Die? Of course not! I never heard of such nonsense! Please . . . please try to control yourself, Lura!"

"*Aw*, he won't die!" spoke up Watson. "I've seen dogs eat lots of them. It's only cats they hurt."

"But you said so!" accused Lura, clutching the dog to her breast. "You said if he et one, it would kill him!"

"No, I didn't," retorted Cal. "I said sometimes too many lizards killed *cats*."

"Oh, come, come, now!" protested Polley, laying his hand on her shoulder. "Please don't be unreasonable, Lura. Buster looks all right to me . . . just set him down a moment and see if he shows any signs!"

"You get away from me!" she cried, shrugging her husband's hand aside. "I know you . . . you *want* him to die!"

"I do not!" declared Polley, but she knew it for a lie.

"Well, then, get out the automobile!" she commanded, going wild. "I'm going to take him to the dog hospital in Los Angeles!"

"Oh, fiddlesticks!" exploded Polley. "I'll do nothing of the kind. Missus Polley, you're just a plain fool."

"Well, I may be," she flared back, "but you're an *old* fool! I hate the very sight of you!"

"No! Never!" he went on, ignoring her retort. "I'll never dance attendance on a dog!"

"Then I will!" she came back, starting over toward the car. "You're just waiting and hoping that he'll die! And that worthless Emily . . . I told her to watch him . . . but he caught a big lizard, and et it!"

"Well, do as you wish!" returned Polley with asperity. "You may have the use of the car."

He looked on gloomily as she sent the servants flying, fitting up the big car for the trip, and, when she had departed, with Buster on her lap, Polley swore.

211

"Damn a woman, anyway!" he ended up fervently. "Did you ever see one that wasn't a fool?"

"They can make a lot of trouble," observed Watson with a sigh, and followed him into the house. But Polley's line of thought was hopelessly broken—all he could think of were his troubles with his wife—and after a couple of drinks he dropped down into a chair and sat gazing stonily into space.

"Impossible!" he burst out after a minute of staring silence and rose up with sudden decision. Ignoring the startled Willis, he strode into his study and returned, tearing a paper into fragments.

"What's this?" demanded Cal as Polley handed him the fragments—but he knew. It was the option on the Golden Bear.

"It's no use!" declared Polley. "I'm not going to buy your mine! I'm going to sell out and quit this cursed place. It's been nothing but trouble and worry and expense . . . and what has it brought me in? Not a dollar . . . not a dollar . . . and do you know how much it's cost me? Sixty thousand wouldn't begin to cover it!"

"Yes, but look what you've got," protested Watson encouragingly. "Look at all this rich ore that's coming in. You've got a good mine and if you keep on sinking. . . ."

"Oh, bosh!" exploded Polley. "Every dollar that I spent here is lost. But I'm going to show the world that I'm still a good businessman. How much will you give me for my mine? Yes, I mean it . . . the whole mine . . . the lock, stock, and barrel . . . the house, the hoist, and the hole! Speak quick . . . how much will you give?"

"Well," began Cal, after an instant of rapid thinking, "I'm not in a position to buy. You know that as well as I do. But that doesn't prove that the Thousand Wonders isn't a mine. . . ."

"Bah!" exclaimed Polley, striding angrily up and down. "You are trying to rob me of my money. Two hundred and fifty thousand for the Golden Bear! It's an insult, I say, to my intelligence! Oh, I see it all now, but you can't dupe me, my bucko. I have a test for such cases as this. How much will *you* give *me* for the Thousand Wonders mine? I will sell it for one thousand dollars!"

"Well, you've sold it, then," said Cal, making a grab for his roll, and he laid $1,000 on the table.

"Why . . . why . . . !" began Polley, his neck puffing with excitement, and then with savage decision he accepted the money and scribbled out a quitclaim deed. "I beg your pardon," he said at last, "if I've seemed to reflect upon your integrity. Now, what are you going to do with your mine?"

"I'm going to work it," answered Cal, "and I'm going to make it pay. Have you ever been down that hole? Well, what do you know about the mine? I'm just the same as broke, but I wouldn't sell out right now for a hundred thousand dollars, cash."

"And why not, pray?" questioned Polley, his red eyes beginning to gleam. "Have you been down the shaft yourself?"

"No," said Cal, "but I'm going down right now. I always knew the Thousand Wonders was a mine."

"Well, well," fumed Polley, beginning to pace the floor, "perhaps I have been too precipitate. You don't want to sell the mine back? No, no . . . quite so . . . of course not, of course not. Well, I wish you the best of luck, Mister Watson."

He shook hands gravely, but his weasel eyes were watching, and, as Cal started to leave, he beckoned him back.

"Tell me the truth," he wheedled. "You're welcome to your buy. What is it that you know and I don't?"

"I can't tell you," answered Cal, "but if you want to take a flyer . . . well, how about Johnson's claim?"

"Do you advise me to buy it?" burst out Polley eagerly. "Say the word . . . that's all I ask!"

"Advise, nothing," returned Cal. "You're a hard man to deal with . . . been spoiled by having your own way. What I say is . . . well, use your own judgment."

"One thing more," asked Polley, "is the Golden Bear for sale? It is not? Well, that is my answer."

Chapter Thirty

ONE DOLLAR—MEX

A man must be agile to keep up with a millionaire who is subject to brainstorms and repentance, but Cal Watson flattered himself that he had whipsawed Mr. Polley even if he did claim to be a world beater. There had been some quick turns, and Cal had come there to sell, but the next thing to a good sell is a good buy. The machinery and improvements at the Thousand Wonders were worth twenty thousand, laid down, but Cal had had in mind that vein of native silver that Duffy's crowd had been so industriously high-grading. He might not be a miner, according to Peggy McCann's lights, but he was getting on in the realm of high finance.

He found Peggy McCann at the collar of the shaft, but at the guileless grin on the old miner's face Watson hesitated to come out with the truth. Peggy was, indeed, getting old, although his hair was just turning and his inch-long eyebrows were still black. It was just that the years had made their mark on his rugged countenance, for he had lived hard, asking odds of no man. Yet his black eyes still snapped with the unquenchable fire of youth and in his heart he was still a boy. But the time would soon come when old age would claim its toll, and Peggy had not saved a cent.

"Well, Peggy," began Cal, "how's the high-grading coming along . . . have you got any samples in your leg? That last was a good one, but I noticed you took it back. Come through now . . . haven't I always been your friend?"

"You have that," conceded Peggy, "but you're always gitting arrested . . . and, when a man's irritated, he's searched!"

"You're a deep thinker," acknowledged Cal, "but tell me this, Peggy. How does it come, if you're so smart, that you're always broke?"

"Heh! Broke, is it?" gloated Peggy. "You ought to see the rat's nest that I've got in me leg right now! Would ye be wanting a hundred or so, for that trip across the line into Mexico? If that's all it is, stop bating about the bush, because I've niver had sich a fartune befoor."

"No, and you never will again," answered Watson soberly. "Hard luck, Peggy, but it was too good to last. The Thousand Wonders Mine has been sold."

"Sold, ye say!" cried Peggy, suddenly losing his benevolent smile, "and who was the gomerel that bought it?"

"A first-class mining man," boasted Cal, handing over his deed. "The native sons have rustled, Peggy."

"Hooh, and what's this?" scolded McCann, fumbling helplessly for his glasses. "Well, me glasses are garn, and I can't read a word. But d'ye mean to tell me, Cal, that you've bought this old mine back? Curse the day that I showed ye that rock!"

"Oh, I don't know," soothed Cal. "You may be luckier than you think . . . the news was liable to break any day. And I'll tell you what I'll do . . . you gave me the tip . . . you can keep all the ore you've got."

"Kape nothin'!" exploded Peggy. "It was the opportunity of a lifetime, and I ruint it by dropping that rock. What'll the byes say to me now, after all I've been telling them? Ah, Watson, I niver thahrt you'd do it!"

He regarded him mournfully and Cal let him run on until his reproaches and lamentations had ceased. It would be difficult, indeed, to convince Peggy of his innocence, and especially while the blood was in his head, but after McCann had quieted down, he explained to him carefully the circumstances that led up to the sale.

"Ah, well," complained Peggy, "that's always the way . . . I niver can hold me luck. It's been this thing and that thing, ever since I was a child and got caught staling milk from Pat's cow. But what shall I tell the byes underground . . . will they roll up their blankets and go?"

"I'll tell you," proposed Cal. "I've got no love for those lads . . . they ganged me and did it dirty . . . but, if they'll keep their mouths shut and do what I say, I'll let them keep their pickings . . . whatever that is, even if it runs up into thousands. But the first man that blabs, I'll trim him. Now this is a case where we're out to clean Whispering Johnson, and that's as much as I'll say. What we need is a little time to frame up something deep, and, in the meantime, here's my proposition to you. I am needing, Mister McCann, the services of an expert to prospect the Golden Bear for silver. A practical mining man preferred, and, if he's got a wooden leg, it makes no difference to me. He'll need a few assistants, and, if they happen to be high-graders, there'll be no kick coming there, either. The ore is what I'm after, and the men that find it will get one month free lease, to make a clean-up. Do you know where I'll find such a gang?"

"R-right here, and thank ye kindly!" answered Peggy with a grin. "Good bye, Cal, and kape out of jail."

That was the main thing, after all, to keep out of jail. Yet, as Cal cut across Dry Lake for Soledad, his thoughts were not on his trial. He had made a wonderful buy, even if the Thousand Wonders was barren, but with that vein of native silver it was worth $100,000 and maybe up in the millions. Still, wonderful buys were not what he had come for—he had gone out to make a sale—and that $1,000 had been like part of his lifeblood, for he needed it to pay for his defense. Yet a man must play the game or crawl under the table, and he had called Peggy's bluff like a sport. The next thing was to cash a few chips.

A feather of dust, coming through the pass, caught his attention as he rode somberly on. Then, leaving the road, a jack-rabbit car came rushing toward him and he knew that Wiggins had heard. He came speeding across the lakebed like a tumbleweed before the wind and threw a wide circle to stop.

"What's the matter?" he demanded. "I met Missus Polley down the road, and she said she was going to the hospital!"

"The dog hospital," corrected Cal. "The whole deal has gone to hell . . . it takes a woman to dish things."

He drew out the fragments of the torn-up option, and Wiggins threw up both hands and swore. It was startling, coming from him.

"Never again," he declared, "will I go into a deal where there's a woman even remotely involved. And so her dog ate a lizard . . . well, if that don't beat Hades. And he tore up the option, right there?"

"Right there," assured Cal, "and told me I was a crook. Said he was wise to the whole dirty deal. But he said he had a test for a case like that . . . offered to sell me the Thousand Wonders Mine."

"I get you." Wiggins sighed. "Well, that dog eating the lizard has cost us a tidy sum."

"Sure," agreed Cal, "but I haven't quite finished. I bought him out . . . for a thousand dollars!"

"You did!" shrilled Wiggins, opening his eyes up wide. "My boy, you're wasted on mining. Did you ever think of trying my line? But what did the old four-flusher do then?"

"He tried to buy it back." Cal grinned. "And then he asked about the Golden Bear. Got a hunch we've found something good."

"Well, have you?" inquired Wiggins, but Cal evaded the question, although why he could hardly say. Surely, of all the people he had turned to in his difficulties, there was no one who had responded like Wiggins, but Cal's only answer was an enigmatic smile and a shrewd glance up the road.

"Here comes his truck back," he said. "The old boy is marooned. I wonder if he'll go in as freight or wait for the limousine?"

"It'll be a long wait," opined Wiggins, "if I know anything about women. But what is it, Cal . . . what's on your mind?"

"Oh, nothing," responded Cal. "Only Polley is thinking of buying Whispering Johnson's claim."

"No!" exclaimed Wiggins, and his canny smile came back. "Well, what's the next move? I suppose you figure on beating him to it?"

"You're wrong," answered Cal. "I'm through with these millionaires . . . they're too damned swift for me."

"What!" snapped Wiggins. "You don't mean to say you're going to let him buy it, straight out? And not make him pay you your cut? Well, I must say, Watson, after making such a start, your game seems to be falling off. Because the first rule in mining is to make the rich man pay . . . the poor man has nothing to pay with."

"True enough," admitted Cal. "Only I happen to be poor, too. I need all my money to hire lawyers."

"Why, my dear boy," protested Wiggins, "haven't I always been your friend? Just tell me . . . how much do you want?"

"I need five thousand dollars," ventured Watson at last, "but you've already put up ten thousand for bail."

"I'll tell you," suggested Wiggins, "I'll turn that over to you. It'll be released when you surrender for your trial. Just a moment and I'll write you out an order." He scribbled a hasty note, and handed it to Cal. "Now," he said, "to return to Polley."

"Wiggins," began Cal, after a thoughtful silence, "I can't help likin' you, somehow, and yet I hate to pull this stuff. Of course, Polley is crazy, and it's a crime to be rich, but . . . well, I don't want to trim him again. He's treated me right, according to his lights, and I've been there and drunk his champagne. . . ."

"Yes, yes," prompted Wiggins as Cal came to a stop, "very creditable, I must say, to your heart, but you're young, Watson, you're young. Have you anything to suggest?"

"I've got a scheme," said Cal, "to trim Whispering Johnson, but that's as far as I'll go. I'll fix him so he'll sell for one dollar, Mex. You buy it, and *keep* the mine."

"And the profits?" hinted Wiggins.

"You keep it," reiterated Cal. "There'll be profits. No, I'll tell you," he burst out, "you've been so good to me, Wiggins . . . Polley's miners have made a strike. All the time he's been fuming around, they've been digging out native silver and selling it for five dollars a pound."

"I happened to know that." Wiggins smiled. "Part of my business, you understand, but I thank you just the same. We're going to get along, Watson."

"I believe it." Cal laughed, reaching over to shake hands. "But let's play the game on the square. That Gold Dollar claim is good enough to keep . . . the thing is to grab it quick. Now you ramble back to Soledad and get Johnson's best price, and about the time he thinks he's made a sale, I'll blow into town with the news. Then the price will be one dollar . . . Mex!"

A gleam of understanding came into Wiggins's quiet eyes and he leaped out to crank up his car, and, as Cal followed after him, he saw his streak of dust rushing up through the pass like a meteor. Cal jogged on more sedately, and, when he rode into Soledad, the jack-rabbit car was parked by the store. Wiggins was sitting on the boardwalk, whittling shavings and listening to Johnson, who was expatiating on the glories of his mine.

"Oh, Mister Watson!" called Wiggins as Cal rode past, and Johnson glanced up wrathfully. "Just a moment," explained Wiggins, "a question of information . . . how long is the Gold Dollar claim?"

"I don't know." Cal shrugged. "Fifteen hundred feet, I guess. Why don't you ask the owner of the claim?"

He glanced fleetingly at Whispering Johnson, who rose up waspishly and the battle of words was on.

"I done told him," grumbled Johnson, "but if he values the word of a. . . ."

"Well, say it," challenged Cal, "you can't hurt my feelings. I always consider the source."

"You damned cow thief," bellowed Johnson. "You been knocking my mine again . . . I say it's worth twenty thousand dollars. Ain't it on the same lead as the famous Thousand Wonders? Well, and look at the ore they've found!"

"Since when?" mocked Cal. "The Thousand Wonders is closed down. Didn't you see Missus Polley go by?"

"You shut up!" warned Johnson. "Now I've had enough of this, savvy? Don't you say another word against that mine!"

"A-all right," hailed Larry Kilgallon, as he came in the door, "if here isn't Cal Watson! What's the good word from up above?"

"Oh, nothing much," said Cal, and, after buying the drinks, he ordered a hearty meal. But news travels fast in a string town like Soledad, and soon a breathless idler came up from Johnson's store with the news that the Thousand

Wonders was closed down. Cal ate on soberly while the discussion raged behind him, replying to chance questions with grunts, but, when he stepped down from his tall stool at the lunch counter, it was Larry himself who posed the question.

"What's this I hear" he said, "about the Thousand Wonders closing down? Did you happen to come that way? Then Peggy and the byes will be coming in on the truck to . . . ?"

"They're working for me," returned Cal.

"For you, eh?" Larry beamed. "On the Golden Bear, ye say? *A-ah*, there was a wonderful mine! But what was the mahther with old Polley all at once . . . they say that his wife has left him."

"Maybe so," answered Cal, "she didn't like it out there. Anyway, he got tired and sold out."

"Sold out!" cried Larry as the crowd gathered about, and Cal laid down his quitclaim deed. "Howly Moses!" exclaimed Larry. "And did ye buy it yerself, now? A thousand dollars down and no more! Well, well, think of that . . . and the machinery and iverything. But I always said he was touched. He ain't right, byes, I tell ye . . . drinkin' that piscn French champagne . . . did ye moind the look in his eye? Well, well, closed down . . . this'll be a hard blow for all of us . . . but I heard the byes had struck ore?"

"It pinched out," returned Cal. "Never had a real ore body. Left Polley sixty thousand in the hole. I just bought it for the tools and material. Well, I'll put my horse in the corral."

He went out into the sunlight and looked down the street to where Whispering Johnson was gesticulating. Wiggins sat bowed over, thoughtfully whittling long white shavings—the price would be one dollar, Mex.

Chapter Thirty-One

EXHIBIT A

All the desert side was there when Cal Watson came to trial for stealing Sol Barksdale's calf—Whispering Johnson, Bill Beagle, Sol Barksdale and Armilda, Wayne Crump and Polley and his wife. Little Buster had survived the lizard he had eaten, but the Polleys had moved into town; the desert was too lonely, and, besides, there were more lizards, so Lura had had her way. She was driving her new automobile, a peace offering from her husband, and attracted more attention than the trial.

Whispering Johnson wore his soiled shirt and his vote-getting overalls, still draped according to custom below his paunch, and in a voice like the rumbling of a mountain bull he announced that they had caught Watson in the act. Bill Beagle was subdued, chewing tobacco and spitting somberly. But Wayne Crump was in his glory. He wore a new velour hat, a fancy shirt with pink armbands, and a pair of short-waisted pants. His curly black locks were oiled and patted down until they stuck to his bony brow. But although he swaggered about gaily in his polished, high-heeled boots, the scared look was still in his eyes.

There had been a chance meeting between Crump and California Watson just before the case was called, and since then Crump had been nervous.

"Well," he had said, "have you got that ten thousand?"

"No," answered Cal, "I gave it to a lawyer. How's your

223

forgettery?" he inquired as Crump stood watching him, and Crump had smiled at him slyly.

"All right," he hinted. "Make it five."

"You'll get life," stated Cal, "if I told what I know." And he went off and left him, staring.

Now the trial had begun, not a dollar had been passed, and Crump was a little wild. The jury had been drawn, after a searching examination from the beetle-browed Anson Jeffreys, and, as he looked at this man who was destined to cross-examine him, Wayne Crump put his forgettery to work. Anson Jeffreys, it was claimed, was a lineal descendant of Judge Jeffries who had conducted the Bloody Assizes, and in repose he looked like a ruffled lion in the presence of yapping curs. In action he was a human volcano of words, spouting demands, innuendoes, and accusations, a man who ran roughshod over witnesses and opponents in order to get his man. If that man did not respond with the truth and the whole truth, he shook the truth out of him by force. He had a voice like a rapier's flash—and he had cost Cal $10,000.

Abe McKinney was there with his files of notes to supply the salient facts for the defense, and every time he looked at Crump, he seemed to be waiting to stab him with his long forefinger. Between them sat Cal Watson, very quiet and self-possessed, never doubting the outcome of the case. When Cal glanced at Armilda, sitting with her father and Crump, he prayed that his lawyers would win. If not, if the lie held and they could not controvert it, he would have to rise in his place and denounce Crump as an ex-convict whose word was not good in any court. That would end the case, right there, as far as he was concerned—and it would end Armilda's romance, too. Yet, as he looked at her furtively, he could not believe that she had ever been really in love with Crump. She looked too clean and wholesome to have been capable of it. Yet he had seen her with his own eyes, butchering a calf in a sandstorm. Cal had never quite recovered from the shock of that strange scene and the sense of its unreality. He had almost thought at times that he had dreamed it in some way, after his exposure in riding through the storm. But it was Armilda, he knew it, and she had shot and skinned the calf exactly like Crump's other dupe. Lester Wood had not wanted to skin the calf below Cal's house, but he had bowed to a stronger will. Perhaps Armilda had done the same. In the background of his mind Cal never quite forgot Armilda's mother who had run away and died in old Mexico.

It was afternoon when the jury was sworn and the district attorney opened the battle. He was a handsome young man with a wealth of black hair and a nose like a Roman senator, and in spite of the presence of the formidable Anson Jeffreys he began his case with assurance. The law and the evidence were all on his side, the defendant had been caught in the act, and, besides that, he had the moral support of Whispering Johnson and his friends. They had crowded into the courtroom until the bailiffs had brought more chairs and the judge had finally ordered the doors closed, and in the tense silence that falls when a man's freedom is at stake the district attorney called his first witness.

Sol Barksdale took the stand and testified, among other things, that on account of losing cattle he had employed Wayne Crump as a detective. Having thus paved the way for his principal witness, the district attorney excused Barksdale. As Wayne Crump, slightly pale, took the witness chair, every eye in the courtroom was upon him. He had failed in his attempt to extort money from Watson, and now there was nothing but his revenge. His eyes were a little wild and he glanced often at the door, but he told a straight story and stuck to it. He had been employed to watch Watson, he had been hiding near his house, and, upon hearing a shot, he had hurried down the cañon and discovered the defendant, skinning a calf. It was a solid-colored, red yearling, and, after packing it back to the ranch, he had removed the skin and delivered it to the sheriff as evidence.

"Bring on that skin!" ordered the district attorney, throwing back his flowing hair and settling himself for a speech. "You have heard, gentlemen of the jury, the testimony of Mister Barksdale, regarding his trouble with the defendant. You have heard the further testimony of Mister Crump. He is an officer of the law, a cattle detective by profession, and he was accompanied by a town marshal, Mister Beagle. The witness has stated that he caught the defendant in the act of skinning this J Prod calf, and that the brand of the animal had already been mangled in an effort to conceal its identity. Such an act, if it can be proven, is *prima facie* evidence of the intent to commit a crime . . . and we have this animal's skin to prove it. Bring on Exhibit A!"

Dave Johnson himself brought the exhibit into court, and at a sign laid it down on the table. The district attorney knew the value of suspense, and he did not unfold the hide.

"Your honor," he declaimed, "and gentlemen of the jury, I am aware that all men are fallible. We are all swayed by passions that are liable to warp our judgment, even to influence our testimony under oath. But a fact is a fact, a brand is a brand, and a knife cut speaks for itself. I am aware that the learned counsel for the defense is prepared to question the witness' testimony, to cross-examine him regarding the facts which he has stated, but I ask you, gentlemen of the jury, can he controvert *that?* Can he question this hide and this brand?"

He unrolled the stubborn hide and pressed it against the table, then held it out in one hand.

"I will ask the witness," he said, "if he can identify this hide. Is this the skin you refer to?"

"That's the skin," reassured Crump, barely glancing at the exhibit that had buckled back into its folds. "And I turned over to the sheriff as Exhibit B the knife that the defendant was using."

"Bring in that knife!" thundered the district attorney, turning the hide inside out in order the exhibit the brand, "and here, gentlemen of the jury, are the signs of his handiwork. . . ."

He stopped and looked about, glanced down at the hide again, then gazed inquiringly at the sheriff.

"Sheriff," he began, as the crowd rose up to stare, "are you sure you have brought the right hide?"

"Yes, that's it," asserted Johnson. "Exhibit A. I've had it locked up in my vault."

"Let me look at that exhibit!" spoke up McKinney suddenly, and strode over and snatched the hide away. "Your honor!" he barked. "This is not a J Prod brand. I object. . . ."

"Order in the court!" shouted the bailiff, hammering lustily with his mallet. "Sit down there, or I'll throw you all out."

"Let me see that," directed the judge after the uproar had subsided, and then he, too, glanced at the sheriff.

"Sheriff," he said, "are you sure this is the skin that was turned in as Exhibit A?"

"That's the skin!" declared Dave Johnson. "I'd swear to it anywhere. It's never been out of my vault."

"The brand here," observed the judge, "seems to be in the form of a triangle. May I inquire if you know such a brand?"

227

"That's a Triangle Dot!" exclaimed Dave Johnson in disgust, and Wayne Crump leaped down from his chair. One glance was enough for the cowboy's trained eye.

"It's been changed!" he charged. "This isn't the same hide!"

"Let us have order!" commanded the judge, waving them all back to their seats, and Crump dropped back into his chair, dead white. The hide was the same but the brand was different—someone had switched a Triangle Dot skin. As for Watson, one glance was enough for him, also, but he shut down his jaws and smiled grimly. It was not the same skin, but what then? Was he, the defendant, called upon to give testimony that would strengthen the case against him? That was up to the district attorney. The learned Anson Jeffreys, out of his element for once, stared blankly at the scene before him, but Abe McKinney had been a cowman and knew how to read brands, and he waved the hide like a banner.

"Your honor," he shouted, "I move that the court instruct the jury to acquit the defendant for the reason that the evidence introduced by the prosecution does not sustain the allegation of the indictment! On the contrary, it contradicts it, for the indictment alleges the theft of the animal branded J Prod whereas the hide introduced in evidence as Exhibit A shows the brand to be Triangle Dot!"

"I object!" protested the district attorney, but he was beaten, and the judge promptly ruled against him.

"The court instructs the jury," he said, "that, without leaving their seats, one of their number should sign a verdict, as foreman of the jury, finding the defendant not guilty."

Cal rose up smiling, but the pack was at his throat and in the lead came Sol Barksdale, clamoring.

"Arrest that man!" he cried. "My daughter will swear out a warrant. The Triangle Dot brand is hers."

"Can't *you* do it?" urged the district attorney, biting his lips with excitement. "I shall go to the bottom of this matter. You're her legal guardian . . . swear out another warrant, and we'll see who tampered with that skin."

"I would," stated Barksdale, "but my daughter is of age and no longer under my guardianship."

"Well, where is she? Get her up here! This is a serious matter. Mister Watson, I'm going to ask you to remain here."

"Anything to accommodate," answered Watson dryly, and glanced about the fast-clearing courtroom. He saw Wiggins in a corner, talking busily with Polley and Crump, and Mrs. Polley just going out, but no one had rushed up to shake hands with him yet, and Whispering Johnson was furious. He stood just across from him, arguing savagely with his brother who was hotly denying any complicity, and, when Armilda was brought to the front of the courtroom, Johnson could hardly be silenced while Barksdale stated the case.

Armilda stood smiling in the old way she had, even including the defendant in her glances, but when the district attorney brusquely demanded her compliance, she turned grave and shook her head.

"No," she said, "I can't swear out the warrant."

"But why?" raved the district attorney. "It's your duty as a citizen, and you owe it as well to your father."

"I know my duty," she retorted, "without coming to you. But if you've got to have a reason, we've always been friends, and I told Cal he could kill my yearlings, any time he was out of meat, only he had to save the brand . . . so, of course, that explains about the hide."

"It explains nothing!" snapped her father. "Didn't you see him with that calfskin? And wasn't it a J Prod animal? Well, then, perhaps you will explain how it was changed on the way . . . there's something very curious about this!"

"I don't have to explain," returned Armilda sweetly, and went off and left them fuming.

"Well," spoke up Cal, "what are you all going to do about it? You're a bunch of crooks, and you know it. I didn't steal that calf, or any other calf, so you want to be danged careful what you say. I've got a ten-thousand-dollar lawyer just r'aring to whirl into you. Do you want me, or do I go free?"

"You go free," grumbled the district attorney, and went off muttering angrily, while Cal made a break for the door.

Chapter Thirty-Two

THE *POST-MORTEM*

The age of miracles has passed and what would at one time have been a commonplace became now a matter of wrangling and recrimination. In the days of the saints the mere changing of the brand on a calfskin locked up in a vault would hardly have excited comment, but the stiff-necked generation that sojourned in Mojave City was mostly from Missouri. Even the beneficiary of the deed had his shrewd suspicions as to the agency that was behind this transmutation, and, although he kept his face straight, there was a questioning look in his eye as he stepped out of the court-room—free. There was something decidedly fishy about the whole transaction, but if anyone could explain it, Armilda could. One thing was sure, she had never so much as hinted that he was welcome to kill her beef.

She had made up that lie purposely in order to balk her father, and perhaps to save Cal's own hide, but he wanted to let her know that he needed no such protection and that, left to himself, he would have won. It was all very nice and friendly for her to come into court and reel off this glib, convincing lie, but, coming as it did, this switching of the hides had spoiled his plans completely. Here was his $10,000 lawyer, a cross-examiner without an equal, a man who could have torn Crump to pieces, and, before he could come into action and vindicate Cal's good name, the whole case had been thrown out of court. Cal had spent a small fortune to engage Anson Jeffries in order to impugn Crump by his past, and now in a minute the whole case had blown up.

As he came out on the broad steps that led down from the courthouse, Whispering Johnson and Dave struggled past him, and, from the sheriff's office just below, Cal could hear their loud-mouthed wrangling as they held a *post-mortem* on the hide.

"There's something rotten here!" declared Whispering Johnson. "Now, listen, Dave, don't you think you can double-cross me. You've been friendly with Cal Watson, you never shut him up at all, and, by grab, you changed that skin."

"I did not!" came back Dave. "And you nor nobody can say I did. I locked that hide in my vault, just the way it was handed to me, and no one has touched it since. I keep that key myself, never lend it to nobody, and I tell you that's the very same skin."

They were having it back and forth, and Cal was still listening when he saw a handsome limousine at the curb. The door was half open and a woman's face peered out, a face like a Neapolitan flower girl's. It was Mrs. Polley in her stunning new car, and, as Cal watched her, she was joined by Wayne Crump. He had been one of the throng that had gathered about the Johnsons as they were arguing the matter of the hides, but, as he strode out to meet her, Cal saw the look in her eyes—the rest was plain as print. Then the door closed behind Crump, the curtain was pulled down, Buster yapped, and they glided away.

"Good night!" exclaimed Watson, and shook his head grimly. The recreant lovers had fled. Having seen the first act, the finale was plain to him, but he did not feel called upon to interfere. Let them flee, and Godspeed, and, if they never came back, it would be soon enough for him.

He had started out to seek Armilda, but now his resolution failed him. How would she take this sudden departure? How would she greet him if he came hurrying with the news that Crump and Mrs. Polley had fled? For all he knew, they were just riding around the block to give little Buster the air! So many things had gone awry that he felt himself at fault, like a hound that has overrun his trail. When he had come to Mojave City, he had thought he had everything slated, but nothing had gone according to schedule. Crump had not sworn to any lies, Cal's lawyers had not flayed him, Armilda had suddenly befriended him, and now, after a lull, here came Peggy McCann, riding up on the station bus.

"Lave me arf here!" he shouted, and, as he saw Cal on the steps, he let out a whoop of joy. "Come down," he beckoned, "and I'll show ye something gorgeous! Look at this now!" He held up an ore sack. "You're a hell of a miner!" he shrilled derisively. "Look what you had all the time at the Bear!"

He grabbed out a handful of ore and Cal's heart jumped, and stopped—the Irish had struck silver again.

"Now that lease," went on Peggy in his most caressing tones as men crowded in to see the ore, "ye didn't put it on paper, ye know. But it's good, eh, Cal, me bye. Your word's as good as your bond, eh? The byes sent me down to make sure!"

"My word is good," answered Watson shortly. "You've got a lease for thirty days."

"You're arl right, then." Peggy laughed, patting him lovingly on the shoulder, "and a dom good man of your word. But ye'll never be a miner, Cal . . . ye couldn't work for me a day . . . it was right before your eyes, arl the time!"

The *post-mortem* over the calfskin was brought to an

abrupt close by the flash of Peggy McCann's ore. In half an hour the word was all over town that Cal Watson had made a big strike. Cal forgot about his trial and his baffling complications, forgot the men and women who had opposed him—the Golden Bear had made good, his father's faith had been vindicated, there was ore, and it gleamed like jewels. Native silver of metallic white, and ruby and horn silver, too, all set in a matrix of crystal quartz—and the vein was as wide as Peggy's hand. He was the center of a shifting crowd, above which Peggy McCann loomed like a man among dwarfs, big and swollen with huge muscles, his broad face all aglow as he repeated the tale of the strike. But it was Peggy they were listening to, and, as Cal stood dreaming, he was plucked out of the crowd by Wiggins.

"Come over here," he said. "I've got a buyer for your mine. Make it steep . . . a half million, at least."

Cal followed him reluctantly—he did not want to sell his mine, he wanted to keep it and develop it and make good, and, when he saw Polley, his eyes shining expectantly, he stopped and jerked away.

"No," he said, "I don't want to sell the Bear. My old man told me to keep it."

"Well, sell him the Thousand Wonders," hissed Wiggins in his ear. "He'll give you two hundred thousand."

"Nothing doing," announced Cal. "Absolutely!"

"Ah, but everything has its price," Polley reminded him, smiling fatuously, "and I want to own the Golden Bear."

"You'll never do it," replied Cal. "And I want to correct you, right there . . . there are some things that are beyond price, Mister Polley!"

"Ah, yes," beamed Polley. "What is that the Bible says about a virtuous woman? And by the way, have you happened to see Lura? She went out a while ago in her machine."

"I saw her." Cal nodded, and something in his tone caused the millionaire to forget the Golden Bear.

"I hope," he frowned, "she wasn't driving with that cowboy? I forbade it . . . absolutely! As long as she is my wife. . . ."

"Well, she was," said Cal ruthlessly, "and if you'll take my advice. . . ."

"Advice! Advice!" burst out Polley in a passion. "This affair has gone beyond that. I warned her only yesterday that he was a low, unprincipled hound who would bring her name, and mine, into disrepute, and that the next time I caught her. . . . But by the way, Mister Watson, did you happen to notice the dog?"

"He was with 'em," answered Cal, and Polley's eyes flashed sudden fire.

"Let them go!" he burst out hoarsely. "Let them go!" He began to pace up and down, talking excitedly to himself, and then suddenly he threw up his hands. "Let them go!" he repeated. "She'll make his life a hell. And now what about the mine?"

"I'm sorry," reported Wiggins, "but Mister Watson refuses to part with it. But I suppose you know, Mister Polley, that the original strike of the silver was made at the Thousand Wonders? There's an eighteen-inch vein. . . ."

"I knew it!" exploded Polley. "Didn't I pick it for a winner? Well, who says my system doesn't work? Mister Watson, what is your price on that mine?"

"Two hundred thousand dollars," returned Watson evenly, and Polley snatched out his checkbook.

"It's sold," he said, "without another word. I've gone against my hunches long enough."

Cal glanced across at Wiggins who responded with his quiet smile, and they went in to draw up the papers. Watson pocketed the check with a strange sense of unreality. His mind had become immune to surprise, and a flash of white passing into Johnson's office had led his thoughts astray. Armilda Barksdale had gone by with the Johnson girls—and he wanted to find out about those hides.

They were talking and laughing when he came in behind them, standing in a bevy around Dave Johnson's desk.

"You lost your witness, Dad," teased Mary. "He eloped with Missus Polley . . . and what do you think Polley said? 'Did she take that dog?' he asked. 'Well, let 'em go!' he said. How's that for a gentleman, Dad?"

"Pretty good," responded Dave, looking up to nod at Cal, "but here, now, you girls run away. This is the sheriff's office. What can I do for you, Cal? Come to get your property back?"

"Why . . . yes," assented Cal, greeting the young ladies impatiently. "There's somebody calling for you, Dave," he added.

The sheriff rose up, grumbling at a summons from the cell room, and the girls looked at Cal and smiled. The moment was strangely psychic and something in their eyes hinted to Cal of a friendly conspiracy.

"Shall we tell him, girls?" whispered Mary, and, when Ellen nodded, they turned and glanced knowingly at Armilda. "You do it," they said, and slipped out of the door, looking back over their shoulders as they went.

"Anything serious?" inquired Cal, but Armilda only laughed.

"They're making an excuse to go."

"Yes, but what were you going to tell me?" he went on eagerly. "Say, was it you that switched those hides?"

"Oh . . . goodness!" she gasped, beckoning him frantically to stop. "They could send us to the state prison, if

236

they knew. Oh, if Uncle Dave had heard you. . . ."

"Well, come over here," he suggested, stepping back into the corner, "and whisper it in my ear."

"You aren't mad?" she asked as she followed him into the corner. "Well, we took an impression of his key . . . in a cake of soap . . . and sent it to Los Angeles to a man that makes duplicate keys. And then one day, when uncle was called out of the office, we put the other hide into his vault, and I nearly died laughing when that district attorney looked down and saw my brand. And Whispering Johnson . . . did you hear him?"

"Pretty rich," acknowledged Cal, smiling back a trifle grimly, "but where did you get that other hide?"

"That's my business," she answered. "I . . . I guess you know why I did it?"

"No, I don't," returned Cal, "but I can guess, Armilda. I thought . . . well, I was afraid you'd gone back on me."

"Well, did you care?" she asked, and her smiling eyes lit up suddenly with a glow of wrath. "Why didn't you come back and see me?"

" 'Fraid to do it," he confessed. "They were all out to get me. And there was another reason, Armilda . . . I didn't know, you see, and . . . I wanted you to be happy, if you could."

"What . . . with him?" she exclaimed, and pushed him away scornfully. "You're hopeless," she declared, smiling wistfully.

"Oh, I don't know," he said, drawing her gently to him. "Say, is that what you've been doing all the time . . . trying to get me going?"

"Why, sure." She laughed. "You wouldn't come near me. I thought it might make you jealous."

"It did," acknowledged Cal, "more jealous than you'd

think. But I'm glad you still like me, Armilda."

"Who said I did?" she demanded, looking up and blushing shyly.

"I know it," he said, "so there's no use pretending. I happened to see you in a sandstorm, when you killed that Triangle Dot cull."

"Oh, you know *everything*," she sighed, brushing her hair against his cheek. "Will you come around and see me . . . soon?"

"Right now is soon enough for me," he said.

And Armilda smiled to herself.

DANE COOLIDGE

THE WILD BUNCH

Abner Meadows is only trying to get out of the storm when he seeks shelter in the cave. One of the most notorious bandits of the West, Butch Brennan, just happens to be in the same cave...with the loot from his latest holdup. Meadows knows better than to accept Brennan's offer to join his gang, but he is still stuck with the robber's recognizable horse and a few gold pieces.

Back in town, the sheriff raises a posse, and when they catch Meadows on Brennan's horse and then find his double eagles, they're convinced they've got their man. But Meadows will do anything to prove his innocence, including risking his life to track down the wild bunch that framed him.